HEART
of
DUTY

NATALIE
DEBRABANDERE

DEDICATION

For L.B.

ACKNOWLEDGMENTS

Thanks to Peter again for a wonderful cover design!

And to all my readers:

Thank you for reading and reviewing in all the good places.

I appreciate you greatly!

PROLOGUE

She was riding in the lead vehicle when the call came through on the secure channel.

"Eagle 1 – Captain Wesley, do you read?"

Quinn Wesley, the woman in charge of the small elite unit, wiped sweat out of her eyes with her gloved hands and adjusted her earbud.

"Loud and clear. Go ahead, Control."

It was 106°F inside the truck and no AC, of course. Outside, a barely marked gravel track snaked its way through a barren landscape. Just the odd goat, a gnarly tree, and the outline of a farmer's compound appeared somewhere along the sides from time to time. Hazy sky, fine dust in the air. And not a beach in sight: this was typical, Middle-of-Nowhere, Iraq.

"Enemy spotted a mile east of your current position," the radio tech informed her.

Next to Quinn, the team driver Nic Pacioli touched a quick hand to the spare Glock that he kept strapped to the front of his chest for easy access. He narrowed his eyes at the road ahead, sweat also dripping off the end of his nose in a steady stream. On the back seat were Matt Cale and Jimmy Dodds, two of the best shooters on the squad. They both rode with their back to each other and their M27 rifles sticking out of the side windows. Three soldiers, and the only other female on the team, a journalist embedded with their unit, followed close behind in the second vehicle.

"Are they standing in between us and the forward base that we're headed toward?" Quinn inquired.

"Yeah, seems like it."

"Seems?" Dodds snorted from behind her.

"Patch me through to the guy in charge at the FOB," Quinn requested.

"Yes, Captain. Hold on."

"Slow down a bit here, Nic," she instructed. "Let me talk to the—"

But she never got to finish her sentence. All of a sudden, a flash of brilliant light blinded her, and all the oxygen was sucked out of her lungs. As the track in front vanished, replaced by a patch of sky, she realized that they had gone airborne, and what must have happened. *IED in the road. Fuck!*

"HOLD ON!" Nic shouted.

Quinn braced herself for impact. Not long to wait for it, and more than just one as well, as the vehicle rolled and bounced along the track like a dice out of control. Quinn felt a burning pain in her shoulder when she was thrown against the door. Her head smashed against the reinforced side bar of the window. She wore a helmet, but it still shook her. As the truck came down for the final time, and rested on its roof in a heap of twisted metal and broken glass, Quinn exhaled. She slumped for a moment in the body harness that kept her in position. Metallic taste in her mouth. Smell of blood and diesel fuel in the air. Disconnected, and barely conscious, she floated on the edge for a while... Until a wall of dancing flames in front of her eyes jolted her back to reality. *Our damn truck is on fire!* Quinn jerked forward in instant reaction, forgetting about the safety harness that kept her in place. *Shit, shit, shit!* This was bad.

"Guys?" she coughed. "Nic! We have to get out of—"

But as she turned to check on her driver, she realized that Nic was already gone, dead from an arrow-like chunk of glass lodged in the middle of his throat. Quinn shot a wild look over her shoulder.

"Dodds?"

Jimmy was no longer inside the vehicle. Cale was bleeding and unconscious. Or something worse. *What about the second team?*

"Embling," she called. "Do you read? Control!"

Her comms were off. Quinn moved trembling fingers to the release buckle on her safety harness. Now the damn thing was stuck! She reached for the trusted blade in the holster attached to her leg. In the distance, she could hear the sounds of gunfire getting louder. Closer. Again, there was only one word for this. *Fuck.*

CHAPTER
1

Quinn stared at the luminous dial on her battered G-Shock. Four a.m., her usual time to wake up on any day of the week. She lay on her back with a hard exhale and stared at a random point on the ceiling, catching her breath as the nightmare slowly faded. Always the same one, always hard to shake off. She often woke up with a sense of puzzlement. Sometimes, disappointment. *I'm still here.* Before thinking could get too heavy, Quinn swung her legs over the side of the bed. She went to the bathroom, brushed her teeth, splashed water over her face; put on a pair of shorts, sports bra, and running shoes. She grabbed her backpack with a change of clothes, weapon, and bits of gear, and headed out into another perfect July morning.

"Hey, Quinn."

Her neighbor, Janet Foxx, was a resident neurosurgeon at the local hospital. Neither followed a traditional work schedule, and they often bumped into each other at odd times of the day or night.

"Hey, Janet," she nodded.

One evening, following a stressful round of duty, Quinn had allowed the surgeon to bump into her in a much more intimate way. Only a one-off, but Janet was a relentless flirt, and she did a lazy double-take now as Quinn went by.

"Mm... You look good, Wesley. I'd lick those abs of yours, you know?"

"Uh. Thanks," Quinn grumbled, as a memory arose.

Janet had done exactly that, actually; licked the sweat off her quivering body. She had pressed her mouth over sensitive parts, whispered naughty things in her ear, and pushed her repeatedly over the edge. During her weaker moments, Quinn was tempted to let her do it again. Janet was a fantastic lover. Sexy, smart, and willing. But still... *No.* Quinn did not want to fall into a routine, with her or anyone else. The good-looking surgeon burst out laughing.

"Thanks?" she snorted. "Hey, you're lucky I'm so tired after night shift, otherwise I'd drag you in and have my wicked way with you, Officer. Give you something a bit more tangible to be thankful for."

Amused against her will, Quinn flashed a brief smile and she dropped her sunglasses over her eyes. Janet was one of a kind. Funny. A good human being.

"Get some rest," she advised.

"You stay safe out there, Quinn," Janet winked seductively in reply.

Quinn settled into the three-mile run that would take her to the station. All quiet at this time along the beach trail, but it was bound not to last for long in other parts of the city. Lewiston used to be the kind of place where the worst thing that might happen was a punch-up between surfers after someone got cut-off on a wave. *Old*-Lewiston remained, but it was now only the tip of a sprawling urban centre, with all the usual trouble going on. It was intense. Gritty. The perfect place for a cop like her, who liked to stay busy. Twenty minutes later, Quinn reached the station and the entrance to the gym at the rear of the building.

She liked to start her day with a run, a lift, and a cold shower. Then, rivers of coffee. She scanned her badge and was about to push the door open when a heavy hand landed over her shoulder. Quinn reacted instantly, instinctively. *Drop out of his hold, grab his legs, put him down.* She executed those moves in less than a split second, and heard a satisfying *Woosh* when all the air flew out of her attacker's lungs. She squeezed one hand around his throat to keep him down, and cocked her fist, ready to punch his lights out.

"Urgh!" The man gurgled, his face already turning purple.

Quinn held back, suddenly bewildered.

"Ethan? What the hell, man?" she exclaimed.

At six-foot-three, and built like a small mountain, a string of freckles and his clean-shaven face still made him look too young to be a cop. Especially now, while he stared at her with startled eyes.

"Wh... What?" he groaned. "You asking me?"

Unbelievable! With an irritated shake of the head, she got off his chest and offered him a hand up.

"You should know better than to jump me like that."

"Yeah, obviously!"

She wiped dirt off his uniform sleeve. He rubbed the back of his neck, wincing.

"You okay?"

"Yeah. Just winded. Sorry for grabbing you." He shrugged, a goofy smile blazing through his apology.

"What?" she chuckled.

"Quinn, I got news."

It suddenly dawned on her. This weekend was going to be his jumping-off-a-cliff moment, as he'd described it to the squad.

"Oh, you did it?" she prompted. "Jenna said yes?"

7

"Yeah!" He laughed. Flushing again, not because of being strangled this time. "Can you believe I'm so lucky? I asked, and she said yes. We're doing it. Getting married, me and Jen!"

Grinning, Quinn raised her hand for a fist bump.

"Ethan, that's awesome."

He grabbed her for a clumsy bear hug, which she allowed. Getting married. *Wow.* Hell of a thing.

"You'll come to our wedding, won't you?"

"Of course. Wouldn't miss it for the world."

"Damn, I'm so happy! I was so fucking nervous!"

"I wasn't." Quinn laughed with him. "Jenna's crazy about you, and it shows."

"So am I. Crazy about the girl. Hey, I got donuts and things in the break room. Help yourself, okay?"

"Alright, I will."

"So happy," he repeated, and slapped her shoulder with a delighted grin. "Jen and I will be at Murray's tonight, for beers and stuff, if you can swing by."

"Sure. Are you just starting on shift?"

"Just about, yeah. Gotta calm down before I hit the streets."

Just like that, Quinn's mood took a nosedive. All it took was a second of inattention for everything to change. For life to kick you in the face, and for everything you cherished to be taken away. She suppressed a shiver, managed not to let him see.

"Yeah, stay focused out there," she instructed.

"You too." He bumped her shoulder. "You stay sharp, uh?"

Quinn got the subtle hint. She'd been distracted as well, lost in thoughts. The parking lot was inside the perimeter of the station, technically a safe place to be. And she'd reacted well. But none of that really mattered. Anyone could have been out there, waiting to put a bullet through her head or sink a blade into her kidneys. Lucky it was only Ethan, but he'd caught her with her pants down. And why? Because she was thinking about Janet, kissing her in forbidden places. Totally unacceptable.

"Roger that," Quinn nodded, and she went inside.

••

Lia Kennedy was parked across the street from the station when she spotted the short-haired woman approaching on the other side. *Wow...* She grinned at the sight, a welcome distraction from trying to dissolve the bunch of nerves in her stomach. This one was no tentative jogger, but a full-on runner. Dressed in shorts and a sports bra, half-nude, really, and with a rucksack strapped to her back, the stranger whizzed past the car in a blur of golden skin and hard muscles. Not even breathing hard. Lia dropped her gaze to the side mirror, and she watched her turn left around the corner, heading into the station lot. Another cop then. Possibly. *Probably.* The woman kinda looked the type, as well as incredibly sexy, and Lia suddenly grew impatient. Another glance at her watch told her that it was only six in the morning. For sure, a ridiculously early time to show up to the new job, but: A) She had not been given an exact time to present herself, just told to check in before 8 a.m. B) Waiting alone in the car was making her feel anxious. And C) She was keen, indeed. So, why hide it? *Let's do this thing.* Lia got out of her car, shouldered her backpack, and crossed over to the station. Quick sign-in at the desk, and she followed directions to the admin wing. She was passing in front of an open door when a voice called to her.

"Hello?"

Lia popped her head in and spotted a short brunette with wire-rimmed glasses and a mop of curly black hair piled on top of her head, peering at her from behind a computer screen.

"Hi. I'm Lia Kennedy. Looking for Demi Adjimitrios?"

"You've got her, darling." The woman waved her in with a friendly smile. "Hi, Lia! Boy, you're early. Couldn't sleep?"

"Too excited," Lia admitted. "Nice to meet you."

Demi pumped her hand enthusiastically.

"You too. And good to hear. It's exciting and rewarding working here, and you'll be on the front line with the guys and girls, so to speak. Coffee?"

"Oh, yes, please."

"Help yourself to a donut if you like," Demi offered. With a wink, she added; "Wouldn't be a real police station if we didn't have any of those, right?"

"Right," Lia chuckled. "Thanks."

Not usually a sugar or donut person, she took one anyway to go along with the spirit of the moment.

"I was just getting your badge ready," Demi advised. "Give me a sec."

Lia nodded, as the chief administrator trotted back to her computer. She looked to be in her early fifties, and with enough energy packed into her plump frame to power the entire station. Lia felt instantly at ease with her.

"Are you on your own here?" she asked.

"Everybody else comes in at eight, but I like early mornings alone to get myself organized," Demi replied. "Marie, Tom, and Janice work with me during the day. Good bunch, you'll see. For now, let's get you settled in." She pointed to an empty desk and chair next to the window at the back. "This'll be your station for when you're not out. You've got your own laptop?"

"Yes."

"Perfect. Make yourself at home."

Lia unpacked her things onto her new desk. Laptop, extra keyboard, iPad, camera, a bunch of extension leads, and a photo of her dad. She kept her cell phone, Go-Pro, spare batteries and a drinks bottle inside the bag.

"Here you go, darling. Officially one of us, now."

Lia inspected the new badge that Demi handed to her, with the Lewiston PD insignia next to her name and title. *Lia Kennedy. Press Officer.* She shivered with a rush of satisfaction and a good dose of relief, too. This was quite different from the career she'd planned on, but she was excited about the position nevertheless. And a fresh start, which was everything.

"Are you okay, darling?"

Lia swallowed her emotion and she nodded again.

"Yes. I am very happy to be here."

"Awesome." Beaming in return, Demi laced a friendly arm around her waist to guide her back out of the office. "Let me give you a quick tour of the place and fill you in on the basics."

They walked along the corridor leading back to Reception, and down the other side, past grey-painted walls covered with news bulletin boards, crime prevention posters, or recruitment adverts. Demi introduced her the same way to every uniformed cop they encountered along the way.

"This is Lia, the new reporter."

Everyone welcomed her with a smile and a firm handshake, and Lia worked to commit each name to memory. Losing battle at this stage, but it wasn't going to stop her from trying.

"Canteen's in here," Demi announced, gesturing to a room on the left. "Staff eat for free, so help yourself to anything you want and scan your badge at the till."

"Perfect." Lia planned on spending most of her time at the station when she was not out on patrol, and this would come in handy. "How's the food?" she asked.

"I guess it won't kill you," Demi shrugged.

Lia got the message and she laughed.

"I read you loud and clear."

"And in case you're that way inclined, this here is the gym. Also free for you to use."

Lia looked into the large room, and noticed an impressive display of equipment. This was as good, if not better, than any expensive private gym she'd ever used.

"Free food, a place to exercise, and a window desk next to a coffee machine... Hey, I wonder why I bothered to get myself an apartment," she joked.

Whatever Demi said in reply was lost to her when her eyes landed on a woman doing a series of pull-ups in the corner. It looked like the runner from before. She had her back to them, with her ankles crossed and her knees slightly bent, highlighting a perfect butt and powerful muscles in her thighs. Great pull-up technique... Lia lingered over this vision of a sculpted back, broad shoulders, and dark-blond, sweat-soaked strands of hair clinging to her neck. *Mm...* Perfect physique, too. Unconsciously, she touched her tongue to her upper lip.

"...Lia?"

Demi was still talking, and Lia returned her attention to her.

"I'm sorry. What?"

Demi regarded her steadily, dark eyes glinting in amusement.

"I asked if you were single."

"Uh." Lia blushed. *Busted.* "Yes, I am." *Very single.*

CHAPTER
2

Demi's knowing grin, and the question, obviously, told Lia that the administrator knew exactly what she had been looking at so intently. And loving it. Lia just managed to keep a straight face. *First day, Lia. Keep it together!*

"This way, my dear." Still smiling, Demi directed her further down the corridor toward the more secure area where the interrogation rooms and holding cells were located. "You live locally?"

"Yes, I got a place on Franklyn Road."

"Ah, good. Ten-minute drive, nice neighborhood."

"It looks very nice, for sure."

"You and I are practically next door," Demi added. "I share a house on Harris Dr. with my wife Carole and our ten-year-old, Luke."

She was open, forthcoming, and Lia already felt as if she'd known her for years.

"That's great," she smiled.

"Indeed. You should come round for dinner one night, and I'll introduce you."

"I would love to. Is your wife law enforcement as well?"

"No, she's a nurse at Roosevelt General. Same difference."

"Yes, I know what you mean," Lia nodded.

"Do you? How come?"

"My dad was a Boston police officer, and my mother an ER doctor. I grew up surrounded by first responders of all sorts. It's a world that I know well."

"Lovely. An East Coast girl, uh?"

"Yes. Up until now."

"What made you switch over?" Demi inquired. "It's a big jump from Boston, all the way to our neck of the woods."

Fair question, and Lia had prepared herself for it.

"I've been all over the place with the job," she replied. "And abroad. I don't really mind which part of the country I'm in now, so long as the work is good. And I feel it's going to be super-interesting here."

Demi shot her a wondering glance, but she was thoughtful enough not to push for more. Lia was not surprised; she got that easy vibe from her. She did hide another sigh of relief, pleased to be over this first hurdle with not too much trouble. *So far, so good.*

"I'll show you the duty chart," Demi invited, moving on. "I assume you'll be riding with the officers? Or at least, some of the time?"

"Yes. As often as I can, especially in the beginning. Captain Wilson said he'd like to spend the day with me today but, as of tomorrow, I expect that I'll be good to go."

"Excellent. Let me go through the details of—"

"Demi!" an urgent voice interrupted. "Have we got a spare unmarked I can use today?"

Lia looked up, startled. *Her again!* The air seemed to shift in the room, as the woman who'd caught her attention twice before walked in, a frown creasing her handsome features.

"Good morning to you too, Officer," Demi stated with a pointedly stern look at her. "Fell off the bed on the wrong side today, did we?"

"Sorry. Morning."

"What's wrong with your usual vehicle?"

"It's got a leaking tire and the engine keeps making a weird noise. I need something to drive that doesn't sound like it's ready to die on me." The woman glanced at her, nodded just once. "Hi."

"Hello," Lia smiled, feeling unusually shy.

She stared, but it was hard not to. The cop wore tight jeans, Nike running shoes, and a black t-shirt under a light Kevlar vest of the same color. In a holster on her right hip, she carried the standard-issue Glock 19. Various other bits; mini-Maglite, a pair of handcuffs, and her police badge, were attached to her belt. With her CrossFit physique and surfer-blond hair, she looked like a walking recruitment advert for the Police.

"Quinn, this is Lia Kennedy, our new reporter and media person," Demi said.

The officer stepped forward with her hand out.

"Quinn Wesley. Welcome to the team," she offered.

Firm grip, warm fingers, limpid blue eyes in a chiseled face. Wesley was attractive in a rugged, athletic sort of way. Also, Lia noticed, extremely wary despite her words. *I wonder why.*

"Nice to meet you, Officer Wesley," she nodded.

"Quinn."

"Okay."

For a puzzling second that seemed to go on for a lot longer, neither of them moved. Lia stood holding her hand, and Quinn remained, as if frozen in place. Until her gaze fell to Lia's lips, that is, and a muscle in her jaw flicked. Lia suppressed a shiver at the sudden heat that suffused her body. *Can she feel that?*

••

This woman is hot. Quinn let go of her fingers as heat transferred into her forearm. She was used to that from the physio that she went to sometimes, when nervous tension in her shoulders and neck became too painful to simply shrug off and ignore. He said his Reiki practice had given him hot hands. Quinn wondered if Lia Kennedy was into Reiki. She seemed intense... Attentive, for sure. Even as Quinn turned away slightly, to get herself an espresso from the machine, her chocolate-brown eyes continued to track her movements. Quinn was used to getting cruised by all sorts of women, but not many could make her heart race just by doing so. She tried not to stare too obviously in return, although Kennedy's liquid dark eyes begged for another peek.

"Here you go, Quinn." Demi threw a set of car keys like a missile across the room, grinning when Quinn snatched them in her left hand and shot her a disapproving look.

"Are you trying to take my head off?"

"Stop grumbling and take 11. I'll have your ride looked at sometime today."

"Alright. Thanks, Dem. Lia."

Quinn gave her a polite nod and the reporter blinked, as if startled to be caught looking at her still. She recovered quickly, flicked a strand of silky dark hair off her brow, and smiled.

"See you, Quinn. Nice to meet you."

Quinn was on her way out when Demi called her back.

"Do me a favor and show Lia to Mike's office, will you? I forgot I need to jump on a con-call with HQ in thirty seconds."

Quinn suppressed a flash of reluctance. She was going to be late with all those delays. From the reporter's reaction, her lack of enthusiasm must have been evident.

"It's okay," Lia said quickly. "I can find it on my own if you—"

"It's no problem," Quinn insisted, prompted by a warning frown from Demi. "I gotcha."

With a flicker of a smile and a whiff of vanilla shampoo, Lia stepped in front of her.

"Alright. Thanks."

Quinn could not avoid looking at her as she followed her out the door, and she kidded herself that it was the reason why she did it. Kennedy was dressed for a first day at work in black denims, light-grey trainers, and a maroon polo shirt tucked in. A strand of hair was caught in the collar, and Quinn almost raised a hand to set it free, before she remembered that it would be a bad idea. Clearly, Janet's sexy talk must have had more of an effect on her than she thought. She kept her eyes straight and her hands off the woman. As they walked past the gym, Lia glanced at her.

"Saw you in there earlier. You looked good."

Quinn could take the comment one of two ways; as a flirty remark, or a genuine compliment on her form. Kennedy did not look like she was flirting. Quinn relaxed a fraction.

"Thanks," she replied. "Do you train?"

"Yes, but not in the gym. I prefer to swim."

"Open water or pool?"

"Open water whenever I can."

"You know we have a swim group here?"

"Really?"

Quinn smiled at the way that her face lit up. *Dimples. Cute.*

"Yes," she nodded. "A mixed group of officers and medical personnel from Roosevelt Hospital. All kinds of abilities. I think they train twice a week at the beach near Murray Pier."

"That's perfect. I live on Franklyn, just a five-minute walk from there. Do you swim too, Quinn?"

"Not seriously, no. I run on the beach, sometimes."

Quinn spotted a couple of patrol officers up ahead, walking a 'customer' toward the interrogation room. They'd have to pass by on their way, and she instinctively shifted places with Lia. She wanted to be the one on the outside, closest to the suspect. The approaching man had been relieved of his shoes, the belt on his trousers, and his hands were cuffed behind his back. Made safe, certainly, and the second cop, Jed, was holding on to him. It did not stop the guy from glaring at them as the group drew close, dark eyes shooting daggers from a snarling face covered in tattoos. Quinn rested a gentle hand on Lia's arm and guided her to stop next to the wall.

"Just a sec," she murmured.

••

Lia was not sure what surprised her more. Her intense reaction to the sexy cop, or the fact that she did not mind all that much that it was happening. Really... *Not at all.* When Quinn touched her arm, it was all she could do not to reach out and take her hand. To lace her fingers through hers. *This is nuts!* Lia had been prepared for a lot of things this morning, but definitely not this. On top of it, if anyone else had reacted the way that Quinn did when the officers appeared, Lia might have elbowed them in the ribs and stepped back in front. Just to prove a point. She may not carry a badge, or a gun. And as for the art of pull-ups, forget it!

But she could hold her own on a judo mat, and she was tough in other ways too. Resilient, physically and mentally. Yet, when Quinn moved so protectively in front of her and the group of men, Lia noticed her heart skip a beat. *Oh, for god's sake!*

"Captain's office is this way. Lia?"

The men had passed and Quinn was on the move again. Or rather, stopped in the middle of the corridor, waiting for her. Lia hurried to catch up.

"So, you been doing this long?"

"What?" Lia inquired. *Lusting after you?*

"Being a police reporter."

"Oh, uh... Yes and no. Kinda."

Quinn's blue eyes skimmed over her face, her expression a mix of amused and wondering.

"I see. You don't have to tell me."

"No, I—" Lia started to say more, but sounds of struggle, soon followed by a guttural scream, cut her off.

"Argh... Stop! STOP!"

From the first interrogation room in the back stumbled one of the officers they'd just seen, and the tattooed guy that they had in cuffs at the time. Except that he was no longer restrained. Now, he was ferociously trying to pry the cop's weapon out of his hands. No sign of the second officer. *Oh, Jesus.*

"GUN! GUN!" Quinn shouted.

She took three running steps and launched herself at the pair. In the melee, Lia could not see clearly who was holding the gun at this point. She knew that at any moment, a shot might be fired that ended someone's life. She watched anxiously as Quinn helped to bring the man down. But he was still fighting.

"Drop the weapon," the male cop grunted.

"Fuck you!"

Quinn did not bother to speak. She used her legs to try to keep the guy still, and punched him on his side with her free hand. Coming at it from an awkward angle, and the hits did not look as effective as they needed to be. Lia screamed down the corridor.

"Help! Help us over here!"

Two more officers came charging down the other end. A high-pitched whine rose from the floor. The suspect was literally frothing at the mouth, half screaming and half hissing.

"Kill you! Fucking kill you all! ARGH!"

Barely five seconds had elapsed since Quinn had jumped in to help, yet it felt like ages, as if Lia were watching it happen in slow motion. Quinn groaned when the suspect snapped his head back and smacked her in the mouth.

"Get him," she growled at her backup.

Another cop smashed a meaty fist into the suspect's face. Not enough to fully knock him out, but at least this got him to let go of the weapon. Through a mouthful of blood, eyes wide open and full of fury, the man uttered a wounded scream as the cops dragged him away.

"Murderers! Murderers!"

"Shut up."

Lia watched Quinn, who did not pause even a second to rest. She rolled over and pulled the first officer up onto his feet.

"Jed, you okay?" she inquired sharply.

"Yeah... Yeah. Fuck!" With shaking hands, he secured his weapon into his holster. White as a sheet already, his face turned grey when he looked back inside the interrogation room. "Ah, shit! Joseph."

CHAPTER
3

In the zone, with tunnel vision, hyper-aware of even the slightest shift in the fabric of her universe... Quinn had sensed the gun angle toward her in the struggle. She felt the muzzle dig into her pelvis, below the protective hem of her bulletproof vest. With the intense clarity brought on by heightened levels of adrenalin, she knew that if the perp managed to squeeze the trigger, or if any sudden movement caused a shot to be fired, she was the one who'd be hit. And it wouldn't be pretty. *Not gonna let that happen.* Nothing would make her loosen her grip on the man, not even when the back of his skull connected harshly with her mouth and split her bottom lip open. If anything, the familiar taste of iron on her tongue only served to focus her more. *Nobody's going to die. Not on my watch.* Sadly, it might have already happened.

"Joseph. Joe, open your eyes!"

She knelt next to the other cop's still form and pressed two fingers over his carotid artery. No pulse. *He's not breathing.*

"Ambulance," she snapped. "Somebody, call—"

"On it," a female voice replied, and Quinn was surprised to discover Lia Kennedy kneeling next to her, her eyes wide but otherwise totally in control.

21

Quinn ripped her colleague's shirt open and she started CPR on him. *One, two, three, four, five…* Jed had slipped a hand under his partner's neck, tilted his head back, and opened his mouth. On the count of five, he blew air into his mouth.

"Come on, Joe… Come on, man! Breathe!"

Quinn continued to pump his chest, all the while aware of every movement around her, and of Lia speaking quickly on the phone.

"The police station on Maddison. Male. No pulse."

"Not breathing," Quinn said tersely.

"He's not breathing," Lia relayed. "No visible injuries."

"Perp punched him in the chest," Jed volunteered.

"Looks like a cardiac arrest," Lia transmitted.

Nice assessment, Quinn reflected. The reporter certainly was on the ball.

"Three minutes, okay." Lia repeated what the operator told her. "Yes, we're doing CPR. I'll stay on the line."

Quinn focused all on the job at hand and on continuing her steady rhythm of compressions. A small crowd had assembled. She was vaguely aware of her colleagues in the background, and of Demi, asking everyone to back off and give them some space to look after Joe. It was hot in the room. *Stifling.* Quinn flicked droplets of sweat out of her eyes. She thought of Joe's wife and kids; twin boys under five. Her arms had started to shake, more from tension than the effort involved in what she was doing, and her vision narrowed slightly. *Just keep going.* She glanced down. Joe's face was ashen. Still not breathing.

"Wake up," she muttered. "Come on, Joe."

Flashes in front of her eyes, as she recalled faces and smiles. Friends. Partners. Her brothers and sisters in uniform, some of whom she was not able to save. *Not today again. Never again.*

"Quinn..."

As well as blood, she could taste grit and sand in her mouth now. Feel the scorching sun on the back of her neck, the smell of tires burning. Acrid smoke in the air made it hard to breathe.

"Quinn."

Bullets whizzed overhead and on the sides, kicking puffs of dust all around her, and she knew it was only a matter of time until one found her.

"Leave me here. Please… Save yourself!"

Quinn tightened her grip on the wounded woman in her arms. Her own injuries might have allowed her to crawl away in search of a bit of cover, but they made it impossible to carry someone else. And what cover, anyway? There was only open ground now, on all sides. She was out of ammo and it looked like Air Support was not coming. They were on their own here. And yes, they were going to die. Quinn brushed reassuring fingers over the woman's cheek. She managed a genuine smile for her.

"It's okay," she promised. "I'm not going anywhere."

"Are they… close?"

Blood bubbled out of her mouth with every out-breath. It would not be long now.

"No," Quinn lied. "We're fine. Close your eyes. When you wake up, we'll be back at Base and everything will be alright."

"WESLEY!" Quinn landed back in the real world with a jolt, as her captain grabbed her shoulder and pulled her off Joe. "Let the paramedics handle it now."

Feeling sick, dizzy from the flashback, Quinn pulled back to let the medical team gain access. In next to no time, the medics attached defibrillator leads to Joe's chest and they shocked him twice. The verdict soon came, and it was good news.

"He's back! Let's get him to the hospital."

Quinn leaned against the back wall and closed her eyes as she exhaled. *Man... It was close.* The next thing she was aware of, warm fingers circled around her wrist, and she looked into a pair of the warmest brown eyes.

"Hey," Lia whispered. "Are you okay?"

"Yeah." Quinn swallowed hard. "I'm fine."

"Quinn, you're shaking."

It was the craziest thing, but Lia's secure hold on her wrist, and the calm yet concerned way that she regarded her, flooded Quinn's system with another major load of adrenalin. Damn if her teeth had not started chattering.

"I'm alright." Admitting to anything else never crossed her mind. "I just—"

"Wesley," Wilson called. "Have a medic check you over."

"It's not necessary, sir, I'm—"

"Not a request." His tone was sharp, but his expression softened as he came over, and he clasped her on the shoulder. "Hey, good job."

"Thank you, sir."

He turned to Lia.

"Ms Kennedy, are you alright?"

Quinn shivered as Lia let go of her wrist, confirmed that she was fine, and exchanged a few words with her new boss. Quinn remained standing with her back to the wall for support, feeling both cold and feverish at the same time. Lia's fingers on her arm had sent heated tingles all over her body. Their absence left her feeling strangely disconnected and... Lost. Lonely. *What the hell is—*

"Wesley," Wilson called again, and she jumped.

"Sir?"

"Get moving."

24

Knowing that arguing was a losing battle, Quinn pushed off the wall.

"Hey, Quinn," Lia called.

Quinn glanced back at her, her heart instantly doing a nice little flip.

"Yes?" she prompted.

Lia flashed her a gentle smile.

"See you later, okay?"

It sounded like a promise, although of what, Quinn had no idea. All she knew was that the prospect of spending more time with the beautiful reporter, perhaps one-on-one, soothed an ache inside her that she had not even been aware was there. Mindful of Wilson's presence, she just nodded.

"Yeah, see you."

••

Not surprisingly, Wilson got tied up dealing with the aftermath of the incident, and Lia's meeting with him would be delayed. Not a problem; she was used to working alone, and she knew how to keep herself busy. She drifted back to the office, keen on meeting the rest of Demi's people and getting more of a feel for the workings of the station, when she noticed a flash of an already familiar figure walking past the door. Lia flew after her. Quinn had already disappeared outside when she rounded the corner, but she hurried through the exit door as well. The parking lot was drenched in morning sunshine. Lia raised a hand to shade her eyes.

"Quinn?"

Quinn halted mid-stride and she glanced over her shoulder. She waited. Once again, that sense of the air growing still under the sheer power of her presence was impossible to ignore. Slightly taken aback, and suddenly shy, Lia paused. But hey. She was committed now and, after all… *I'm just being friendly here.*

"I need to go."

Quinn was clear about her priorities, although she made no attempt to move. Just the contrary. She removed her sunglasses to meet Lia's eyes.

"I know, I just wanted…"

What? Lia wondered. *To check you were okay? To take another look at you? Just to be near?* Quinn took a step closer.

"Everything alright?" she asked, and Lia let out the breath that she had been holding. *Get a grip, Kennedy.*

"Yes," she smiled. "Just wanted to make sure that you are, too."

"Definitely, all systems go." With a smirk, Quinn pointed to the Steri-Strip that covered the cut on her swollen lip. "No big deal, eh? Just to keep the captain happy."

Certainly, this was nothing compared to what it could have been. Still, Lia did not like to see the dark bruise forming on the side of her mouth. It had to hurt. She also recalled the way that Wilson had needed to grab Quinn, literally, and yell in her face to get her to make space for the paramedics and the defib unit. Quinn had been so focused. So intense. *Somewhere else entirely.* Lia had caught her eyes after Wilson pulled her back. Stormy, full of pain. Quinn had looked right through her. She'd been out of breath and shaking when Lia put her hand on her. And Lia was not naïve about these things. Aware that it was neither the time nor place to push, though, she nodded.

"Okay. Great."

Also, it was none of her business. She should go back in the office. Let the woman get on with her day. Or at the very least…

Say something! Quinn beat her to it.

"So, are you going to ride with the guys?"

"Yes. Starting tomorrow, hopefully." *And with you, too…*

"Make sure you wear one of those when you go out."

She knocked her knuckles over the Kevlar that covered her torso, and Lia's gaze dropped to her chest. *I wonder what she looks like underneath.* No doubt it would be spectacular. But the notion was so startling, and the thought, so out of character for her, that she almost burst out laughing. Quinn noticed. Not amused, she was quick to frown.

"I mean it, Lia. It's rough out there."

"Yes." Lia was unable to suppress a smile at that quick flare of temper. Before she could censor her next thought, she'd already decided that it was beyond sexy. "I've done this kind of work before," she added. "Got my own gear. But thank you. I appreciate your—"

"Right," Quinn interrupted gruffly. "Later, then."

She walked away, leaving Lia standing on her own with her mouth open and her heart fluttering inside her chest. *Hell of an interesting start to the new job. Now you'd better regain your focus, Kennedy.*

●●

Mike Wilson was a tall and stocky guy who looked like Jocko Willink; albeit with a full head of curly dark hair and a stylish moustache. Lia met with him at two o'clock that afternoon.

"Yes," he confirmed when she asked. "I'm just back from the hospital. Joe DiMattias will make a full recovery. He suffered a minor heart attack due to being punched hard in the chest, but there'll be no long-term damage for him."

27

"Excellent," Lia approved.

"If anything," Wilson grunted, "it's a relevant warning that he needs to take better care of himself."

Lia did not comment otherwise, although she reflected that the poor guy probably deserved a bit more sympathy after what had happened to him. Wilson himself was supremely in shape, and she knew that people like him sometimes had little patience for the ones that they viewed as less dedicated.

"What happened this morning, exactly?" she inquired.

Wilson narrowed his eyes at her.

"Off the record?"

Lia suppressed a frustrated sigh. Less than a day on the job, and the captain was already trying to muzzle her? She'd have to prove herself. It was as expected and, again, not a problem.

"Sure," she nodded. "Off the record."

"Actually, there's nothing sensitive about this incident." Wilson sat down behind his desk. "The two officers involved were following protocol. They did it by the book, totally. It's all on tape. Turns out their only mistake was to relax a little too much. Can't afford to become complacent in this job. Not even here at the station."

"What was that guy brought in for?"

"Driving on a suspended license with a 20g bag of coke in the glove compartment. Nothing that should justify wanting to kill a cop."

"Nothing should justify that," Lia murmured.

She felt cold as she remembered the painful-looking bruise on Quinn's face. She had seen the terrifying angle of the gun. She knew what had been at stake during that struggle. Quinn had put her life on the line without hesitation. Lia had a feeling that she must be no stranger to such acts of heroism and sacrifice.

Admirable behavior, but another reason not to get too close to her personally.

"Ms Kennedy." Lia focused back on Wilson's face. "The last media person we had in-house was only interested in reporting false truths and sensationalist dirt. He did us more harm than good. I am not so keen to repeat the experience."

Lia grinned, feeling invigorated.

"I understand, sir," she assured. "But it won't be like that with me, I can promise you. I plan to be very useful to this department. Here's how..."

CHAPTER
4

Quinn was driving home two days later, after forty-eight hours of near-solid duty, when the call came through.

"Any available units: suspicious guy seen loitering outside the convenience store on Mansfield Road."

As a supervisor, and late clocking off-duty by a couple of hours, Quinn could have let another unit pick up that call and carried on home. What she should have done, really, was turn her radio off. But she never did, and she'd also just passed the location. She checked that the way was clear before executing a rapid U-turn, and responded with her unit number.

"2-Alpha-7, show me en route. ETA three minutes."

"Ten-four, 2-Alpha. Suspect possibly armed."

Of course... Shower, pizza, and catching up with the latest basketball game on TV would have to wait.

"2-Charlie-9, responding as well. Quinn, I'm right behind you," Ethan advised on the radio.

"Good," she acknowledged.

"Confirmed shots fired at the location," the dispatch officer advised. "Two down. No other info available."

Ah, damn! Quinn stuck her foot to the floor and soon came into view of the store. She performed a quick assessment: people were running in panic out of the Ben & Jerry's on the left side of the road. She spotted a first victim lying in the middle of it, another one staggering down the sidewalk, clutching onto his stomach. And the apparent shooter, carrying a handgun, taking off at a dead run into a side street.

"2-Alpha-7, chasing on foot," Quinn announced in a calm voice, despite a rush of adrenalin shooting through her. "Ethan, get to the other side."

"Gotcha, Quinn!"

Down an alleyway lined with garbage containers and a few makeshift shelters, she managed to keep pace with the fleeing suspect. It would have been nice to put a bullet in his leg and stop him that way, but the street was filled with random people, homeless by the look of it, making it too dangerous to risk a shot. It was dark, as well. Only eight p.m., but a summer storm was on the way and dark clouds had robbed the evening of its light.

"Police! Stop!" she hollered.

By the book, but the man fired a blind shot over his head and kept on running. Clearly, they did not share the same safety concerns. A bushy-eyed guy in a grimy army jacket peered out from behind one of the trash cans.

"Keep your head down," Quinn advised as she raced by.

They were almost at the end of the alleyway now, and the shooter was running just as fast. The issue wasn't that she could not keep up, but that they would emerge out into a much busier street. There would be people there. And an opportunity for this guy to grab somebody and use them as a shield…

"Ethan, where are you?" she snapped.

He sounded loud and clear in her ear.

"Right in front."

In the next instant, the patrol car screeched to a halt at the end of the street, blocking the way out. Very nicely done. Ethan and his partner, Mikey, leaped out of the vehicle. He took cover behind the passenger door. Mikey leaned over the bonnet.

"Stop!" Mikey yelled. "Drop your weapon!"

The shooter slowed down, but he did not stop.

"On your knees! Put your gun down," Ethan repeated.

The man halted and he turned to face Quinn, who stood a short distance behind, weapon in hand and her finger steady on the trigger. She noticed that he was young. Early twenties, by the look of him. He had blue eyes, freckles. A youthful appearance that could have made him appear less dangerous than he actually was, but she was not fooled. The kid had blood on his hands.

"You're done," Quinn informed him. "Settle down."

"Nah... You're wrong."

An eerie smile appeared on his mouth. Suddenly, he did not look so youthful anymore. She saw his eyes darken, and his lips compress into an evil line.

"Don't be stupid. Put your weapon down."

All the while, she could see it taking place almost as keenly as if she had been watching the scene on a screen. She saw him, the gun, her backup. She was aware of herself in the picture too. Feeling equally detached and connected. Ready. When the guy raised the gun to his own head, it was fast, but Quinn was still faster. She delivered only one shot, and made it count. The gun flew out of the man's hand. He grabbed hold of his wrist and howled in pain. Where the palm of his hand used to be, nothing remained now but a smoking, gaping hole. Quinn stepped close, weapon still pointed at the suspect's head, but with her finger on the side of the trigger guard. Just taking no chances.

"Bitch!" he yelled. "Fuck! You shot me? I'm gonna—"

"Get down," Ethan ordered roughly, and he helped him along.

The three officers ignored the man as he went on screaming insanities, mostly aimed at Quinn. While they had him sprawled on the ground, Ethan and his partner cuffed his hands behind his back and checked him for hidden weapons.

"He's clean," Mikey announced.

"Take me to the hospital!" the man hollered. "I'm bleeding to death!"

Astonishing shift of mindset for a guy who had just tried to shoot himself in the head.

"No, you're not," Ethan said. "Calm down."

"FUCK YOU!"

As another unit pulled up, and a medic also rolled on scene, Quinn re-holstered her weapon and she gripped her lapel radio.

"Dispatch, 2-Alpha-7. Shooter in custody."

"Acknowledged, 2-Alpha. Good job."

"Get that guy seen to," she instructed her colleagues. "And book him in."

"Roger that."

"Stay awake, okay?"

The incident at the station was still very fresh in everyone's mind, and Ethan flashed her an intent look.

"You bet. You gonna stick around?"

"Yeah, I'll go check on the victims over there."

"I'll go with you," a clear, confident voice announced.

Quinn whirled around to find herself standing almost nose to nose with the new reporter. Instantly, annoyingly, her heart rate went up. Her pulse was going harder now than it had been during the chase. Even while running or apprehending the perp, Quinn had not felt out of breath. She did now.

"Lia."

"Hi, Quinn," Lia nodded with a smile.

Close enough to kiss, Quinn found herself eyeing a pair of sensual lips. She stared into the woman's eyes, invitingly dark and mysterious. And she froze, in perfect anticipation, when Lia raised her fingers to her mouth. Before she could touch her, the radio crackled to life.

"2-Alpha-7, are you still on scene?"

Lia blinked and she dropped her hand. Quinn took a step back from her. She had to clear her throat before she could reply.

"Roger, I'm still there," she responded.

"Acknowledged, 2-Alpha. Just checking."

Lia, armed with a Nikon camera, fell into step with her as they headed back to the main scene. Quinn did not even think to question her presence. The only puzzling thing about that might have been that it all felt so easy.

"Did you always assume you'd have to shoot this guy in order to disarm him?" Lia asked.

"No. It's not standard MO, and I was hoping not to. I just reacted to stop him making a big mistake."

"That brief stand-off was fascinating to watch. Stressful, but fascinating."

Quinn shot her a wondering glance.

"You saw it happen? All of it?"

"Yes. I spent the day on patrol with Mikey and Ethan." Lia returned her look. "Your reaction was spot-on. Did you think he might try to shoot you?"

"That crossed my mind, yes. He was cornered. Not a lot of

choices."

"And yet, you stood your ground."

"I knew I'd be faster. Are you interviewing me?"

"Not officially," Lia shrugged. "I'm just curious by nature."

She was dressed in cargo pants and a pair of Nike trainers. Dark-pink silk blouse with the sleeves rolled up, and something else which made Quinn grin in approval.

"Good to see you in Kevlar, Ms Kennedy."

"Told you I had my own gear. I am no rookie, Officer Wesley." Lia leaned her shoulder briefly against hers as she said that, perhaps to soften the tone of her statement. "I'll be over there if you're looking for me. Taking a few more shots of our officers at work."

"Alright."

Quinn watched her head toward a cluster of police units and a couple of ambulances, their emergency lights pulsing in the gathering darkness. It was hot in the street, the air thick with the scent of ozone and imminent rain to come. Lia Kennedy did not carry herself as if this were her first gig, indeed. Self-assurance and competence were attractive traits in a woman, and she clearly had plenty of both. Quinn rubbed her arm and shoulder, feeling thoughtful all of a sudden. Her body still tingled nicely with the memory of Lia's skin brushing against hers.

"Hey, Wesley."

Another officer approached, smiling wide.

"Hi, Robson." Quinn stood with both hands on her hips, legs shoulder-width apart. "So, it's good news, is it?"

"Yeah, very good," he confirmed. "The shooter managed to hit and injure three people, but none of them critically, so they should all make a full recovery."

"Excellent." Quinn remained alert despite the reassuring report, taking her own advice about staying sharp and on the ball. She was aware of everyone present at the scene, and of their positions. She kept a watchful eye on Lia, too. "Do we know the details of what happened?"

"Still piecing it together but it appears fairly simple at first glance. The shooter's girlfriend works nights at the convenience store. She dumped him last week and he's been hassling her on the phone ever since. Tonight, he came round in person looking for her, wanting to make up, apparently."

"With a gun?" Quinn snorted.

"Yeah, go figure. She was on a break, having ice-cream next door with her new partner. The guy went ape-shit when he saw them together, and started shooting randomly."

"He shoot her, too?"

"She took one in the leg. Should be fine after they patch her up at the hospital."

"Alright." The last ambulance was driving off, and a small crowd of curious onlookers finally dispersed. Quinn spotted Lia walking back toward them, eyes fixed onto her with singular intent. It almost made her shiver. "Need any help wrapping up here?" *Please, say no!*

"No, thanks," Robson echoed. "We're good as it is."

As he walked away and Lia caught up with her, Quinn felt herself relax. She was tempted to chalk it up to the release that always followed an intense job, but she knew that would be a lie. It occurred to her that she was craving some time alone with the reporter. *Unbelievable.*

"All done?" she asked. "You got what you wanted?"

"Yes." Lia nodded, smiling in satisfaction. "And I feel even better knowing that nobody was lethally wounded."

"Me too." A fresh breeze had picked up. A mass of inky-black clouds hovered low overhead and the temperature, at least on the outside, was dropping fast. "Looks a bit like the end of the world, doesn't it?"

"True." Lia glanced at the sky and chuckled. "Or at least, a downpour of biblical proportions."

Robson rolled by slowly in a patrol car, his partner flashing them both a thumbs-up out of the window. Quinn answered the same way and quickly returned her attention to Lia.

"It's getting late."

"Yes, and I told my ride to go on without me."

"I'll drive you home, then."

"Are you sure you don't mind?"

Are you kidding? Not only did Quinn not mind; she wanted to. *Badly.* Wondering at her unusual reaction to the woman, she just managed to keep her expression neutral and pretended that it was no big deal.

"I'd be driving past your place to get to mine anyway."

A crack of thunder made them both duck instinctively, and Lia flashed a brilliant smile.

"Awesome. Let's get out of here then!"

"Roger that."

The instant they got inside the car, the heavens promptly opened. Spotting goosebumps over Lia's naked arms, Quinn turned the heat on. She was having a similar reaction, although nothing to do with being cold on her side. Her nipples hardened against the soft material of her t-shirt, and she was grateful for the body armor that kept her concealed. *Get a grip, Wesley.*

"2-Alpha-7, logging off-duty," she relayed over the radio.

"Gotcha, Wesley. Let's try that again, eh!" the dispatcher chuckled in reply.

"Why is she laughing?" Lia asked.

"Probably because it's the third time I've tried to sign off today."

"Ah. Busy times?"

"Yeah... The usual, to be honest. How was it for you?"

"Interesting. Intense. And captivating." Lia laughed as her stomach rumbled. "Oops. Yeah, I missed lunch today."

Quinn stunned herself with her next words.

"Want to grab pizza and a beer with me?"

CHAPTER 5

Lia did not reveal that her biggest disappointment over her first few days in the job was that she did not bump into Quinn even once. She heard her on the radio often, as she rode with other officers. But there was no repeat of the other morning, when she had been able to speak with her quite a bit. Lia was grateful for the busy times, as well, and wondering why on earth not seeing Quinn should be an issue. Catching sight of her again for the first time in the middle of that alleyway, facing down an armed guy who'd already shot several other people, had left Lia kinda breathless. Now, she felt that way again.

"I mean, if you like," Quinn shrugged. "We don't have to."

Lia noticed her triceps contract when she tightened her grip over the steering wheel, and she reacted instinctively, by resting a hand on her leg.

"Oh, no," she said firmly. "I'd love to have pizza with you, Quinn."

More jumping muscles under her fingers, and she carefully removed her hand. She was not overly tactile, but Quinn seemed to invite this sort of gesture. *Don't be stupid.* Of course, Quinn did not invite it. Lia just found it hard not to be that way with her.

41

"Okay." The tiny furrow in the middle of Quinn's forehead disappeared and she grinned, as if the prospect of pizza and beer filled her with the utmost delight. Lia allowed herself a second to fantasize that it may have something to do with sharing it with her. "There's a lovely Italian further down the beach. They do good pasta too, if you're into that."

The bruise was still in evidence on the side of her mouth, but she had lost the Steri-Strip. Lia stared at the small scar on her lower lip, and bit dreamily onto hers.

"Hmm..." she murmured.

Quinn shot her a brief glance.

"You okay?"

"Yeah." Lia straightened. *Just kisses on the brain, don't worry.*

She told herself the same. Having this kind of response to a gorgeous woman like Quinn was probably only natural, after all. Lia would have to get used to this sort of thing, and adjust to life in the real world again. She had expected as much. No surprise. *No problem.* When Quinn parked in front of the restaurant a few minutes later, Lia felt perfectly settled, albeit a little cold as she unstrapped her protective vest.

"I think I've got a jumper you can borrow," Quinn offered.

She handed her a faded red hoodie with *LEWISTON P.D.* stenciled on the back. It was a size too big for Lia but clean, soft, with an after-scent of sandalwood and clove cologne. Quinn's scent. Putting it on felt like receiving a hug, and Lia felt instantly warmer. It was dark now, and a bit fresh in the aftermath of the storm. A strong breeze blew in from offshore. The weather made her long for comfy jumpers and closeness.

"Thanks," she nodded. "I feel better."

Quinn smiled in response.

"You look cute."

She had got rid of her own vest and slipped on a well-worn black leather jacket over her t-shirt. Probably more to cover the weapon holstered on her hip than because she was feeling cold. She looked impossibly hot to Lia, and even more so, dressed like this. The faint flush of color across her cheeks as she delivered the compliment was attractive too. Lia would not have taken her for shy. Just reserved and, certainly, not interested. Despite her resolutions, her curiosity was piqued. Quinn Wesley possessed the sort of looks that could be described as lethal, and her personality was just as alluring.

"Shall we?" Lia invited.

"Yep."

The restaurant was cozy and full, always a good sign, and they managed to secure a table at the back near a giant potted olive tree. Lia was not surprised when Quinn chose the seat with her back against the wall and the best view of the room in front. Off-duty or not, she was still a cop. Lia's intuition told her that there might be more to this story as well. Quinn struck Lia as the kind who never fully relaxed. That had to take its toll. As if on cue, Quinn rubbed her hands over her eyes and sighed heavily. She sounded exhausted.

"How are you doing?"

"Me?" Quinn raised a perplexed eyebrow. "I'm fine. Why?"

Before she even realized what she was doing, Lia reached across the table, cupped her cheek in her hand, and brushed a light finger over the corner of her mouth. It was instant. Quinn's clear blue eyes darkened faster than storm clouds rolling in from the sea. Her gaze emptied. Her eyelids lowered and she let out a soft exhale. That sigh was so many things all at once… Hot, for sure. Sexy. But also touching and endearing. *Telling.* Feeling her body react to Quinn's reaction, Lia dropped her hand, just not so fast as to make it look as if she had been burned. Even if she was burning inside.

"Does this hurt?"

Quinn blinked, touched her own lip, and she chuckled.

"Are you kidding? This barely counts as a pin prick in my world."

Relieved to feel them both on steady ground, Lia laughed along with her.

"Oh, I see. Tough girl, eh?"

"Is there another kind?" Quinn teased.

"Well-said," Lia approved. "I'm glad you feel okay."

The waiter delivered two Budweiser in brown bottles and a familiar 'Hey, Quinn', on his way to another table.

"Is this alright or would you prefer wine?" Quinn asked.

"That's perfect. I take it you're a regular here?"

"Yeah, it's convenient after a long shift."

"So, what do you do when you're off-duty?"

"Um..." Quinn frowned as if this were a hard question. Lia watched her take a swallow of beer and pass her tongue over her lip. Just a pin prick? *Yeah, right.* "I catch up on sleep. Recharge. Go running on the beach. Work out. That sort of thing."

She did not mention a partner. Given her looks, this was both interesting and surprising for Lia.

"Basically, you just bide your time until you can get back to it, uh?" she prompted.

"Basically, that's it, yeah," Quinn grinned. "I like my job."

"That's nice. Did you always want to be a cop?"

The waiter came back to take their order, interrupting.

"I'm having all-veggie with added pepperoni. Would you like to share a large one between us?"

"Sure."

"I'm afraid I don't really know what your job entails, Lia," Quinn said after placing the order. "What kind of things will you be reporting on?"

Lia held her gaze as she picked up her beer. She recognized avoidance in the way that Quinn had shifted the conversation onto her. If this had been an interview, she would have pushed. But it wasn't, and she enjoyed the fledgling connection between them a little too much to put it at risk.

"Well, a lot comes into it," she started with a smile.

The flash of relief across Quinn's face was hard to miss.

"Are you a freelancer?"

She seemed very keen to move them on, and Lia went along with her.

"I am freelance in general, yes. But I was hired by the Police Association on this one, so I do have a set of guidelines to follow. My work is two-fold: to report on the activities of Lewiston P.D. in order to give people clear sight of what that all involves..."

"To show where their tax money goes?"

"Exactly. The second part of my job will involve a lot of PR through social media. To be honest with you, that's probably the most important side of it."

"Yeah." Quinn ran a hand through her tangled locks and she sighed. "We need all the help we can get at the moment. Trust in the police is at an all-time-low. It makes our job a lot harder and more dangerous when people think that we're the enemy."

"Trust works both ways," Lia agreed.

"Definitely. We all have to be extremely careful nowadays. I always was, but others, not so much. Anyway." As if aware that this line of conversation might lead Lia to ask more personal questions, Quinn smiled and changed the subject again. "What about you? What do you do in your off-time?"

"Well, I like to swim, like I said. Netflix and cook."

"Is that some kind of code?"

"No." Lia chuckled. "Or if it is, I don't know it. But I really enjoy cooking, and relaxing in front of a good show. Other than that, Demi invited me to a barbecue at her house this weekend, and I also have a ton of unpacking to do."

"Yes, Demi said you're from Boston."

"I am, indeed." *Were you talking about me?* Lia would have lied if she said that part of her did not like the idea. Had Quinn asked about her? She dismissed the notion, even as her heart gave a little jolt of happiness. *Don't be ridiculous.* Yet, there was no forgetting Quinn's reaction earlier on when Lia had touched her lip. Lia knew what arousal looked like on a woman's face, and Quinn had seemed hungry.

"How does the rest of your family feel about your move to the other end of the country?"

"I don't have a family anymore."

Quinn went a little still.

"Ah, sorry. I didn't mean to—"

"No, no, it's okay," Lia interrupted. "I didn't mean to be so sharp."

"Don't worry about it."

It was Quinn's turn to reach over and squeeze her fingers.

"My dad was a cop," Lia volunteered. "Genuine old-school, tough guy with a big heart."

"I see." Quinn nodded in approval of the description. "We have plenty of those in the department. Solid people you can depend on."

"Yes. He raised me single-handedly after my mother died. I was only ten years old at the time. I spent the last three years

46

looking after him. He was ill with dementia. He passed away six weeks ago."

Lia drained the rest of her bottle. Trying not to shake, stunned at her own self. She was usually so guarded with the things that she revealed to other people! Such a private person. And Quinn had not even asked. *I just threw it all out without any restraint.* Lia looked at her, worried that she may have gone too far with the personal. Quinn's expression was impossible to decipher.

●●●

What am I doing? Holding hands with a woman I barely know, asking her things I wouldn't even want to answer? Why are we even here? Usually, the last thing Quinn would be looking for after coming off duty was this kind of emotional interaction. She liked to switch off after work and keep it simple. Sometimes, this meant wandering off to one of the lesbian bars downtown where other female officers, firefighters, or medical personnel went to relax after hours. Quinn preferred her hook-ups hot and simple. She was clear on the fact that she did not want a relationship, and never encouraged extensive pillow talk. But something about the reporter made it hard not to want to remain right where she was, and carry on listening and talking.

"Gosh, Lia," she murmured. "I'm sorry about your dad."

Lia closed her fingers over hers.

"It's okay. Thanks."

She sounded in control but there was no hiding the pain in her eyes. Quinn did not let go of her hand. Mistaking the sudden intimate vibe between them for a romantic one, the waiter ran over to match the ambience by delivering a lit candle, albeit stuck in a less than inspiring Orangina bottle, to the table.

"Bella, bellissima, amore mia—" he purred.

"Cut it out, Alex," Quinn muttered.

He shot her an exaggerated offended look, grinned at Lia, blew her a kiss, and scampered off toward the kitchen.

"Is he Italian?"

"Nope, third-generation Russian. And that's the only Italian he's managed to learn, even after working here for over a year. I think he thinks he's fooling the clientele."

Lia's face lit up beautifully when she chuckled, and Quinn could not help but feel pleased that she had contributed to it, at least in some small way. Pizza arrived. Conversation centered on easy topics while they ate, like other good places to have a meal in Lewiston, or Quinn's favorite running routes along the coast. After a coffee, it was time to go. The storm had passed. It was warm again, with a full moon shining over the ocean. Lia took a few steps out onto the beach. Quinn, never one to tag along aimlessly, followed close behind, as if drawn to her by invisible strings.

"It's so beautiful out here," Lia sighed.

"Yes." Quinn stared at her profile edged in silver. "It sure is nice." She caught Lia stifling a yawn. She did look cute in her oversized police hoodie, but Quinn had already let that slip once, and it was time to get a grip. "You look beat. Come on, I'll drive you home."

"Okay." As if it were the most natural thing in the world, Lia laced her arm around her waist as they headed back to the car, and she shot her a smile. "Aren't you tired yourself, Officer Wesley?"

Quinn momentarily lost her breath at the feel of Lia leaning against her side, especially as it left her little choice but to rest her arm around her shoulders. For a moment, heat was all she felt, and she struggled to form a full sentence.

"No," she replied. "I am wide awake."

CHAPTER
6

They drove in silence for a while. Quinn knew it had to be in her own head, but she felt as if the air were tingling between them both. A vague sense of anticipation lingered. She felt tight. Hot. Hyper-aware of Lia sitting beside her. Part of her wanted to find some kind of excuse not to let her go just yet, and another could not wait to get home, and take care of the ache between her legs. Either that or do push-ups.

"This is me right there," she nodded as they drove past her own place.

"Oh, leave me here then, Quinn," Lia answered. "I can walk the rest of the way."

"No, no, I'll drive you."

"Is it not safe around here?"

"It's okay. But you know how it is: every place is safe until it's not."

"Mm. Can't be worse than Iraq," Lia mused.

It was like being hit. Quinn felt the back of her neck tighten to the point of seizing, and the same happened to her shoulders. For a brief but alarming moment, her vision narrowed and she had to shake her head to bring it back to normal.

"Quinn? Everything okay?"

"Yeah. I—" Quinn lost her voice and she had to swallow. "Fine."

A mile further on, Lia pointed to her apartment building.

"I'm in here. Top floor, corner apartment."

"Right."

Quinn barely glanced at it as she parked in front. She was still feeling as if she'd been zapped by lightning. When Lia rested a soft hand over her thigh, she actually flinched.

"You've gone very pale, are you sure that you're okay?"

"Yes." Quinn turned to her with her heart racing. Lia had noticed her reaction; it was too late to deny it. Also, she just had to ask. "Why did you say that about Iraq? Were you there?"

"Yes, for a year."

"When?"

"2005 to 06."

Oh, Jesus! "As a reporter?"

"Yes." Lia nodded softly. "I spent time at Camp Bastion and also at a British FOB run by the Royal Marines. I went on several patrols with them, learned the basics."

Quinn was no longer aware of the clean scent of the ocean carried on the breeze. Other smells assaulted her; smoke, sweat, blood. *Fear.* Only memories, she knew, the lifeless recollection of sensations. Not real. *Memories can't hurt you.* She forced herself to relax, as the often-rehearsed phrases drifted automatically across her mind. *I'm okay. I am safe.* She had learned to stay in control and grounded. She knew how to deal with the disorienting rush of feelings and emotions that anything related to Iraq often brought on.

"I came back with a kind of sixth sense about safety," Lia concluded. "Street-wise, you might say."

Her hand was still resting on her leg, and Quinn tried very hard not to tremble. She failed. Everything was a little too much.

"Quinn..." Lia murmured.

Quinn felt the familiar impulse to run. She was vulnerable at this point, whenever the topic of Iraq came up in conversation. It was rare that it did, but it always left her feeling open and raw. Lia seemed like the sensitive and intuitive type. She was staring at her as if she could see right inside her head, every traumatic memory. Quinn felt exposed and, for sure, did not like that one little bit. *I really have to go...* Paradoxically, though, the urge to stay, and even to return Lia's touches, had increased by a good order of magnitude. Quinn was not foolish. She recognized the warning signs, she knew what was going on. Stress and low-level adrenalin simmered in her system. Fatigue, too. Mixed with healthy sexual arousal at the feel of a beautiful woman's hand on her leg, paying attention to her, and all the ingredients were there for a big mistake to happen. It occurred to her that she might drive downtown after this. With luck, someone would be up for some quick relief. Better than push-ups or solo play time to distract her from the memories. She knew she would not be able to sleep either way.

"I'll see you to your apartment," she invited.

Lia held her back as she reached for the door handle.

"You were there too," she said.

Just stating the obvious. She had already guessed. It was too late to change the subject, or try to deny it. Quinn realized that she only had herself to blame for ending up in the hot seat now, anyway. *I should have let it slide when she made that comment earlier.*

"Yeah, I was there," she admitted.

"When?"

"2004 to 07."

"Three years?" Lia stared at her intently. "What? Full-time? In what capacity?"

"Um…" Quinn could feel her reluctance rising. "I was an Army captain. I did two rotations during the three years."

"Oh, right! What was it like for—"

"Lia." Quinn was careful to keep her voice steady when she interrupted, and she even managed a small smile, but she could not go there. Not even with a woman who may be able to relate to her experience in some small part; and especially not this one. She raised her eyes to Lia's and was startled by the intensity of her gaze. "I'm sorry. I don't want to talk about it, okay?"

••

At 06:15 the next morning, Lia headed to the beach for her first swim with the group. It was a little chilly, but she felt fine in a layer of neoprene wetsuit. The sun was already up. Before long, sand would be too hot to walk on. Her mind immediately leaped from one hot topic to the other. *Quinn.* Lia had gone to sleep thinking about her, and woken up in the middle of the night, wanting. With the sheets tangled around her legs and remnants of an erotic dream flashing across her mind, she was swollen, aching for release. The intensity of it surprised her. Of course, being aroused was not the issue. She took care of herself when it happened, without fuss. Just satisfying natural physical urges and moving on to more important things. This time though, she wanted to take her time. She lay back on her stomach, stroking herself. Quinn was such a study in contradictions. That she was strong, skilled, and excelled in her chosen career, was obvious for all to see. But Lia had not expected the layer of vulnerability that rose to the surface during the conversation. Something must have gone seriously wrong for Quinn in Iraq. *I don't want to talk about it.* Quinn had spoken in a normal voice, but Lia had felt the faint tremor still in her leg. Was she aware of how deeply sad and wounded she appeared in that moment? It was only for a second, before her walls came up, but Lia had seen it all. So much going on under the surface... So much that Quinn did not want to show, and maybe not even acknowledge. It had to be hard. Lonely. Lia understood a lot more about that than Quinn would know. She'd ached to take her in her arms and kiss her then, to take some of her pain away, in the best way that she knew how. Hours later, alone in bed in the forgiving darkness, Lia allowed herself to fantasize about what may have happened if she had reached for Quinn in the car. Not just a friendly hug, for sure. A kiss... Maybe more? Sex with the woman would be passionate and wild, Lia was certain of it. First of all, Quinn looked like it. Also, the sort of woman who was able to maintain such control over her emotions was bound to be spectacular when she finally let go...

"Hey there!" A smiling brunette came to stand in front of her, dressed in a similar wetsuit. "I'm Janet. First time with us, is it?"

"Yes." Lia grinned in return and she shook the hand that the woman offered. "I'm Lia."

She did not miss her appraising glance. *Ah. Right.* Plenty of good-looking lesbians in Lewiston then, apparently. Or at least, women who were open to same-sex connections. Lia was pretty sure that it was the case for Quinn too. She had felt her vibe, and no way was she straight. That did not necessarily mean that she was after a relationship, of course... Lia reminded herself that she was not in town for this kind of thing either. She'd come here to work. Hard. And to put her career back on track.

"Morning, ladies."

Mikey and another officer smiled hello as they walked past, both in *Lewiston P.D.* wetsuits and goggles around their neck. Seeing the branded gear reminded Lia that she had kept Quinn's hoodie. In spite of herself, her heart leapt at the notion that she'd have an excuse to go looking for her at some point. *For god's sake, Lia!* She shook herself. Now was not the time. *Not ever.* Several more swimmers had arrived now, and started a round of stretching.

"I'd better warm-up too," she said.

"Yes." Janet joined her in that. "So. New in town?"

Even at six a.m., and ahead of a bracing swim, the woman managed to make it sound like a pick-up line she'd deliver in a club, perhaps after a few drinks. Confident, for sure.

"Yep, a transfer from Boston," Lia offered.

"And you know Mikey. Are you a cop?"

"I'm a police reporter attached to the station. You?"

"I work at the hospital. I'm a neurosurgeon."

Lia smiled, genuinely impressed. Not just good-looking, but accomplished women around here, too...

"That's great," she nodded.

Janet stretched her arms above her head.

"Yeah, I like it. So, you know Quinn?"

Lia caught the subtle hint of impatience in her voice and she suddenly realized what this was about. Did Janet view her as competition? She held her gaze with a steady smile.

"Yeah, I know Quinn."

Before Janet could reply, Dave Myers, another cop from the station, bellowed a greeting.

"Alright everyone! Good morning!"

Lia turned to him. She was eager to focus on her swim and

not get involved in any discussions about the nature of her relationships. If she were honest, too, the idea of Quinn seeking solace in the arms of the beautiful surgeon did not sit well with her at all.

"So, welcome to the new guys," Dave said. "Todd, Lia..."

Lia gave a little wave to the group.

"Remember the safety rules: remain within the perimeter of the red buoys. Keep an eye on each other as you go. And have fun!"

"Well, it was nice to meet you, Lia," Janet said. "I'll see you later."

She sounded nice, albeit a little wary, and Lia flashed her a genuine smile. She was new in town, yes, and definitely not after ruffling people's feathers. Whatever Janet's connection to Quinn may be, it really was none of her business.

"You too, Janet." She squeezed her arm briefly. "Have a good swim."

Lia did enjoy her time in the water. For her, there really was nothing better than spending time in the middle of the ocean, connecting to raw nature, to feel grounded in a new place. She went home after the session, showered, ate a bowl of muesli, and turned on the News in the background. Then, she took her time unpacking. She did plan to spend a lot of her time at the station, but she understood the importance of having a welcoming place to go back to after being out in the field. Once everything was in place and the apartment tidy, she got on with some cooking. It was always nice to have meals ready in the freezer, as well, for when she felt like being lazy. Demi called just as she got started on a spicy bolognese sauce.

"Hey, girl. How you doing?"

"Great, thanks. I'm getting organized at home."

"Excellent. Just making sure you remember the barbecue is tomorrow?"

"Oh, sure, I wouldn't miss it." Lia meant that. Demi was lovely. Lia had enjoyed meeting her wife and kid and, although she used to prefer spending time on her own when she was not working in the past, she knew what would be best for her at this point. "What would you like me to bring?"

"Your choice of naughty," Demi laughed. "Alcohol or cake, you decide."

"I'll bring both," Lia declared.

"Perfect. See you tomorrow, darling."

CHAPTER 7

Demi's barbecues were always popular affairs, and a lot of fun for adults and younger ones alike. Mid-afternoon at her house, at the bottom of the spacious yard, a group of hardened cops were getting their asses kicked by a bunch of under-tens in a game of soccer. Swimming lessons were in full swing in one corner of the pool, supervised by Demi's wife, Carole, and one of her nurses friends. A few guests had laid out beach towels in a circle on the grass to enjoy a few drinks and a chat. Quinn did not mind socializing, but she preferred being busy. She had shown up at her friends' house early that morning to help with food prep and cleaning. Now, she was stretched out on a deck chair by the side of the pool, eyes closed behind her sunglasses, and drifting into a delicious torpor after only drinking half a beer.

"Hello, gorgeous…"

Quinn half-focused on the warm breath against the side of her face. A caress started on the sensitive spot behind her ear, went along her jaw, and trailed softly across her mouth. When fingers slipped under her t-shirt to caress the muscles in her stomach, she shivered in reaction.

"Don't wake up."

In addition, a gentle hand started to stroke the back of her neck and the top of her shoulder.

"Wanna lie on your stomach, baby?"

Quinn had put herself through a punishing workout first thing in the morning, and she was sorely tempted to move into position. Those talented fingers slid into her hair. *I should move.* This sort of treatment would make her drool if she was not careful, and probably something else, too. Yet, it felt too damn nice. The buzz of alcohol that she was not used to, sunshine, a sweet massage. She could not stop it yet. *Just another few sec—Oh, fuck!* Quinn bolted upright.

"Nice," Janet laughed. "Very nice!"

"Christ, Jan! Don't do that!"

"What, baby?"

Quinn whipped her glasses off to glare. Janet may think this was funny, but she did not.

"Grab me like that in front of everyone," Quinn enlightened her. "And kids!"

"No one's paying attention to us, don't worry."

"Well, no matter. Get your hand off my crotch, thank you."

Grinning, Janet released her, although her smile widened.

"Your nipples are hard, you know. Let's go home and I'll take care of you."

"No."

"Why not?"

"Because I'm not in the mood."

"Liar," Janet teased. "You can deny it all you like, but your body's talking loud and clear. I know you need this, Quinn, and so do I. Come on, let's go! I'm back on rotation tomorrow and I want to have fun today. With you."

"Jan, I really don't feel—"

Quinn froze in mid-sentence when she caught sight of Lia in the distance. She stood with Ethan and his soon-to-be-wife, Jenna. Ethan had his back turned, talking. Jen was laughing at something that he must have said. But Lia was not. *Not at all.* Her eyes were fixed on her and Janet, her mouth tight, her face a picture of disapproval. *Shit.* She looked pissed-off. Quinn had no idea why it should matter, but her stomach dropped.

"What?" Janet said impatiently. "Can't you at least—" Her eyes drifted to the group and back to Quinn, flashing in sudden curiosity. "Ah. I see. You're into the new woman in town?"

"Don't be ridiculous."

"Ooh." Janet grinned, back to teasing. "Twitchy, uh. You do have a thing for her."

"No, I do not," Quinn repeated, and she stood up. "I don't enjoy being fondled in public, that's all."

Before she could react, Janet grabbed her by the front of her t-shirt and landed a daring kiss over her mouth.

"You should chill, Quinn," she declared. "Really."

On that profound statement, she headed off to try her luck with one of the nurses. Meanwhile, Quinn watched Lia sit down with Jenna to enjoy the soccer game. She debated joining them, but decided it would be best not to. Feeling more irritated than she knew she should be at the little episode, she went to the kitchen in search of distraction.

"What can I do to help, Dem?"

Demi shot her a puzzled glance as she closed the fridge. She was holding a plate with a giant piece of cake in one hand, and a glass of wine in the other.

"Nothing!" she laughed. "Or do like me: grab something to eat, have a drink, and enjoy. That's the whole point of today, my dear; not endless chores, okay? Plus, you deserve it after all the work you did for us this morning."

"Uh-uh." Quinn zeroed in on an obvious task. "I'll take out the trash."

"What's wrong with giving yourself a break, for a change?"

"Nothing. And I was, until Janet assaulted me."

"Oh, is she on the prowl?" Demi chuckled.

"Yeah. On fire."

"You know she likes you, don't you?"

"Oh, really?" With an ironic snort, Quinn pointed through the open French doors. Out on the patio, Janet now sat straddling another woman's lap. She was alternating between feeding her pieces of strawberry, caressing her face, and nibbling at her mouth. "Janet likes women, period. Nothing to do with me specifically."

"Do you mind?"

"Of course not."

Demi nodded in approval at the two women.

"Seems like a lovely way to spend the afternoon, if you ask me." Quinn did not reply, although she agreed. It would be an exceedingly fine way of doing it, but not with Janet. Not today, anyway. She was wide awake now. Feeling restless. "Speaking of fine women, where's my wife?" Demi added in a mischievous tone.

"In the pool. Luke's playing soccer."

"And where's Lia?"

Quinn paused as she picked up the trash bags.

"Lia?" she repeated. "Why?"

"Not a trick question, Quinn," Demi shrugged. "She's new, and I just want to make sure she's enjoying herself and making friends."

"She seems to be doing just fine, yes," Quinn muttered.

"Everything okay between you two?"

"Of course, it is."

"She's nice, don't you think?"

"Yeah, very nice."

"Hold on," Demi said.

Quinn stopped again, met her friend's gaze, and found her grinning from ear to ear.

"What?" she prompted.

"I get the feeling that perhaps you wouldn't mind so much if it was our lovely Ms Kennedy assaulting you," Demi grinned. "Is that what's got you roaming around the place like a brooding lion? Sexual frustration?"

Quinn shook her head, laughing, even as her body agreed with the statement.

"Knock it off, Dem. I'm not roaming, I'm just being useful."

"Uh-uh, that you are. But I'm just wondering. I don't know, you seem kinda edgy."

Demi was only teasing. *For now,* Quinn reflected. In truth, the woman had a knack for reading people and figuring things out. She was also kind, and tremendously easy to talk to. Demi was the only person in fact, apart from her captain, who knew the story of what had happened to her in Iraq. Quinn both loved and trusted her, but she did not want to give her a chance to probe too deep under the hood. With a confident glance that she hoped did not reveal anything too compromising, she nodded.

"Go find your wife, Dem, and stop projecting on me."

"You're not leaving, are you?"

"No, I'll just do this and come join you."

"Alright, then," Demi approved. "Hurry up."

Quinn took her time with the job, actually. She was feeling unusually thoughtful. She'd been looking forward to seeing Lia again at the barbecue. This was strange in itself, and also tinged with trepidation. *So damn weird.* Quinn did not look forward to social events. And she certainly was never nervous ahead of one! Outside of work, she met women for a specific purpose, which did not involve much talking. But the conversation with Lia the other evening had been intense. The vibe, close and intimate on both sides. Quinn flashed a brief, pensive smile at the memory of Lia's touch. The woman was either naturally very tactile, or it was something else. Maybe both... Quinn had felt the heat of Lia's fleeting gestures. There was a hunger there. Obvious need, simmering just below the surface. Mystery, and her own secrets. When it came to that, Lia had challenged Quinn's usual reserve. In the car, after dinner, Quinn had been tempted to open up to her. She'd told Lia about Iraq, and being in the army... Only a few headlines, but it still felt like too much. In spite of that, Quinn had come to the barbecue looking forward to another encounter. Hoping... For what, she was not too sure. Perhaps, to experience more connection. Or to feel more butterflies in her stomach, whenever Lia rested her deep dark eyes on her. Quinn had caught her staring at her mouth a few times during dinner at the pizza place. Maybe, Quinn just wanted to feel warm fingers around her wrist again, as if Lia perceived her need for groundedness. And her craving to be held.

"Stop that, you idiot," she muttered.

Quinn wished that Lia had not witnessed Janet's antics with her and, even worse, her own initial reaction. Once again, she tried to convince herself that it did not matter. Or that it should not. But of course... It did.

••

Demi settled in between her wife's legs on the grass, and all but purred at her slice of carrot cake, hidden under a ton of added cream. She took a bite, closed her eyes, moaned in satisfaction.

"Ah... Yes! Isn't that the most delicious thing you ever put in your mouth, Car?"

Carole raised an interested, laughing eyebrow.

"Well," she mused. "Are we talking about food, or—"

"Stop," Demi warned. "Don't answer that question. Not in front of guests."

"You don't know what I was going to say, Dem."

"Nipples!" Demi giggled. "My nipples, to be precise. Am I correct?"

Carole bent to kiss a tiny spot of cream off her lips, and she grinned at Lia.

"She's right, you know. My gorgeous wife tastes better than cake, better than whisky, better even than—"

"Enough!" Demi ordered, shaking with laughter. "Be good, now. Sorry, Lia! We try to behave, but it's very hard. And I'm not often very motivated."

"No," Lia smiled. "Don't apologize for being so in love and letting it show. You two are gorgeous and a real pleasure to be around. Also, I like nipples too, you know."

Demi sat up, eyes twinkling in curiosity.

"Whose?" she demanded. "Tell me, I won't repeat."

"No specifics at the moment," Lia chuckled. "But I'll keep you posted." She spotted Janet in the distance, kissing a woman who was not Quinn, and felt instantly better. "Janet's a bit of a flirt, isn't she?"

"You don't say." Carole glanced over her shoulder, and she turned back with a gentle smile. "That's typical Jan for you. She plays hard but trust me, she's also an extremely gifted surgeon.

God forbid but, if anything ever happened to me or my family, I'd want her in charge. No question."

"That's great to hear."

"How do you know Janet, Lia?" Demi inquired.

"I met her before a swim with my training group the other morning. She asked me if I knew Quinn. I got a feeling the two of them might be close."

"Huh-uh." Demi grinned, neither confirming nor denying the feeling. "I see."

Lia realized that she was being less than subtle about it, and it was outrageous to even be asking; but she could not help it. She wanted to know.

"I just wondered," she shrugged.

"You're interested in Quinn?" Carole asked.

"No, no..." Lia winced when she noticed the defensive tone of her own reply. "I, uh... I'm just curious, I guess. Getting to know people."

"Right." Carole flashed her a warm, if slightly disbelieving smile, and squeezed her shoulder as she stood up. "Excuse me, ladies, I'm just going to go and check on our young Luke over there."

Once she was gone, Lia must have looked miserable enough that Demi decided to put her out of her misery.

"Quinn is single," she declared. "But only human, if you see what I mean, and despite what she seems to believe. She and Jan also happen to live in the same apartment building. I think they had some fun, once or twice. But nothing serious or long-term between them other than friendship."

"I thought it might be something like that," Lia murmured, as Janet and her conquest headed out with their arms around each other. She thought of making it clear, again, that she was not interested. In Quinn, or anyone else. Happily single, too. But something Demi had said made her ask. "What do you mean, *'she's human despite what she seems to believe'*?"

"Oh, just the usual," Demi smiled. "Look out there today: we've got cops, firefighters, docs, nurses... All wonderful people. The selfless, heroic kind who think nothing of putting their own life on hold, or even on the line, in service to others. Janet may appear a bit wild, but don't let that fool you. She's always ready to go at a moment's notice and do what it takes to save a life, no matter what. So is my wife..."

CHAPTER
8

Lia noticed the sparkle in Demi's gaze when she looked in the distance to where her wife stood with their young son. Carole was making sure that he stayed hydrated, by the looks of it. And nodding enthusiastically, as well, as he demonstrated to her a good pass that he had made. Demi's expression was a mixture of fierce and loving, affectionate and proud. Lia felt her heart tighten and she averted her eyes. The woman that she wanted to marry had never looked at her like this. Not even once. *And neither did I.* Not for the first time, Lia reflected on how lucky she actually was that the relationship had not survived her father's illness. Better to be on her own than settle for less. If she could not have what she saw in Demi's face for her wife, she wanted none of it.

"...Quinn, you know?"

Lia jerked her head up at the mention of Quinn.

"Sorry, Demi. What was that?"

"I said, Quinn is one of the worst for that, going all-in for the greater good. If it was up to her, she'd live at the station." Demi gave a gentle chuckle. "She was on her way to doing just that, actually, a little while back. But the captain intervened. He's a good guy, too. Takes care of his troops."

Lia looked at her, biting on her lip.

"Quinn seems very intense."

"She is. You two are very similar in that way."

"Oh?"

"Yes." Demi's eyes crinkled as she smiled. "Intense and mysterious. That's okay, by the way. But you know, we're a tight group. And you're with us now, Lia. I hope you know you're among friends."

"I know, yes." Lia actually felt it deep inside, a wonderful sense of belonging. "And in no small part thanks to you, Demi. Thank you for inviting me today. And for making me feel so welcome at work too."

"No problem. I know what you intend to accomplish with your work, and I am one-hundred percent in support. Now then, would you mind if I—" A sharp cry interrupted, both women turned to look, and all the color drained from Demi's face. "Oh, no!"

They rushed over to where Luke, and a girl of about his age in a Manchester United shirt, were on the ground. Both looking slightly dazed and confused, although not crying yet, but with blood running down their faces.

"What happened?" Demi exclaimed.

"One ball, two heads going for it," Mikey explained, as he held his daughter. "They almost knocked each other out. Can't fault 'em for enthusiasm."

The girl's left eye was almost swollen shut already, and she bled from a cut on her forehead. As Demi cradled their son in her arms, Carole performed basic neuro-checks on them both.

"How you feeling, Skyler?" she asked.

"Okay," the girl sniffed. "I'm sorry I hurt Luke…"

"Don't worry, sweetie, Luke will be fine," Mikey promised.

But when Carole carefully palpated the sides of her son's bloody nose, he screamed and burst into tears. Demi winced.

"Shh... It's okay, baby, it's okay..."

"I don't think your nose is broken, son," Carole advised in a soothing voice. "But we'll swing by mommy's work and make sure of it, okay?"

"'Kay," the kid murmured. "Can Skyler come with us?"

"I think that's a very good idea, yes. Mikey?"

"Roger that," he nodded. "I'll drive. Kids, we'll get you ice-cream afterwards, okay?"

"Ben & Jerry's?" Skyler asked, squinting hopefully through her swollen eye.

"Anything you want."

Lia smiled as both kids flashed a thumbs-up at each other. Perking up now that treats had been mentioned. They made for a cute pair, despite the blood involved.

"Car, you go ahead with Luke," Demi said. "I need to take care of things here before I can—"

"Leave it with me, Dem," a warm, strong voice replied. Lia almost held her breath as Quinn materialized by her side. "I'll tidy up and lock the house for you."

"I'll help," Lia offered.

"Thanks, girls," Carole smiled. "Appreciate it."

Walking off with Luke in her arms, Demi shot them both a wry look over her shoulder.

"Have fun, you two!"

●●

Not surprisingly, more people volunteered to help with the tidy-up, and it was quickly done. After everyone left, Quinn finished hosing down the patio. She locked the backyard door, wheeled the Traeger that she had just cleaned into the garage, and turned at the sound of someone dribbling a ball. Lia was still there.

"Hey, Quinn," she smiled.

She looked lovely in a pair of cargo shorts that highlighted slender, athletic legs, and a red Nike tank top that did the same for her upper body. Quinn tried not to linger in contemplation, although it was hard.

"Hey," she nodded.

Lia bounced the ball one last time, lined up a shot from the three-point line, and sent the ball clean through the hoop. Quinn caught it on the rebound.

"Nice."

"Yep," Lia grinned.

Quinn chuckled at her smug tone.

"Can you do it again?"

"Want to try and stop me?"

"You're on," Quinn approved. "My start."

Quick as a flash, still grinning wide, Lia stole the ball before Quinn could even complete a second bounce. She dropped her shoulder, skipped past her on the left, aimed, and let her fly. The ball did not even touch the sides of the basket.

"Too slow," she laughed.

"I wasn't ready, to be fair."

"That's a poor excuse."

"Oh, you think so?"

"Yeah. Try harder."

Quinn grabbed the ball as Lia attempted to sneak past her a second time, she spun around, and dunked a perfect shot. She chuckled at Lia's outraged expression.

"What? You said try harder."

"Alright. Now, we're on!"

The next fifteen minutes had them matching each other shot for shot, until the final one. Quinn was in possession of the ball. She was about to shoot a three-pointer, and Lia jumped to intercept. She managed to get her fingertips on the ball and send it off wide, but stumbled upon landing and started to fall backwards. There would be no coming back from that one. Quinn realized that, and tried to catch her; but unfortunately, she also lost her balance in the attempt. She was just able to slip an arm around her waist, and cup the back of Lia's head to protect her from contact with the tarmac. They hit the ground hard and rolled.

"Uhmpf!"

Quinn could not suppress a groan, as red-hot pain erupted in the middle of her elbow and shot down the length of her forearm. Her stomach twisted in response, and she gritted her teeth to contain the reaction.

"Quinn? Hey, are you okay?"

As Quinn refocused, she found Lia's eyes on her. Burning. In spite of the pain, she instantly became aware of a whole different set of sensations in her body. Lia had wrapped her arms around her neck during the fall, and she still had her in a tight lock. Her right hand moved to the side of her face.

"Quinn?"

Quinn remained speechless. She lay on top of Lia with her right leg sandwiched in between hers. Pressing close. And once again, as fate would have it, close enough to kiss as well. She did her best not to stare at Lia's mouth, but it was a losing battle at this point. If she lowered her head a bit more, their lips would be touching. If she moved her leg, even just a fraction upwards, the contact would become even more intimate. Quinn tried to stay still but that was a problem, too. She could feel her own heart pounding. Her cheek was on fire where Lia's fingers were still resting, and all she wanted to do was to close her eyes, and lose herself in the feeling. In feeling *her*.

"Quinn," Lia repeated. "Are you hurt? Talk to me."

••

Quinn had just saved her from smashing her skull on asphalt. Rough landing, all the same, and she had absorbed a lot of the impact. So, Lia wanted to make sure. When Quinn did not answer, she stared into her eyes and attempted to make sense of it. Like watching summer clouds rolling over wide open country, every tiny shift in Quinn's mood and feeling was expressed in a subtle change of color. Her eyes went from limpid blue to stormy, transparent to hazy, back to fierce and hyper-focused. Lia had caught a flare of pain in her expression earlier. It was gone now, and Quinn was watching her almost as if she'd gone into a trance. With her emotions in plain sight for once, and a flush of color in her cheeks, she was even more gorgeous than usual. When Lia shifted under her, Quinn almost gasped. Lia ached for more contact. She wanted to rub her thumb over her lips. Hook her ankle behind her leg. Lift her hips and roll on top of her. Good thing her concern kept her sane. Good thing also that Quinn showed restraint by remaining so still. Lia moved her fingers off her face. Dropped the arm that she'd kept around her neck. And felt instantly cold when Quinn rolled off of her.

"Let me see," she demanded.

"I'm fine," Quinn finally answered.

She sat cradling her elbow in her hand, but Lia also noticed that she was watching her with an amused grin. Relieved to see her smile, she pointed her chin at her.

"What?"

"You." Quinn's smile widened and grew thoughtful at the same time. "You're fierce with a ball in your hands, uh?"

"And you're missing half the skin on your forearms," Lia stated, because it was easier to focus on that than on the heat in her belly. "I'm sorry. That's my fault."

"Ah." Quinn slowly flexed her arm. "It's not too bad."

"You need some ice on your elbow. And your knuckles are bleeding."

"Just scrapes, but ice is a good idea. How's your head, Lia?"

"It's fine. I didn't hit."

"Anything else hurt?"

"No, thanks to you. Thank you for catching me." *You felt so damn good!*

"No problem."

Quinn continued to stare as if she could see the thoughts inside her head, and Lia could not resist taking her good hand in hers, to lead her back into the kitchen.

"Do you know if Demi and Carole have a First-Aid kit in here?" she asked.

"Uh, yeah... Under the sink, I think."

"Sit down then, Quinn. I'll get it for you."

"Hey, it's okay, I can—"

"Please, indulge me. I feel guilty."

Quinn chuckled, although she did find herself a stool and waited as instructed.

"Why?" she asked. "I'd understand if you didn't feel good about losing the game, but falling over is nothing to feel guilty about. Oh, don't forget ice, please."

Lia located the emergency kit and found a pack of ice cubes in the freezer. She wrapped that up in a tea towel. Quinn's eyes were warm on her face as she joined her, as was the handsome smile dancing on her lips. Lia handed her the ice, trying not to get caught in her eyes again.

"Here you go. This should help with the swelling."

"Thank you." Quinn placed the improvised ice pack on the counter and rested her elbow on it with only a small wince. "It should do the trick."

"Good. By the way, what makes you think I lost the game?" Lia inquired.

"Um, let's see." Quinn's voice was just the right amount of mischievous. "Keeping score, maybe? I was clear ahead at that point."

Lia opened the emergency kit and she raised an ironic eyebrow. No matter how attractive Quinn may look at that very moment, some things needed to be kept straight.

"Maybe we should check your head if you really believe that," she declared. "We were even at that stage, Officer Wesley, and you missed that last shot. I was about to bury you into the ground."

Quinn's eyes twinkled with amusement.

"Bury me? I don't think so, Ms Kennedy."

She was laughing, obviously having fun teasing and being teased in return, and Lia resisted the urge to grab her chin and kiss her. *What in the world is happening to me?* Her reaction to Quinn was not the norm, and puzzling. *Maybe it's been too long since I was with a woman...* And especially such a good-looking one. Lia put it down to that, and the fact that Quinn Wesley ticked all of her boxes. From her looks to her personality, her choice of career, the protective vibe that oozed out of her, and even the way that she dressed. Lia liked those faded Levis' on her, torn at the knees to offer tantalizing glimpses of tanned skin underneath. The black t-shirt with a local gym logo on the chest, stretched tight across her shoulders, was very nice too. Quinn continued to smile, as if she did not mind being appraised. Lia took a settling breath and she grabbed a spray of disinfectant.

"This is going to sting a bit."

"Yeah. I think I can take it."

"I'm sure you can," Lia smiled. "Be brave and I'll buy you ice-cream afterwards."

CHAPTER
9

Quinn knew for certain that she would not be sitting there still if it had been someone else fussing over her. But it was Lia. And Lia made her feel... *Well*. Perhaps that was the thing. Lia made her feel, period. She was flirting, Quinn knew. The woman may not even be aware of it. It was very subtle; but she was flirting nonetheless. Cracking sweet jokes. Teasing. Showing genuine concern and wanting to look after her. Just being kind, really. It was a very long time since Quinn had allowed a woman to be that way with her. If she ever went back to someone's place, she never spent the night. She did not send flowers the next day or follow up with a dinner invite. And for the most part, no one ever expected any different from her. Once in a while, a woman may suggest something more permanent, but Quinn's answer was always the same. *I don't want a relationship.* Why, then, did she feel the need to linger around Lia so much? The simple fact that she was a reporter should have put her off. Quinn stiffened at the thought.

"Okay?" Lia murmured.

"Yes, fine."

"You've gone very quiet on me."

Quinn registered that she was standing very close again, looking at her with a gentle smile. From her sitting position on the stool, Quinn could have easily rested both hands over her hips and pulled her closer. Her face would be level with Lia's breasts, then. She blinked to clear her mind of that image, too.

"Just pondering which flavor ice-cream to go for."

"Ah, yes." Lia held her gaze, her smile turning wistful. Not fooled by that answer, Quinn realized, but wise enough not to challenge her on it. "Stay still."

Quinn stared at her own arm while Lia applied disinfectant. It would be too rude to indulge in what she really wanted to do, which was to look at her. To study the elegant line of her jaw, observe the mix of gold and green in her irises, and imagine what it would feel like to press her mouth over her full, blood-red lips...

"Now lift your arm a little, so I can see under?"

Quinn flexed her right arm again.

"Gosh, Quinn," Lia frowned in dismay. "Your elbow's all black and blue. And swollen. Are you sure nothing's broken?"

"Yeah, it's fine. The ice is doing its job. I'll just—"

"Hold on." Lia settled both hands over her shoulders when Quinn started to rise. "I don't think we're done yet. Your hand's still bleeding."

Not really... Just a trickle of it, and a few more scrapes. Not worth a second glance, as far as Quinn was concerned. It would not be the first time that her knuckles got smashed. Probably not the last either. But Lia did not ask for permission. She stepped forward to stand in between her legs now, and Quinn shivered a little too hard in response.

"What's going on?" Lia asked.

"Nothing."

Quinn could feel heat coming off of Lia's body. She could smell her: vanilla and sunshine. A hint of lavender. Warm skin. Quinn gripped her own leg with her good hand in order not to reach for her this time. Something told her the gesture might not be well received. Or maybe, it would. But either way... *I don't want to go there. I can't.* She did close her eyes, needing to steady herself. Lia noticed and misinterpreted the reaction.

"Dammit, Quinn, you're not well!"

"I'm perfectly fine." Quinn chuckled, feeling better for it. It broke the spell, which was no bad thing. "Stop fretting, will you? You didn't break me."

Lia frowned, a mix of disbelieving and irritated.

"Then let me finish, please," she argued. "In case you didn't realize, I'm trying to be helpful here."

"I did realize, yes," Quinn grinned. "And you are. I'm very grateful."

"Hold steady."

"Ten-four."

More disinfectant was sprayed, stinging and other feelings stoically endured, and Lia dabbed at her scraped-up knuckles with a cotton ball. Her grip was gentle and firm as she held her wrist, and Quinn could not help looking at her this time. Lia did not seem to notice. She appeared a lot more focused and intent than the injury warranted. Quinn wondered about that, and she recalled the things that Lia had said about her last three years. She had been brief and to the point when talking about her father, emotionless, but it was still enough for Quinn to understand that she must have been very close to him. Only six weeks since he had passed; no doubt Lia must still be grieving. Perhaps this little incident was touching her deeper than it normally would, and Quinn resolved to go easy with the joking.

"There you are." Lia flashed a more hesitant look. "Sorry to make such a fuss."

Because she so readily admitted vulnerability, Quinn found it easier to be honest in return.

"No," she murmured. "I appreciate your help."

"Good. I'm no surgeon, but…" Lia allowed that sentence to go unfinished, and just concluded with a brief shrug. "I hope it's not too sore in the morning."

Was she alluding to Janet with that comment? Quinn did not want to presume, or launch into an explanation of the kiss that Lia must have witnessed earlier. Janet also did not deserve to be talked about as if she were just a random girl of no importance. Quinn might not want any long-term thing, but her respect for the surgeon was never in doubt. So, she remained silent. But as Lia started to let go, she held softly onto her fingers. Lia had grown withdrawn all of a sudden. Distant. Sad, even. Quinn did not want to end on this note.

"Are *you* okay, Lia?"

"Yes… Thank you for asking."

"Of course. No problem."

"You should ice that elbow again when you get home."

"I will. Let's have a rematch soon," Quinn added, hoping to get back onto happier ground. "So that there's no doubt in your mind who's the better player."

Good attempt, and Lia's left eyebrow shot up in reaction.

"If you like," she said. "But your first attempt to prove yourself left you bleeding on the floor, so…"

Ah, welcome back. Quinn smiled, knowing it was probably safe to answer that one.

"Only because I had to save you from falling," she retorted. "I am sworn to serve and protect, as you well know."

"Uh-uh." Lia finally laughed, and something inside Quinn's chest settled nicely. "Okay, we'll have a rematch if you insist. At the risk of breaking your heart, Quinn, or making you cry."

"Don't worry, I'm tougher than I look."

"Good. You'll need it. For now, I should go."

"Sure."

Quinn released her and stood up. But although Lia had just announced that she was going, she did not move or take a step back. The two women stood in silence, gazes locked, their thighs almost touching. Quinn unconsciously held her breath while she watched Lia's lips slowly part and her eyelids grow heavy. Lia's eyes were fastened onto her mouth again, her expression intent. Quinn could not fail to recognize the signs of arousal, and her legs wobbled in response.

"Lia."

"Quinn…" Lia murmured.

"Ladies!" a voice boomed out from across the kitchen. Quinn jumped, startled, feeling as if she were waking from a dream. She glanced aside. Demi was leaning against the door with her arms crossed and a smug expression on her face. "Sorry to break the spell, but we're back."

●●

A few days later, in the office, Demi came to find her.

"So, how are you surviving, my dear?"

Lia looked up valiantly from her laptop.

"Ah… Pretty well, I think. I'm updating the website and our social media accounts with some of my latest footage. Also, I'm working on my pitch for a series documentary that I'd like to introduce to Captain Wilson. How are you doing, Dem?"

Demi laughed, face glistening with the effect of AC failure at the start of what the met office promised would be a killer of a heatwave.

"Sweltering, like we all are, but in awe of your trooper's attitude! The AC company confirmed they'll have a team over ASAP, which could mean everything from today to sometime by the end of the week, knowing them."

"Ah," Lia shrugged diplomatically. "Okay." She had all but forgotten about the heat while focusing on her work, and now she accepted the ice-cold can of lemonade that Demi handed to her with a grateful nod. "Thanks."

Demi sat in front of a free-standing fan in the middle of the aisle.

"Glad the job's going well for you," she approved. "Is it all you expected it to be then?"

"Turning out to be even better, actually," Lia reflected.

"Awesome! How come?"

"Well, virtually no constraints or censorship..."

"Always a good one," Demi chuckled.

"Yes. And I am finding my feet with social media as well. I was never a big fan in the past, but I'm discovering new ways to use those tools that are beneficial. Our YouTube channel needs dusting out and re-branding, by the way."

"It sure does. And then?"

"Short, impactful videos focusing on the day-to-day life of our officers should help to create a sense of community with our viewers," Lia stated. "What do you think?"

"For sure," Demi approved. "Mainstream media are often less than kind about the police and the work that we do. Even to the point of outright bias. It's harmful... Sometimes, I wonder if it's even legal!"

Lia recalled a similar conversation she'd had with Quinn on the subject.

"I agree, yes," she nodded.

"If you allow a sort of behind-the-scenes look at us," Demi smiled, "I think it would be very helpful to encourage a sense of connection between the public and our officers."

"That's it, yes. Quite different to the way I approached my work before, when I was shooting segments for the networks..." Lia did not linger on that. New life, new ways. And she meant it; this job had a lot of potential, she'd been given free rein, more or less, and it was up to her what she made of it. "There's so much I can do here. I'm excited. It's going to be good."

"Fabulous. And that idea for a series?"

"I'd like to focus on specific officers..."

Lia paused to listen to a burst of radio chatter on the police scanner in the background.

'All units: prowler reported at 410 Nelson Rd. Female caller says a white male is circling the house and has now entered the yard. He's wearing jeans and a red t-shirt. Around 6'3. No weapon seen.'

'Roger, Dispatch. 2-Alpha-7, on my way.'

Quinn was responding, and Lia's attention sharpened. She liked to leave the scanner on when she worked in the office. It kept her connected to the officers on the ground, and informed of what was going on. She would hear Quinn from time to time, and that was nice as well. Her voice always stood out from all the others. As this reminded Lia of the other night, after the barbecue, she felt uncomfortable with the heat for the first time. Demi needed no other prompting to shift the conversation.

"Have you seen her recently?"

Her. Lia considered asking who, playing innocent, but Demi was no fool. So, she tried for a casual shrug instead.

"I bumped into her a couple of times, yes."

'Dispatch, I'm at the property.'

"Ten-four, 2-Alpha. Caller says she lost sight of the guy. She's armed, by the way.'

'I'll have a look. Please make sure that she knows I'm here, and tell her to stay inside.'

'Roger that.'

Quinn sounded in control, as always, but Lia tensed in spite of herself. This call might turn out to be absolutely nothing, but she knew that every single one was potentially dangerous. She thought of a spooked stranger armed with a gun, and the things that might go wrong.

"How's she doing?" Demi asked, oblivious.

"Uh, fine," Lia replied. "But we didn't chat for long."

Just barely enough time to exchange a few words, nothing of substance, and Quinn was flying out the door again. Lia knew not to take it personally. She was busy as well, and liked it that way. But she could not deny that the more those brief moments happened, the more she craved longer times with Quinn.

'2-Alpha, the caller advised that she can hear noise near her back door now,' the dispatcher announced. A bunch of static ensued. '2-Alpha-7? Wesley, do you read?'

Lia held her breath.

CHAPTER 10

Quinn spotted the guy by the back door, crawling in the bushes on his hands and knees. Tall, blue-jeans, red t-shirt. She stopped, weapon drawn but pointed at the ground. Ready for anything, as she announced her presence, but not overly aggressive, which never helped.

"Police," she warned. "Turn around slowly."

"Come on, baby," the guy crooned.

Frowning at the unusual reply, Quinn glanced toward the house to catch an old woman peering through the window, and pointing at the guy with an irate finger. Quinn acknowledged the gesture, and she was about to repeat her order when the man did turn around to face her.

"Say hello, pup," he grinned. "Hello, Officer! Woof!"

In his arms, the so-called dangerous intruder held the cutest puppy. Now, he took hold of his paw and made it look as if the puppy were waving at her. Quinn suppressed an amused smile and a roll of the eyes. She slowly holstered her weapon.

"2-Alpha-7? Wesley, do you read?"

"Yes, situation all clear," Quinn replied, and she nodded to the guy. "Lost your dog, sir?"

"Yes." His grin turned sheepish. "Sorry, Officer. This bad boy ran off across the street, and I was just—"

"What are you doing in my yard?" an angry voice shrieked. "Oh my god!"

The man paled and he promptly stepped behind Quinn for cover. Probably emboldened by her presence, the old woman had come out of her kitchen. She was now waving an ominous-looking Colt .45 in the air. Not looking too steady with it either, and Quinn realized that she may have spoken too soon with the All-clear. She turned to fully face the furious home-owner and raised a calming hand.

"Ma'am, put that down."

"That's mine."

"Fine. Just put it down for me please."

The woman lowered the weapon slightly and glared past her at the puppy hunter.

"What you got there? I don't want cats in my backyard!"

Christ! She can't even see that far? Quinn was done asking, and she knew it would not take much to disarm this one. Without hesitation, she stepped forward, grabbed the Colt, and twisted it out of her hand.

"Ow!" the woman screamed. "What are you doing?"

"Ma'am, get back in the house, please."

"I'm the victim here, Officer!"

"Hey, can I go?" doggie-man inquired glumly.

"Wait for me out front, please," Quinn instructed.

"Give me my weapon back, or I will report you to Internal Affairs," the woman threatened, as she led her back inside the house.

Clearly still scared, she was shaking like a leaf. Quinn was keen not to upset her even more.

"Have a seat for me, please," she invited with a smile. "Can I get you a glass of water, or anything else? How are you doing, ma'am?"

Her respectful tone finally resulted in the woman calming down a bit.

"I was so frightened," she admitted, on the verge of tears. "I live on my own since my husband passed away. The fence needs fixing. I saw this man crawling around, and I... I was so scared; I didn't know what to do!"

"You did the right thing by staying in and calling us. Now, about this gun..."

"It's my husband's. My dear Anthony was an army guy." She smiled at a picture on the windowsill. "Ain't he handsome in his uniform?"

"Very handsome," Quinn approved. "I was in the Forces for a while, too."

"Really? Good girl!"

Pacified now, the woman all but patted her on the head.

"Thanks. Do you have a permit for this weapon, ma'am?"

"No... I'm afraid I don't."

"Then you know what I'm going to say, right?"

The woman nodded with a tired shrug.

"Sadly, yes. Although I think it might be for the best, if you took the darn thing away from me. Knowing my luck, I might end up shooting myself in the foot. Or someone else. I don't see all that well."

"Yes. We don't want an accident."

"But if I need to defend myself..."

"If you do, then call us," Quinn said softly. "We'll be there quick, like I was today."

"Yes... Yes, you did okay. Thank you, dear."

Quinn got her a glass of water and a blanket. She checked that the Colt was the only weapon registered at the house, and took it with her when she left. Puppy-guy was waiting next to her car, and keen to find out what was going on.

"Is she okay?" he asked as soon as Quinn joined him.

"Yeah, but not thanks to you, uh?"

"I'm sorry. I just didn't think."

"Yeah, I get that. It was an innocent mistake but you scared her out of her wits, and you could have got yourself shot." She scratched the puppy under his chin and got herself a lick. "Keep this one on a leash, from now on, and stay out of people's yards, okay?"

"Sure. Thank you. I think I'll buy some flowers and go over to apologize, in a bit."

"Nice one," Quinn approved. "Make sure to use the front door this time."

"Ah! You bet!"

It was nice, every once in a while, to be able to help genuine people who got into trouble for doing dumb people things. Like running after cute puppies. Easy stuff. *Lia would have loved to witness this one...* Quinn headed back toward the station as she approached the end of her shift. She'd been thinking of Lia at odd times. In between jobs. While she ate lunch in her car, or during her morning runs to work. Late at night, too, when she lay naked in her bed. The memory of that evening at Demi's was firmly imprinted on her mind. They'd been about to kiss when Demi had walked in, Quinn was sure of it. Hell, she still wanted to! If she let her mind wander, she could imagine even more. But where her usual fantasies stopped with the physical, it went far beyond that when she imagined spending more time with Lia. The reporter had been to Iraq. She would know— *No. Don't.*

Quinn gritted her teeth and forced her musings to a screeching stop. No, actually. Lia would know nothing about what it had been like for her over there. Quinn blew air out to steady herself as she turned into the station lot. *Just drop it.* The urge to open up and share was probably only natural. Lia was a powerful trigger, after all, just for being an attractive woman who seemed to like her. Nobody's fault. Quinn headed straight to the locker room, changed into her running gear, and headed home to cool off. *No problem.* And indeed, the next morning started off just fine. Good workout, nice strong coffee, and the AC was back on. No difference to Quinn, who spent her days out in the heat anyway, but Demi and her people were pleased, and it was nice to see them all smiling. Lia sat at the front of the room during morning briefing. Quinn remained standing at the back the way she often did. Just a regular morning, and nothing of note to report from the previous shift. Wilson was about to send everyone to their duties when he nodded to her.

"Oh, Wesley."

"Sir?"

"Take Kennedy with you today."

Quinn flinched and almost dropped her coffee at the order. She opened her mouth to speak but nothing came out. She did catch Lia's blazing smile from across the crowded room, and her heart skipped a beat. *Dammit.* Quinn ignored Lia as the room started to empty, and she went straight after Wilson.

"Sir, may I have a word?"

"Sure." He waved her into his office. "What's up, Wesley?"

Quinn did not like to complain, and arguing orders was not her style either. The AC may as well still be broken, too, because she was sweating bullets.

"About Ms Kennedy, sir," she started.

"Uh-uh? Yes?"

Quinn did not often waste her captain's time; as in, *Never*. And she had his full attention now. She swallowed.

"Um. You know, I normally ride alone…"

"Yes," he nodded. "Unless I tell you to do otherwise."

Just stating a fact, as if he were commenting on the weather or something equally inane, but the remark made her feel like a rookie. And if there was one thing that Quinn disliked, it was this. Of course, she only had herself to blame for it. Act like an idiot, get treated like one.

"Roger that," she acknowledged. "Yes, sir."

He called her back as she was about to leave.

"Hey, Wesley." She turned. "Something I should know?"

The question was not unfriendly, but loaded. Even though he left it vague, she still got the message loud and clear. *Can you handle it or not?* And of course, he knew her background.

"No, everything's fine," she assured him.

"I hear she's been excellent with the other teams. She's alert, unobtrusive, and doesn't need baby-sitting. From what I've seen of it so far, she's doing a cracking job, too."

This was praise indeed, and Quinn was pleased to hear that Lia was doing well. There was only one thing left for it.

"I'd better get going then."

"Agreed," Wilson replied.

Quinn found Lia in the office, filling up a bottle of water. No Demi in sight, which was a relief. She could do without any clever remarks this morning.

"I'm ready, Quinn," Lia said as soon as she saw her.

Quinn's mind went blank at the sight of her. It was already hot out, and Lia was dressed like the other day in cargo shorts. Running shoes on her feet, and a white t-shirt, untucked. A pair of Aviator sunglasses hung from her collar, and a black *Lewiston P.D.* baseball cap completed the attire. She looked like a rugged professional. Tough, sexy. Quinn bit on her lip, frowning lightly.

"Something wrong?" Lia wanted to know.

The question brought Quinn back to her senses.

"Where's your Kevlar?" she asked.

Lia picked it up off her desk.

"Just putting it on now." She passed the vest over her head and secured the straps. No fumbling, quick and precise. She was obviously practiced with this sort of thing. Quinn watched her throw her rucksack over a shoulder, and Lia flashed an excited smile. "All set. Shall we, Officer?"

Damn, she was attractive! Quinn was torn between wanting to tell her to stay put, and dealing with her captain's wrath later; and feeling excited as well at the notion of spending the entire day with Lia in the car. *Better get your damn head straight, Wesley.* This was duty, not a day out. Quinn dropped her Oakleys over her eyes and she nodded. *Roger that.*

"Yes. Let's go."

••

Lia buckled up on the passenger seat next to Quinn, reflecting on this sudden twist of fate. She'd been putting off asking to ride with her, because… Well. *Just because.* Lia was no blushing schoolgirl, by any means, but hanging around Quinn still did peculiar things to her system. Every time she bumped into her, her heart raced and she always missed a breath. After the other night at Demi's, she had purposefully avoided her. Not that she liked doing it… Just the opposite. And it left her feeling puzzled, really. How could you miss a woman that you barely even knew? Still, she did. A bit on the pathetic side, but true. And sitting next to Quinn was by far the most exciting thing she'd done in a long time. *Besides almost kissing her...* Lia could not help but shiver at the memory. She stole a glance at her as Quinn drove them out of the parking lot. Hard muscles, strong features, and the often-serious expression on her face went well with the police badge and weapon. But Quinn's windswept blond hair and disarming smile betrayed a different side of her at unexpected moments. A softer, warmer side. Under the Kevlar vest, her conditioning had not erased small but full breasts. Lia remembered the feel of Quinn's body on top of hers after the fall. She'd breathed her in, hot skin and a hint of sweat. She had felt her breasts molded against hers. They fitted together like two pieces of a puzzle. Looking into Quinn's fierce blue eyes, Lia had known for sure that she'd welcome the kiss. Quinn had seemed on the edge of bursting into flames. So had Lia. Even now, she could feel her heart racing. Being alone with Quinn was special. And not just because she was so handsome.

"Everything okay, Lia?"

Lia could not read her eyes behind the sunglasses.

"Yes," she nodded. "And you?"

"Yeah."

Quinn radiated tension. Lia suspected that she knew why.

"Hey, I didn't ask Wilson to ride with you, you know?"

"No. I didn't know."

"Well, now you do. I was planning to ask you first before I confirmed with him." Quinn sighed and she rolled her neck. "Is this not okay, Quinn?" Lia insisted.

"It's..." Another sigh. "I was surprised, that's all."

"It's what? What were you going to say?"

"I like to work alone."

"I won't get in your way, I promise."

"I know that. I just…" Quinn bit on her lip as if she'd again let slip more than she wanted. "Never mind. I guess it's just for today, uh?"

CHAPTER
11

Seeing the incredibly self-possessed woman flustered was a new experience for Lia, and not at all unpleasant. It occurred to her, with a jolt of surprise and pleasure, that she would quite enjoy causing a bit more of this sort of confusion. In a different way, of course... She eyed Quinn's chiseled profile, the strong line of her jaw, and she felt the impulse to caress the strands of rich blond hair at the back of her neck.

"Yes?" Quinn prompted impatiently.

"What?" Lia murmured, startled. *What is she asking me?*

"Just for today. Right?"

"Oh, yeah. Um... Probably." Lia was eager to reassure, but not willing to compromise further needs or opportunities. "You mind if I ask you a question?"

Quinn's body language said she did. Very much so. Yet, she did not admit to it.

"Go ahead," she replied, eyes fixed on the road in front.

"Why do you prefer working on your own?"

"Because I only have myself to worry about, then."

"But you attend calls with other officers, right? All the time. That's how it works."

"Yeah, I do."

"So…"

"It's not the same, Lia."

Quinn spoke in a quiet voice that belied her inner agitation. It also indicated that the matter was closed, and Lia was not foolish enough to try to push. Or at least, not now, or overtly.

"Okay," she nodded. "Well, thanks for letting me ride with you on this one. I appreciate it."

Quinn gave a nonplussed shrug.

"Can't promise it'll be super-useful. Probably just more of the same thing you already experienced with the other teams."

"Hell, no. I don't think so," Lia blurted out.

She could not help herself, nor the look that she gave Quinn at the same time. It was done before she was aware of it, and both words and tone conveyed her meaning loud and clear: *Not the same when I'm with you.* Quinn pushed her Oakleys on top of her head and shot her another glance. This time, an involuntary smile flickered on the corner of her mouth.

"Thanks," she murmured.

It required every ounce of willpower Lia possessed not to reach over and cup her face in her hand. Everything about Quinn invited this sort of thing. Touching… And lots of it. *Steady up, Lia!* Quinn's intense blue eyes swirled with a bunch of fleeting emotions, all of them too fast for Lia to identify. The Oakleys promptly went down again.

"Let's do this thing, okay?"

"Ten-four," Lia replied, earning herself a smile.

They drove around for fifteen minutes before the first call came through. Something about two women involved in a fight at a nearby gas station.

"Any available units, please respond."

"2-Alpha-7, taking this one," Quinn relayed.

Lia quickly secured the GoPro to the front of her protective vest with tried-and-tested Velcro. Quinn did not bother making eye contact when she said:

"Don't you need permission for that?"

"I would have asked," Lia grumbled.

"When?"

"What?" Lia stared, not sure if she was imagining things or if the conversation had just turned confrontational. "What do you mean?"

"I'm just wondering," Quinn continued evenly, even as she swung the car wildly around a tight corner. "We record on dash-cams and body-cams all the time, but you're not technically a police officer. So..."

Lia gripped the sides of her own seat as they flew over a series of speed bumps. She felt her breakfast come alive and start to kick in her stomach.

"Oh," she gasped. "You mean asking the people that I film?"

"Yes. Who did you think I meant? Me?"

"Uh... Yeah."

"I don't mind what you do," Quinn assured. "But even if I didn't want you to film me, I wouldn't be rude about it. I just want to be prepared, and aware of what you'll do when we get to a scene, okay?"

"I understand. Well, stay out of your way is first on my list. Then, I focus on the officers doing their job in my line of work, not on the public. If I wanted to interview someone, I would ask, but not usually at a scene. My work is focused on observing the police, not any victims or perpetrators."

"Good. Thank you." Quinn slowed down as the gas station

came into view. "When we get there, or anywhere, I want you to stick to me like glue, okay?"

Like that's going to be a problem. Lia almost laughed out loud.

"Got it," she said instead in a steady voice.

"And if I tell you to get back to the car, you do it."

"Fine." Lia swallowed her reluctance. "But I'm hoping you won't, okay?"

"Yes, I hear you."

Quinn stopped in front of the station.

"2-Alpha-7, at location," she advised.

"Ten-four, 2-Alpha," came the standard reply.

A small group, five men and two women, stood outside. As Quinn took a moment to observe their surroundings from the car, one of the men waved a friendly hand in their direction. It all looked pretty civilized to Lia.

"Doesn't look like a dangerous situation," she remarked.

"Yeah, well. You never know."

"Yes, I'm aware of that."

Quinn briefly clasped her hand.

"I know you're no rookie. Watch your six. Let's roll."

Lia stayed close, but she also tried to fade into the background. It was a skill and she was good at it, getting people to forget that she was there. Quinn did not strike her as one who easily would, but Lia hoped that she would relax a little bit as the day went on. Right now, she observed her on this first call, took mental notes, filed away questions to ask later. She already knew that Quinn was an ex-army captain. This might explain the dominant vibe that she caught from her now. Or perhaps it was just natural ease and authority, combined with the badge on her belt. But everyone definitely went very quiet and alert as she approached. Quinn addressed the groups in a friendly voice.

"Hey, everyone. What's going on here?"

"I called you," a guy started. "I work this station, and—"

"Officer," one of the women cut in sharply. "I'll fill you in."

She was dressed impeccably in a tailored silk business suit. So was the other woman, who also came to speak to Quinn now. Both did not look like the type who'd throw punches to solve a disagreement... Although, as Quinn had just told her, you never knew. Lia remained politely standing off to the side.

"We're colleagues," the first woman announced.

"Friends," the other one indicated. "Very good friends."

"Fighting friends?" Quinn prompted.

"I pushed her," the first one said.

"I threw a carton of oat milk in retaliation," the other stated. Both women exchanged a glance and grinned at each other. "We knocked down an entire stack of soup cans."

"It was beans," the station manager interjected.

"And done by mistake. You understand, Officer."

Quinn nodded and she looked to the guy for confirmation. "Is that correct?"

"Well, sort of," he grunted. "But they did knock down my entire display."

"And we told you we'd pay for any damage." Both women were glaring at him now.

"There's no damage, to be honest. But—"

"Okay, so there's no problem then, is there?"

That shut him up. The blond-haired woman turned steady eyes toward Quinn.

"I'm sorry for wasting your time, Officer."

This one was clearly used to being in charge, and regarded Quinn as her equal or slightly below. Lia was amused. Quinn's expression did not change.

"You're alright," she nodded.

Ignoring her and everybody else now, the women turned to face each other.

"I am so sorry, Kim. This is so stupid... I really don't want to let work come in between us."

"Oh, honey, I'm sorry too! You take the lead on this deal, okay?"

"Are you sure?"

"Yes. I'll take the next one."

"Okay, darling. Hey, I love you."

"I love you too."

When both women kissed, Lia noticed Quinn avert her eyes and grin, briefly. Her game face was back on when she took the station manager aside for a quick word.

"So. No damage, is that right?"

"Yeah, that's right. Guess I didn't really need to call you in the end, but when these two started knocking stuff down, I didn't know what else to do."

"That's okay. Better safe than sorry."

"No harm no foul," he finally smiled.

"There you go." Quinn turned back to the women and she gave each one an assessing glance. No doubt as to who was in charge here, and Lia enjoyed witnessing her easy confidence. "You two going to be okay now?"

"Yes, Officer," the one named Kim grinned in reply. "Very fine."

You bet. Lia wanted to laugh. The sexual energy between these two was palpable. On that note, the duo headed to a black Mercedes convertible parked on the side, got in, and swiftly departed. Once back in the cruiser, Quinn reported the situation to Dispatch as resolved.

"Interesting call to begin the day, uh," Lia commented, keen to see what she would say.

"Hot-headed lovers throwing things." Quinn nodded with an amused chuckle. "I'm glad I didn't have to jump in between the two."

"I'm not. It would have made for entertaining footage."

"For outtakes, you mean?" Quinn laughed. "Officer Wesley getting her ass kicked by two businesswomen in heels?"

"That would do nicely," Lia teased. "Thanks for the tip."

"You're welcome. But don't hold your breath."

••

Quinn was not enjoying herself; not exactly. This was duty, and she took it extremely seriously. As always, she was focused and ready for anything, and today even more so because she had an untrained ride-along with her. But it was hard not to feel like smiling at times. Lia brought a different quality to the day. Something intangible yet undeniable. Warmth. Sure strength. A grounding presence. Quinn did ride alone most of the time, but not always, and even the most experienced officer she'd been paired with did not have the same effect as Lia. Was it because she was female, and Quinn just happened to be more sensitive to a woman's energy? Maybe. *Or maybe that's because it's her.* Quinn would rather settle for a punch in the face than to admit it, but she was happy to have Lia with her. She studiously avoided thinking about what this may mean, and the schedule definitely helped. The morning went by in a flash and, after the first solo call, was spent mostly in support of other crews.

"Yeah, I float around quite a bit," Quinn replied in answer to one of Lia's questions. "I'm a senior officer, so helping out on sensitive jobs or being there to mentor the guys is part of what I do."

"How often do you deal with an extreme call like the other day? The shooter at the store, I mean."

"Thankfully, not often, although we encounter quite a lot of angry or scared people. Or both. Drunks. Addicts. Nobody calls the cops when everything's going fine, right?"

"For sure."

"It can get pretty bleak. But sometimes we get lucky, and people end up kissing and making up."

"Happy endings," Lia mused in a wistful tone.

It sounded as if she may be talking about something other than police work, and Quinn did not prompt her for details.

"Happy endings are always nice," she simply said. "So. Do you fancy having lunch at the beach?"

"Is it that time already?"

"It's almost two o'clock, actually, and I'm so hungry that I could faint."

"Wow, I didn't realize... But now that you mention it, I'm starving as well."

"Good. Let's find a place to fuel up then."

They settled for hot-dogs, fries, and a pitcher of ice tea to help combat the blistering heat. Lia asked a few more questions while they ate, but she stayed well within the realm of procedure and Quinn's experience as a cop. She never once mentioned her time in the army, or ask any other personal questions. Quinn was grateful for that but also weirdly conflicted once again. The more respectful Lia was of her boundaries, the more the impulse to talk to her and open up manifested. Not necessarily about the army and Iraq, all that sensitive stuff... But in general. Lia felt solid to her, and in a good way. She seemed like the kind of woman who could be caring and tender, but who was also strong and independent, able to handle her own stuff. Quinn quickly recognized that she wanted to know about that too. Put simply, she had the urge to know her. Intimately. As this became fully clear to her, even pouring straight ice down her back may not have been enough to soothe the rush of heat that she experienced. *You're on duty. So is she. Get on with it.* She reached for her sunglasses, pulled her credit card out of her pocket.

"I'll get this. Let's get back on the road, shall we?"

"Sure. I'm ready for Round 2."

It happened as they were leaving. The sound of screeching tires as brakes were applied. A series of impacts. Breaking glass. There were screams, an explosion, and a thick column of smoke started to rise from a nearby street.

"Quinn?" Lia queried.

"Stay close to me," Quinn advised, and she started to run toward the smoke.

CHAPTER
12

Lia felt her heart sink as they approached the scene of a major accident. In the middle of the three-lane highway that led back into the city, a bus was on its side. Behind it, through a wall of smoke, she could discern the outline of several more cars all enmeshed in a mass of destruction. She stuck with Quinn, the first official responder at the scene.

"Five vehicles, maybe more," Quinn relayed rapidly over the radio. "Casualties unknown as yet. Yeah, send us all the support you can."

Lia turned on her GoPro and she remained close with her.

"Look!" she pointed.

A single man was crawling out of a broken window on the bus and attempting to slide down the side. Quinn grabbed hold of him as he fell off and she quickly steadied him.

"Hey, you okay?"

Blood trickled down the middle of his face from a cut on his forehead, but the injury appeared only superficial. He regained his equilibrium.

"Yeah, yeah... I'm fine."

"Are you the driver of this bus?"

"Yes. I don't know what happened. I—"

"How many onboard?" Quinn interrupted sharply.

Lia could not believe how lucky it was when the driver said that he was the only one. The bus had not been in service at the time.

"Can you walk?"

"Yes."

"Then get yourself to safety," Quinn instructed. "As far as you can, okay?"

As he took off, Lia moved on ahead slightly to help another person slide out from inside an overturned car. It was another single driver, also able to move on his own. More people started crawling out of other vehicles. She heard sirens in the distance. People crying. There was blood. Suffering was palpable. Above, the sky was no longer visible. Smoke had obliterated everything else, and Lia experienced a sudden sense of disorientation and helplessness.

"Lia."

Quinn's hand on her shoulder was like an anchor to solid reality. Lia clasped her arm in return.

"Quinn, this is bad!" she exclaimed.

"I know, but help is coming. Go back."

It occurred to Lia that Quinn's face had turned very pale. Her usually clear blue eyes were darker. In a flash of intuition, Lia realized the probable reason why. If this entire scene reminded her of Iraq, which it did, very much, then it must be the same for Quinn. Perhaps even worse. Lia's heart swelled with the need to protect, to shelter, and she tightened her hold on her.

"Quinn, are you alri—"

"Lia, get out of here," Quinn snapped.

"But we've gotta help!"

"I'll help. Go back."

Before Lia could reply that there was no way in hell she'd leave her on her own at this point, she heard a cry further down the line of cars.

"Oh, my god! Somebody, help!"

A pickup truck had caught on fire, and a woman appeared to be trapped inside.

"It's gonna blow!" someone shouted.

"Go, Lia!" Quinn grunted, and she flew toward the vehicle.

Stunned for a split second, Lia soon took off after her. Heart pounding to breaking in her chest, but determined to stay by her side... *I'm with you. No matter what.*

••

Quinn was acutely aware of the fire, the danger it represented, and of time running out, but it did not stop her. She scrambled on top of the truck, which had ended up on its side as well. Only one way in and out of the vehicle, and she pushed inside of it through the side window, avoiding lethal shards of broken glass as best she could.

"My baby!" the woman screamed from behind the wheel. "I can't get her out, I'm stuck! Please get my baby out, please!"

"Are you hurt?"

"No. Just get her out, PLEASE!" The woman was hysterical.

"I will," Quinn promised. *Or fucking die trying.*

She squeezed between the seats to reach the back of the cab. The baby bucket seat remained in place and the baby was still in it. Red in the face, crying her head off, but alive. Quinn struggled with the clasp on the safety belt. She ended up reaching for the military KA-BAR knife that she always carried holstered to her leg to release the baby.

"Here you go, sweetie," she murmured.

She could feel and see the flames at the back. The smell of gas was strong. As memories arose, she gritted her teeth and focused only on this moment. *Stay sharp.* People's lives were at stake, including her own.

"Hurry! Please, please, save my baby!"

Quinn managed to turn around, cradling the crying child in her arms. She glanced up toward the exit, just as two hands reached inside the truck.

"Give her to me," Lia instructed.

Goddammit. Quinn would have given anything in her power not to have it be Lia there, at risk, but there was no changing this situation. She lifted the baby.

"Take her and go!" she hissed.

Lia's eyes locked onto hers briefly, sparking hotter than fire in her resolve. Quinn felt her deep in the center of her chest, as if she'd been touched.

"I'll be right back," Lia said, before disappearing from view with the child.

Maintaining control and her concentration, Quinn bent over the mother.

"Where are you stuck?" she asked.

"It's my leg. Left leg caught in something."

The something in question turned out to be a large piece of the chassis, which had broken through the floor of the vehicle. This driver was damn lucky it had not pierced any further in, or she'd be dead. Quinn did not share her conclusion out loud. She leaned both hands against the metal piece instead, and pushed with all her strength.

"Any give?"

"Yes! Do it again!" An explosive sound in the background made the woman flinch. Small explosion, but close. "Oh, god!"

"It's okay," Quinn reassured. "Relax, I've got this."

She lay on the floor under the woman's legs, her shoulder against the obstructing piece of metal. She found solid purchase for her feet, and pushed even harder. Once. Twice...

"Yes! I'm free!" the woman yelled on the third attempt.

"Get out then, quick," Quinn ordered, and she gave her one last helpful shove upwards.

Once the driver was out, she attempted to follow after her. In doing so, she inadvertently sliced her arm on a fragment of glass. The pain was intense, enough to make her vision blur and narrow. Tiny dots danced along the edge, and she fell back against the side.

"Quinn!" Lia reappeared at the window. "Grab my hands! Come on!"

The sight of her was like a shot of adrenalin. Quinn's vision sharpened. She launched herself toward the exit and scrambled out of the cab. Lia caught her around the waist as she landed, a look of absolute relief on her face. Something else too; something warm, deep, and grave, which made Quinn want to grab her and kiss her until they both ran out of oxygen. For now, she just held tightly onto her hand.

"Lia."

"Yes?"

"Run!"

They were not very far from the truck when it blew. From the intensity of the energy wave that followed, Quinn suspected that it was not just the truck. Perhaps another car as well. *Damn!* She hoped that everyone had got out... Sadly, there was nothing else she could do at this point. When the explosion occurred, she also had no time to cushion Lia's fall, or her own. They were both flung to the ground hard, covered in a shower of grit and flaming debris. *At least no one's shooting at us here.* This was no flashback either; just an automatic thought, easily dealt with. Quinn remained in control, although this was sorely tested when she turned to help Lia and found her lying on her back with her eyes closed. For a second, fear made her vision blur.

"Lia!" Quinn knelt over her and passed a supportive hand under her head. She recognized the warm sticky substance over her fingers before even looking. Lia was bleeding. "Open your eyes," she prompted.

Lia blinked, blindly reaching for her.

"Quinn," she groaned.

"Yeah, I'm here. You've got a cut on your head. You okay?"

Lia felt for it with her fingers and instantly tried to play it down.

"Yes, I'm fine. Just a scratch."

"Let's get you up. Hold on to me."

Emergency rescue services had arrived on scene; three fire engines, the technical rescue team, ambulances, and more police. As Quinn supported Lia toward an ambulance, Ethan appeared in front of them.

"Wesley!"

"Hey, Eth," Quinn nodded in relief. "Help us out here."

He slipped on the other side of Lia, passed his arm around her waist in support, and glanced sharply at them both.

"You guys look rough. You need a medic."

"No, I don't need a—" Lia started weakly.

"Yes," Quinn countered. "You're bleeding."

"Well. So are you."

She sounded miffed, and Quinn chuckled with another rush of relief that Lia could feel this way, that she was not too badly hurt, that she was still here. *With me. I didn't lose her.*

"It's not a criticism." She smiled in reassurance. "We'll both get checked, okay?"

"'Kay... Make sure you do."

Ethan flagged down a paramedic for them. While she was seeing to Lia's head, Quinn sat at the back of the ambulance, in the open door, and had her arm looked at by her colleague.

"You're going to need stitches," he declared.

"Can you do it here?"

"Sure thing," he approved.

"So, what's the score?" Quinn asked Ethan.

"Two dead," he replied. "One hanging in the balance."

"Ah, shit."

She was glad when he did not immediately rationalize it by saying that it could have been so much worse, even if that was true. In the aftermath, Quinn observed the scene. The bus, still on its side. Ten cars, as she counted them, all in various states of annihilation. And the pick-up truck that she had just escaped, a smoldering metal shell now. *Another three or four seconds, and I would have been toast...* She shivered, gladly accepted the blanket that the medic offered her.

"How are the woman and her baby, Ethan?"

"They were taken to the hospital as a precaution. But okay, I believe."

"Great."

"Yeah, it is. So, I need to get back out."

"Sure. You can go, we're fine here."

He clasped her shoulder warmly and smiled.

"Good job, Quinn. You made it count today."

113

"Thanks, buddy. I'll see you later."

As the medic finished bandaging her arm, Quinn glanced behind her to check that Lia was being treated as well. She was. *All okay.* She started to relax.

"Any other injuries?" her helper inquired.

"No. I'm good."

"Go home and get some rest," he advised.

"Thanks," Quinn replied absently.

She was still on duty, no reason not to be, so resting would have to wait. She stood up and stretched, carefully, turning back just as Lia reached the door to the ambulance. Her sidekick for the day still looked a little pale, she was covered in dust, but her eyes blazed as they settled on hers. Quinn forgot to breathe.

"How are you?" Lia inquired intently.

"I'm fine." Quinn stepped forward to help her down. "And you?"

"Like I got my head cracked."

"Ah. Well, it's—"

"Quinn." Lia said her name, and only that. She cupped her face in both hands. Her gaze grew even more intense. "Quinn..." she repeated in a raw voice.

Quinn looked into her eyes, glistening with emotion, as Lia caressed her face. Did she know what her touch made her feel? Did she have any idea of the sort of reaction that she provoked? Quinn suspected not. And she knew what this was, too. Coming down off a huge adrenalin high after a potentially devastating event. Danger shared and overcome; feelings heightened in the process... This could all produce a significant emotional drop afterwards. She wondered if Lia had experienced this kind of thing before. Whether or not she had was irrelevant, in a way. Quinn knew that it would not make the moment any less real for her, or impactful. Hell, even she was used to this, but she was still feeling it now. Big time. And Lia's injury would not help.

"It's okay," Quinn murmured. "Don't worry."

She took her hands and held her gently. Lia rested her forehead against her chest. For a minute, neither of them moved. Lia was the first to stir.

"What time is it?"

Quinn checked the G-Shock on her wrist.

"Three-forty-five."

"Feels like years since we had lunch..."

"Would you like another hot-dog?"

"No, I mean..." Lia raised confused eyes to her, but quickly recovered and smiled. "You're teasing me."

"Not really. I just wanted to see you smile again."

Lia lingered, still watching her intently with eyes full of unspoken questions. Until she looked away, and Quinn noticed the corners of her mouth start to tremble. Emotion rising again. Too much of it. Lia looked like she was going to burst into tears. *She's exhausted.*

"Come on, I'll drive you home," Quinn invited. "You saved some lives today, and now you need to look after yourself. That means a shower, clean clothes, and some rest."

Lia went from looking a little lost and tender, to suspicious, in a flash.

"What about you?" she asked. "You're not going to carry on with the day, are you? Not after this. Not on your own. Right, Quinn?"

Normally, this would not even be a question. Quinn would go back on, of course. She'd swing by the station for a scrub and a change of clothes, maybe a coffee and a protein bar, but a few stitches would never justify ducking out of shift early. Not in her world. Having accurately guessed what her answer would be, Lia dug her heels in.

"Fine. I'm going back with you," she declared.

CHAPTER
13

A request from Dispatch to 'Ten-Nineteen', meaning Return-to-Station, as per captain's order, interrupted what might otherwise have turned into a heated exchange.

"I don't know what makes you think I can't handle stressful situations as well as you do," Lia muttered.

"Because a hole in the head is not the same as a scratch on the arm. Did you lose consciousness out there?"

"No, I didn't. And how many stitches did you get?"

Whatever tender mood may have arisen had now shifted to bickering about who was toughest, apparently.

"Two stitches," Quinn sighed.

"Well, I only got one."

"Good for you."

"Hey."

Quinn glanced aside, irritated. But Lia was smiling.

"What?"

"Thanks."

"For what?"

"Caring. Looking out for me."

Quinn reached over to clasp her hand.

117

"I do care. Of course, I do."

Lia was quiet for the rest of the short drive back to base, thoughtful. Happy in her own silence for a bit, Quinn did not push her for more. Wilson welcomed them back in his office with a smile of approval as he took them in.

"Looks like you two earned your pay today."

"Today?" Quinn grunted, and he chuckled.

"Good answer. So, how are you doing?"

"We're fine," Lia assured. "Absolutely perfect."

Quinn knew that her captain was after an injury report, not this kind of careless brush-off, and she gave him an accurate rundown.

"Take the rest of the day off," Wilson instructed. "Both of you. Go home and take it easy, alright?"

"Yes, sir. Will do." Quinn would have argued if she'd been on her own, but she wanted Lia to switch off, so she decided to lead by example. On their way to the locker room, she asked if she might need a ride home this time.

"Yes, thanks." Lia unstrapped her vest and the GoPro. "I'll just drop this off in the office. Take your time. Grab a shower if you like."

"What are you going to do?" Quinn inquired. Her turn to be suspicious.

Lia flashed a sheepish smile.

"Download today's footage."

"Lia…"

"No, look: I just want to make sure it's saved on my hard drive before I log off for the day. That's all. I won't be able to rest if I don't do that."

"Right. Okay. Ten minutes, then?"

"Excellent," Lia approved. "Thank you."

When Quinn joined her in the office, she found the admin team crowded around Lia's monitor, watching the recording of the rescue. They all turned and clapped when she walked in.

"Here's the hero of the day!" Demi beamed.

"Yeah, alright, take it easy," Quinn muttered.

"All in a day's work for you, eh?" Demi laughed.

"Yep. Just doing my job. Lia?"

"Yes." Lia closed her laptop. "I'm ready."

●●

It hit her just as they were crossing the parking lot. Maybe it was the heat... General fatigue, stress, and/or the crushing headache that made her vision blur. But her legs suddenly gave way from under her, and she would have collapsed if Quinn had not been there to catch her. *Not again!* The last thing Lia wanted was to appear weak in front of her.

"Sorry," she blurted out. "I'm—"

"Lean on me," Quinn instructed.

"But your injury..."

"It's no big deal, Lia. Really. Lean on me."

Quinn laced a strong arm around her waist, and Lia had no option but to rest against her side.

"Do you feel faint?"

"Uh... Little bit. I've got a headache."

With not much of a choice in the matter, Lia allowed her to support her to the cruiser, and to help her onto the passenger seat. Quinn lingered in the door with one hand on her shoulder, blue eyes heavy with concern.

"Do you need to go to the hospital? Maybe you should get a second opinion, eh?"

119

"No, no. The medic warned me this might happen."

"Really?"

"Yes. It's hot, and the headache... It's all just... You know?"

Too exhausted to say the rest, Lia rested her head back and made a vague gesture in conclusion.

"All of it, yes," Quinn nodded. "Let's get you home so that you can lie down."

"That... would be good," Lia confessed.

She kept her eyes mostly closed on the way over, focusing on taking deep breaths and staying relaxed. She was aware that Quinn was driving extra-carefully, but every tiny bump and pothole along the way still made it feel as if she were being kicked in the head.

"Lia?"

Not conscious of having drifted into a sort of in-between sleep, Lia opened her eyes to a soft caress across her arm, and Quinn's patient eyes on her.

"Ah..." she mumbled. "We there?"

"Yes. Same maneuver as before. Put your arms around me."

By then, Lia was in too much pain to pretend or protest that she could do it on her own. Without another word, she wrapped her arms around Quinn's shoulders and allowed her to pull her upwards.

"Can you walk?"

"Yes. I'm sorry about this, Quinn."

"Don't apologize, please. We're partners. I'm happy to help you."

Lia was not prepared for how this would make her feel, but it was powerful. *Partners...* Wow. She told herself not to read too much into the word, and she averted her eyes to hide sudden tears.

"Okay," she murmured. "Thank you."

Quinn's body was hard in all the right places, although she was not all tight muscle under her clothes. Lia noticed again the rise of her breasts under her clean cotton t-shirt. Quinn held her close enough for Lia to see that she was bra-less, and that her nipples were hard. A fascinating discovery, for sure. Lia had no trouble picturing her naked. No doubt Quinn would be stunning... She shivered.

"Almost there," Quinn advised, probably thinking that her reaction was due to pain.

Lia was not going to enlighten her, but her nervous system was overheating, and she stumbled again as they boarded the elevator. As Quinn tightened her hold, Lia steadied herself by placing the palm of her hand on her stomach. She felt Quinn's muscles tense in reaction, and her sharp intake of breath. Damn, she was hot! As in, really hot, physically. And that breath… Just as erotically charged. Lia suppressed another apology. She could not take her hand off. Nor did she want to do it. *This is crazy! What the hell is happening to me?* Still, she remained.

"Top floor?" Quinn inquired.

Her voice was huskier. She was breathing faster. Lia could feel her reacting to her touch, and she unconsciously moved her fingers a little lower, caressing her at the same time. She pressed harder, and Quinn did it again; she almost gasped. Lia raised her eyes to her face. Quinn was staring straight ahead. Her jaw was locked tight. Frowning lightly, she was obviously struggling for control.

"You're so gorgeous," Lia mumbled.

Those storm-blue eyes whipped back to her face as if Quinn had been shot.

"What?" she blinked.

"Uh. I'm so grateful. You must be tired…"

"I told you, I'm fine and happy to help. Now, where to?"

"I'm number 7."

Lia let them into her apartment, a bright open-plan space filled with all the things she loved: plants, books, photographs. Quinn took in her surroundings with the speed and practice of a cop accustomed to checking out places.

"Nice. Bedroom?"

"I'll be fine on the couch."

Actually, it was a lie. Lia realized as soon as Quinn moved away that she'd felt much better in her embrace.

"I'll get you some water."

Quinn navigated herself to the kitchen and came back with a bottle of Evian. She set that on the coffee table in front of her, knelt, and started to undo her laces. Lia rested a careful hand on her shoulder.

"What are you doing?" she murmured.

Quinn paused to look at her, her expression searching.

"Helping you. Is that so strange for you, Lia?"

"It's unusual," Lia admitted frankly. "I'm used to taking care of myself. Doing it on my own."

"Or helping others?"

"Yes."

"Well. I'm here now, so you can relax."

Lia stared into her eyes, baffled. Did she have any idea of what she was saying? Or how it sounded? Quinn returned her gaze intently, warmly. She stayed with one hand on the back of her ankle, holding her leg gently. Waiting. Watching her. Lia swallowed.

"I need a shower."

"Yes. I can help you with—"

"No, stay here!" *Oh, damn!* "I mean: you should go, Quinn. Thank you for escorting me home, really, but I can take it from here."

Quinn smiled, clearly amused at her discomfort and doing nothing to hide it.

"You think I'm going to leave you here on your own when you have a hole in your head, and almost fainted on me a couple of times?"

"It was the heat. And again, my head is not that bad when I can be still."

"Okay." Quinn shrugged again as if she did not believe that for a second, but she skipped arguing and just carried on briskly. "Sorry, but your escort is not going anywhere at this point. At least, not until you've had your shower and are in bed where you belong."

Lia stood up on trembling legs, which again had nothing to do with her injury.

"I won't be long."

"Take as long as you need."

"There's food in the fridge, Quinn."

Quinn flashed her a look that said she was hungry, but not for items in the fridge. Everything about her screamed danger to Lia at this point, but also wickedly delicious. She hurried to the bathroom, out of sight for a few precious moments, and grateful for an opportunity to regroup. *Just relax.* Okay – she would clean up, put on some clothes, and get in bed if she had to; but Quinn would have to go. Right now, she was too much of a temptation. Lia stripped off her clothes, still wondering about herself. She did like women, and appreciated a beautiful body when she saw one, but it usually took longer than this for her to feel the first stirrings of desire. She did not look at a woman and instantly feel aroused. Curious? *Yes.* Interested? *Sure.* Ready to talk more? *Absolutely.* But not this incredible simmering heat in her blood every time that she was close to Quinn. Lia was already way beyond the stage of wanting to talk. She wanted to grab hold of Quinn, fist her fingers into her thick hair, and kiss her until she dropped. She wanted to make her lose her breath, all her layers of control, and lose herself in the process. Lia *wanted.* She craved. Very badly. And the feeling was both exhilarating and scary at the same time. She groaned when it occurred to her that all her clothes were in the bedroom, and that she would have to wrap herself in a towel and walk across the lounge to get there. *Just get on with it.* Mindful of the hole in her head, as Quinn insisted on describing it, she washed grit out of her hair and rinsed dust and dirt off the rest of her body. Then, clad only in a towel that barely covered everything that should be, she wandered back out. As expected, Quinn was still there. On the couch, dozing with her eyes closed. She looked at peace there. Younger, and attractively vulnerable in her moment of rest. Lia took hesitant steps toward her, even though it was away from the bedroom, and the clothes, and safety, that she told herself she required. She did not mean to linger there, although she did, and Quinn suddenly opened her eyes.

"Hi." Lia tried to smile, feeling breathless.

The look on Quinn's face went from dazed to hyper-alert in the blink of an eye. She leaned forward.

"Hey, Lia. Everything okay?"

Lia pressed her lips together. She gripped the towel in both hands, and attempted not to blurt out the thoughts bouncing across her mind. *No. Not okay. You're too nice and too handsome. Please, go now...* In the time it took her to formulate a response, Quinn stood up and moved to her. With each step that she took,

Lia observed her expression go through a series of swift changes. There was concern, caution, wonder... And certainty. When she stopped in front of her, Quinn's blue eyes were smoldering. Her face was tight, but not in worry. Not anymore.

"You're gorgeous too, Lia," she said.

Lia watched her hands rise as if it were happening in slow motion. Maybe Quinn was just giving her a chance to pull back, but Lia found herself incapable of doing so. She did not tell her to stop. Wherever this was going, she wanted it. Quinn touched her face, making her shiver. She brushed her thumbs over her cheeks. Hot fingers, and such a gentle caress. Lia was so close to doing something she could never take back...

"Quinn," she murmured.

Quinn grazed her fingertips over her naked shoulders. Lia watched a small vein pulse urgently on the side of her neck. She was seized with the impulse to put her mouth over it, and suck.

"Quinn?" she repeated, almost in a pleading tone.

"Mm," Quinn said in a low voice that was almost a growl.

Her gaze dropped to the top of Lia's breasts, visible above the line of the towel. She licked her lips, moved her right hand to the back of her neck. *I can't. I can't!* Lia thought.

CHAPTER 14

Quinn had not planned any of this; not even fantasized about it. But then, that moment in the elevator happened. Lia went from leaning against her side, as anyone would do when they were not feeling too steady on their feet, to downright caressing her. *Sexually.* And suddenly, Quinn's own desire to be that way with her increased by a full order of magnitude. It was just fingers on her stomach, of course. A light press of Lia's hand over her abs. With any other woman, Quinn might have just smiled, and felt good at the recognition of possibility. Somehow, the fact that it was Lia doing it sent her into a spin. All of a sudden, she was hot, tight, wet. Fucking ready. And then this happened. The sight of Lia standing barefoot, skin still flushed from the shower, in nothing but that fluffy white towel was... *Well.* Outstanding. Spectacular. Such a gift to behold, and Quinn was dying to unwrap it. She wanted that towel gone.

"Hey." Lia rested both hands on her chest.

"Hey." Hoarse. Aroused. Quinn sounded like it. She knew it. Lia knew it. She gave a weak chuckle. "I'm sorry, I can't stop looking at you."

Lia moved her hands to cup her face.

"Quinn. Don't be sorry. Neither can I."

"I was just going to drop you home…"

"Yes, I know. I want you to go. Leave now. Please."

Quinn stilled her hands. She stopped admiring the rise of Lia's breasts under that damn towel and she met her eyes. She would do whatever Lia wanted her to do, but…

"Are you sure?" she murmured.

"No." Lia whimpered. "Not at all."

She leaned into her, unconsciously asking for reassurance. Quinn held her. Kinda needed some of that too. For the first time in a long while, she felt nervous. This was different in ways that she could not have explained, but sensed instinctively.

"Lia, you're trembling."

"No, *I* am not…"

Damn, it's me. The way Lia resumed touching her also did nothing to help with that. Quinn worked to stay in control as Lia slipped her fingers under her t-shirt again. She caressed her lower back, moved around, pressed a firm palm over her stomach. Yeah, Lia seemed to like that spot. Quinn closed her eyes when she felt her own muscles twitch. She liked it too. Her control was slipping. Warm breath fluttered on the side of her neck as Lia spoke.

"You feel so good."

"Lia, if you want me to leave, you can't do this to me."

"I don't want you to leave."

"But you just said—"

"Shhh…"

Lia moved so that they were nearly cheek to cheek. If Quinn turned her head just a few millimeters, their lips would touch. She was careful and slow when she initiated the movement, giving Lia a chance to pull away if she really wanted to. But Lia also turned her way and, in the next instant, they were sharing the same breath. The first contact obliterated everything else for Quinn. She forgot about the nerves. The roaring in her head, which she had not even been aware of, stopped as well, to be replaced with blessed silence and astonishing peace. Just feeling. Just this. Only now. That first moment of connection was brief but electrifying. When they met each other's eyes, Quinn saw her own experience reflected in Lia's face. No words required. Lia kissed her again, and there was nothing hesitant or unsure about her manner this time. The kiss was deep, thorough, possessive. All of that and more. Lia sank her fingers in her hair and leaned into her as if she were laying claim to her entire being. Quinn kissed her back with absolute concentration and dedication. A nuclear bomb could have gone off under her feet, and she would not have noticed. It was that kind of kiss. It left her breathless and wanting more, even as her legs wobbled and her heartrate sky-rocketed through the roof. When Lia pulled back from her, Quinn groaned in protest and she almost tipped forward in her attempt to chase the kiss.

"We need to slow down," Lia murmured.

"I want to rip that towel off of you."

Lia shot her a combination of a warning look and heated smile that made Quinn want to both laugh and plead for mercy at the same time. She suspected that Lia would be able to reduce her to that sort of behavior pretty quickly if she did not allow another kiss.

"I think you're making me a little crazy."

"Feeling's mutual, I can assure you," Quinn mumbled.

Please kiss me... Or get dressed... But don't stand there looking at me like that... It was a real effort, but she took a step back. Lia had just said stop, and Quinn would comply with whatever she said she wanted in the moment. Even though twice already, Lia had told her one thing and done the opposite.

"Are you okay?" she asked.

"Yes. Okay. Great."

"Then I'm glad," Quinn smiled.

Lia's expression turned sheepish.

"Quinn, I'm sorry. I know I'm all over the place..."

"No, you're fine. I need to slow down too."

"Really?"

"Yeah. Unbelievable, I know, but..."

Quinn gave a self-deprecating shrug, but her surprise was genuine. She did not often start things that she could not finish. She *never* started things that she could not finish, or follow someone else's lead in uncertain territory. This was so new to her... Quinn looked at Lia, wondering what it was about this woman that made her feel so impossibly unlike herself. A little crazy, indeed. And loving it.

"Alright," Lia nodded.

She appeared relieved but also ready to jump into her arms and start all over again. Quinn waited, knowing despite her own words that she would not be able to resist if Lia did that. Only one thing for it... She squared her shoulders.

"Okay. I'm going."

"No, please," Lia exclaimed, once again contradicting her own self. "I'll throw on some clothes and be right back with you. Yes?"

"Um... Yes. Okay. I'll wait then."

Quinn went to sit on the couch. She rubbed her face in both hands. Feeling demolished after just a single kiss, and what was up with that? What was up with kissing Lia Kennedy, period? She smirked in amazement and a touch of frustration at her own self. All she knew was that the impulse to do so had been irresistible, and that she wouldn't mind doing it again soon. No, strike that. Was dying to do it again, actually. *Right now.* She sighed.

"Quinn?"

Lia was back. She stood slightly off to the side, fully dressed in jeans and a t-shirt. Watching her intently.

"Hi." Quinn nodded. "You look nice."

*But not as nice as you did before…*She knew for sure that the image of Lia in that towel would remain imprinted on her brain for a long time to come, and that she'd be taking it off her in a variety of ways in her dreams for probably even longer. Quinn tried her best to keep her cool when Lia sat next to her. Hard not to react though. She was close enough for their legs and shoulders to be touching.

"So…" Lia murmured.

"So?" Quinn prompted.

"How do you feel?"

"Weak from that kiss."

She could smell Lia's shampoo. Sense the heat of her body even through her jeans. Her own skin felt electrically charged. She was hyper-aware once again, almost painfully attuned to the fascinating woman by her side. Lia leaned her shoulder against hers, making it harder still not to shiver. But in a good way.

"I don't know what to say, Quinn."

"Is there something specific you should say?"

"No… But I wish I could explain what just happened and I'm not even sure that I can do it to myself."

Quinn shrugged.

"We kissed."

"Yeah." Lia smiled. "But you know what I mean."

"Well, if by explain you mean apologize," Quinn prompted, since it sounded that way, "you really don't need to. I wanted to kiss you, Lia." *I still do.*

"Me too," Lia murmured, staring at her mouth.

Quinn held her gaze, enjoying feeling close to her.

"Am I to understand that you don't often feel that way?"

"No... Not recently. Not for the last three years, in fact."

The thoughtful response, and a tiny frown over her face, both seemed indicative of some inner reflection going on which Quinn did not assume that she was invited to query. And to be fair, only one thing mattered at this moment.

"How are you feeling, Lia?"

She passed her arm around her shoulders, feeling the need to be closer still, and affectionate. Lia seemed to understand and welcome the gesture. She smiled softly, and squeezed her leg in the same way.

"I think I feel great, Quinn."

"Good. You know, this is not the norm for me either."

"No?" Lia sounded both hopeful and gently dubious.

"What?" Quinn laughed. "Did you hear otherwise?"

"I didn't, but Janet seems a bit territorial about you. And the other day, at the barbecue..."

Lia gave a small shrug and she left her sentence unfinished. Even though Demi had already told her that nothing was going on between Quinn and Janet, she still felt the need to confirm.

"I'm single, Lia," Quinn stated. "And I don't hook up with women just for sex as often as people think."

Quinn also rarely felt the need to make that clear to anyone. The women she took to bed usually only cared about one thing: that she was available right here, right now. Intimate talk, before or after play, was not usually a requirement.

"I'm not looking for a relationship, you know," Lia blurted out.

"Neither am I," Quinn replied, thinking this was her line.

"And I'm not up for a quick thing either."

"No. I know."

"Really? You do?"

"Yes. And that's not what I would want with you anyway, Lia." Quinn immediately froze, in surprise, when she heard her own words. Perfect check-mate, and she'd done it to herself with that careless statement. "I mean..."

••

Lia was having the strangest day... It felt like ages since being assigned to ride with Quinn out of the blue that morning. She had completely lost track of time as they responded to one call after the other until early-afternoon. Then, lunch at the beach was so lovely and normal, yet followed by that crazy crash and an even wilder rescue. Lia would never forget the fear that she'd experienced when she'd watched Quinn race back into a wall of smoke and flames, and disappear inside that burning truck. That she had managed to save both mother and child, and come out of it pretty much unscathed, felt a lot like some kind of miracle. *Angels on her side...* Lia looked at her again. The most intense blue eyes she had ever seen, tousled blond hair, full lips and a bold mouth. Officer Wesley looked like the devil, at least the tempting part, and she kissed like an angel. *And what did she just say?* Lia struggled to make sense of the sentence, but never mind that, actually. More importantly... *What am I doing, grilling her about her relationships?* What Quinn chose to do in her off-time, and with whom, was none of her business. *Focus on your own, Lia.*

What are you doing here, uh? Lia knew that she had only been one heartbeat away from whipping her towel off and begging Quinn to take her to bed. Maybe just to take her, period. She shivered with a combination of desire and astonishment at her own self. It was true: she did not want a relationship. No involvement or complications either. And especially not with a woman as devastatingly handsome as Quinn, who clearly was an object of lust for so many others. *Heartbreak material. Don't go there. Okay, but... What about just once?* The voice inside her head was relentless, and Lia massaged her temples as her headache returned with a vengeance. The laceration on her skull, which was not a hole but still felt as wide and open as the Grand Canyon at the moment, was throbbing. She winced.

"I should get you into bed," Quinn said.

Lia flinched at the words that so reflected her deepest wish, spoken with the utmost gentleness. Quinn was too much for her right now. In all the best of ways, for sure, but... Still too much. Lia rubbed her eyes and she started to laugh. She wanted to tell her to leave, but she needed her to stay. And everything else in between...

"Oh, man," she groaned.

"Come on," Quinn instructed.

CHAPTER 15

Next thing Lia knew, they were in the bedroom and Quinn was all business.

"Have you got any headache pills here? If not, I'll go and buy you some."

"Yes. In the kitchen drawer," Lia replied.

"Okay. Get undressed and into bed while I get them."

By then, Lia had given up protesting and claiming that she was okay. Quinn was clearly determined to stay and help, and Lia was not feeling well. Not being alone for this, and especially having Quinn with her, was beyond comforting. Carefully, so as not to make the room spin, she got out of her jeans and t-shirt, hesitated about slipping into bed with nothing but panties on, as she normally would, and put the t-shirt back on. Having Quinn in her bedroom felt a bit too dangerous for full nudity. It was definitely exciting, and probably only as risky as Lia wanted to make it. The police officer seemed both hungry and respectful in equal measures; as in, extremely so. Lia knew that she could be trusted. Quinn would not push for more than Lia was ready to give her at this point, and that was another incredibly appealing trait about her. Right on cue, she called from the door.

"Ready for me?"

"Yes, come in," Lia invited.

Quinn carried a serious expression on her face as she did so, which quickly morphed into a smile.

"You're in bed," she remarked.

"You told me to," Lia nodded.

"As if that would sway you much, uh?" Quinn chuckled. "Here's a couple of pills and the water that you haven't touched yet."

"Thanks. That'll do for now."

"Uh-uh. I still think we should get you to the hospital, just in case you've got a concussion."

"The medic said I'd get a ferocious headache."

"It's up to you, Lia. But I can drive you if you need."

"Let's see how I go with the pills, okay?"

"Okay. Move forward a little bit."

When she did, Quinn surprised her again by sitting on the bed and shifting behind her. Lia stiffened at the sensation of her hands, so warm and gentle, yet powerful, coming to rest on her shoulders.

"What are you doing?"

"Trying to help the pills along. Is this okay?"

"It's... Um. Yes. Okay."

"Relax against me, then."

Lia was all out of objections. She did lean back and allowed herself to rest against Quinn's strong body.

"Good," Quinn murmured.

She moved her hands to the sides of her arms.

"Reiki?" Lia forced herself to speak, as a way to catch the breath that she was in danger of losing.

"Not really. Just, touch is good sometimes, eh?"

"I can't believe you said that."

"Well, it's true, isn't it? Human touch; the laying of hands. Sometimes that's all my physio does at the start of a session and, I swear, I can feel the tension evaporate. Sometimes it makes me shake, too."

"Shake?"

"Yeah. Some kind of energetic release, you know."

Lia closed her eyes, as Quinn rested the palm of her hands a bit higher on either side of her neck. She could feel one kind of tension go, leaving only delicious tightness in another place. She rested a little heavier against Quinn.

"Why do you need to see a physio?"

"Just general maintenance. I like training hard and that goes with the territory."

"Whatever you do, it looks good on you," Lia murmured.

"Thanks." Quinn's breath, was like a caress on the back of her neck. "What about you? Swimming must leave you feeling sore from time to time, uh?"

"It's not too bad. The last three years, I've not had time for much maintenance of my own. Swimming is the only thing that I did not sacrifice."

Those early-morning sessions in the North-Atlantic Ocean had kept her strong and sane when everything else that she held dear in her life was crumbling.

"I'm sorry about your dad. It's a tremendous thing you did for him."

Lia squeezed Quinn's left thigh on the side of her, and she kept her hand there, as Quinn began to gently press her thumbs up and down her neck. The position was comfortable. Intimate and safe. It made her want to share the same kind of secrets.

"It's been a long time since I felt another human's touch,"

she reflected. "Let alone a woman's."

"Yes. It happens sometimes."

"For you?"

"No…" There was a slight pause, then; "For me, it's a long time since I wanted anything but physical."

Lia closed her eyes at the admission. Quinn was pure flame. Everything about her so heatedly honest and straightforward, and lighting up the edges of Lia's consciousness.

"How do you feel about that?" she asked.

"To be honest… I'm not too sure, Lia."

Lia detected a smile in her answer.

"But you're okay with it?" she prompted.

"Hundred percent. How's your head now? Are the pills taking effect yet?"

"Yes… And what you're doing is pure magic."

"Am I allowed to stay with you a bit longer then?"

"Yes. Please. Can I tell you something else?"

"Absolutely."

"I was engaged… Back in Boston."

Quinn's hands stilled for a second, before she started to rub her thumbs in slow, heavier circles over the center of her back.

"Who was it?" she asked.

"A writer for the New York Times. I met her in Iraq, where we spontaneously paired up for the duration of our assignment. She wrote; I did photography. We became very close."

"I'm not surprised to hear that. Intense work in dangerous conditions often creates extremely strong bonds."

"That's right. Back home, we moved in together."

"And did you carry on working as a team too?"

"Yes. We were considered rising stars in the media world at the time. We started traveling the world, getting hired for all the best jobs, and receiving lucrative contracts from major networks and magazines... Building a stellar partnership in all aspects. Or so I believed. Gosh, you're going to make me drool."

"Good." Quinn laughed. "So long as you're relaxed, I don't mind."

Lia was amazed at the ease of it all. She carried on.

"When my dad became too ill to look after himself, I chose to become his full-time carer. Brooke stuck by me for the first nine months but after that... She made her own choice. I don't blame her for it, you know."

"Sounds like you were on different paths."

"That's right. No one to blame for that, for sure."

"Do you miss her?"

"I did. Like crazy at first, but not anymore. And we keep in touch. A text message here and there, a photo she sends from some exotic place... She's happy and doing well in her career. I'm very glad for that."

"Did you lose touch with your own career?"

"Pretty much, yes. After three years off, it was almost like starting at the bottom of the ladder again. And to be honest with you, I didn't have the appetite for it."

"Exotic places not for you anymore?"

"Well, I think I'd like to stay in one place for a change, and be a part of the community. It feels like I could have that here. I'm happy to have landed on the West Coast, and to be doing this job for Lewiston P.D."

"Even when it gives you a hole in the head?"

Lia chuckled, thinking it wasn't all that bad, actually.

"I think we got off lightly today. Don't you?"

"Yes." Quinn concluded the massage by wrapping her arms around her, and keeping her close. "Thank you for sharing your story with me."

"Thank you for listening." Lia held her in return. "Quinn?"

"Yes?"

"Do you mind if I ask you... What's the real reason that you didn't want me riding along with you today?"

••

Quinn had been able to shut down that line of questioning earlier by simply refusing to engage but, of course, that was before the rest of the day happened, and that gorgeous kiss especially. *Intense work in dangerous situations creates strong bonds.* Was it all it was? Feeling extra-close because of shared adversity? Quinn was not naïve. She'd felt something for Lia even before. Something deep. It made zero sense to her, and she did not enjoy this feeling of not being in control, but she could not deal with this question in her usual manner. Avoidance, deflection, brushing it off with a joke... It would not work this time. Lia deserved better. *Maybe I do, too.*

"Are you okay?" Lia prompted.

Quinn shook herself out of her introspective state.

"Yes. Sorry, I drifted there for a moment."

"I noticed. And I can feel your heart racing."

Lia shifted in her embrace to be able to look directly at her. Quinn stared into her deep-brown eyes, full of genuine warmth and a hint of concern too. *Say something to her, for god's sake!* But her mind was blank. Lia passed her arm around her shoulders. Now she was the one doing the holding. Quinn swallowed. She tried to take a deep breath. Failed. Lia pressed her hand over her chest, frowning now.

"Hey..."

"I'm fine," Quinn said quickly, before she could ask.

"Okay, but forget the question, then. I'm a nosy reporter. I tend to shoot questions first, and —"

"No." Quinn clasped her fingers as she was about to move off. "It's alright."

It was a long time indeed since she had wanted anything but a physical, superficial connection, but Lia made her long for something more. Quinn had spotted the flash of disappointment in her gaze just now, even as Lia used the same tactic as she did to cover it up. Jokes... Pretending that it did not matter. If Quinn let her, she'd probably pull away and retreat behind her own walls, never to be reached again. Forget about a racing heart; Quinn lost a couple of beats at the thought of that happening. Intimacy was a two-way street, certainly. And for some reason that she still did not fully understand, the delicate connection with Lia was too important for her to remain in her lane. Not for the sake of emotional safety. And not for whatever else may be causing her heart to pound. Quinn managed to take a settling breath.

"The last time I had a reporter riding along with me was in Iraq," she said. "The patrol ended in disaster."

Lia tightened her arm over her shoulder.

"Oh, Quinn, I'm sorry. I figured you'd had a rough time of it over there, from some of the things that you didn't say to me the other night. But I wasn't sure exactly."

"Yes." Quinn ignored the familiar twist of pain inside her heart. "It was rough, but at least I came back. She didn't. I lost teammates, too."

"What happened? Are you okay to tell me?"

The combination of fierce and protective in Lia's voice made it easier to carry on. Quinn rarely found herself on the receiving end of this sort of vibe. She was the protector in her relationships, whether professional or private. Demi got mushy and motherly with her sometimes, if she had a little too much to drink. She often treated her like an extra child. Quinn was part of the family. It was fine. Also, Demi was married, and she did not turn Quinn's insides to jelly the way that Lia did.

"We were traveling between FOBs in two separate vehicles when we were ambushed." She was careful not to allow the words to reach too deep inside herself, or images to form in her mind. She remained detached, and safe, from the things that she described. "We went over IEDs in the road. Our trucks got hit and destroyed. Then we came under fire from a group of rebel fighters. They'd planned the attack well."

"The reporter," Lia inquired. "Was her name Evan?"

"Yes. Evan Alvarez." *She died in my arms.* Quinn did not say those words because she did not want to tempt fate. She kept her eyes fixed on Lia's, focused on the tiny changes of color in her beautiful eyes. *Here. Alive. It's okay.* "Did you know her?"

"I'd met her once in Boston, at a conference I attended," Lia confirmed. "She was a sought-after speaker at the time. An experienced reporter, and a very inspiring woman as well."

"Yes." Quinn gritted her teeth. "She was."

"Were you injured in the ambush?"

"I got broken bones from the IED and one of the bastards shot me in the arm. I was lucky though. Air Support showed up eventually and I got Medevac'd out of there. I could have stayed in the army but, like you said before, I'd lost my appetite for it by then."

"So, you got out and joined the police?"

"I took six months off and then joined, yes."

"And did you struggle to recover afterwards?" Lia probed,

only to wince, a little sheepishly, when Quinn shot her a look. "Sorry again. You don't have to answer that."

"I dealt with a bit of stuff." Quinn was amused in spite of herself. Everything about Lia made her feel good. "At first, I had flashbacks, anxiety. For a while, I couldn't sleep. When I did, it was wall-to-wall nightmares. Classic PTSD."

Lia regarded her with absolute warmth and sympathy.

"A bit of stuff, uh... That's an understatement. Is it better now?"

"Yes. The other day at the station, memories came up when I was doing CPR on Joe. But otherwise, nothing. I am regularly assessed. I'm fit for duty."

CHAPTER 16

Quinn did not mention that she had struggled with debilitating guilt on top of the other symptoms she listed. Evan Alvarez was a battle-hardened reporter already by the time she'd embedded with her squad. Street-tough and funny, she felt like one of the guys after her initial two-weeks of tagging along with the team. Yet, Quinn never forgot that she was her responsibility. As well as whatever mission she was tasked to accomplish, she was also supposed to keep the reporter safe. To bring her home in one piece. And she had failed. Before the road transfer to the British FOB, Alvarez had been adamant that she wanted to ride in the lead vehicle. Quinn thought it would be safer for her in the second one. She was correct in theory. They argued, but not for long. Quinn was in charge, of course. *But did Evan unconsciously know?* Could some part of her psyche anticipate what would happen? Was it the reason for her insistence, and would she have survived if she had been riding with Quinn? These were impossible questions that Quinn would never know the answers to, and it also didn't change the situation. Alvarez had been killed. She had lived. End of story. All the Intel reports that she had reviewed before the drive stated that the way would be clear. What ended up happening was out of her control. Quinn knew it for sure; everyone had reminded her of that fact. But it had not stopped her from almost giving herself a nervous breakdown with the What-Ifs at one point.

"You're drifting off on me again," Lia murmured, tracing a light finger over her jaw.

"Sorry." Quinn smiled. "I'm here."

"I'm sorry too if I reminded you of painful times."

"That's okay. I wanted to answer your question honestly."

"Thanks. And I have to be honest with you too..."

"Yes?"

Lia snuggled a little closer.

"I'll want to ride with you again one of these days."

Quinn rolled her eyes and she chuckled, as much to lighten the mood between them as to hide the sudden rush of desire that washed over her. Talking about Iraq had made her forget where she was for a moment, but now she was very aware of it, and of Lia in her arms.

"You're not telling me anything I don't know," she said.

"Am I really that easy to read?"

"Well, you're a reporter."

"And?" Lia pushed her with a grin.

"Stubborn. Obstinate. Bull-hea—"

"Hey!"

Laughing, Quinn caught her wrist just as Lia tried to flick her on the chin.

"Careful. I'm injured too."

"Oh, are you now?"

"Yep."

"Thought you were just busy being a bossy cop."

"Well, if you want me to shut up, you should—"

Lia swallowed the rest of her sentence with an impetuous kiss that had the same startling effect on Quinn as the first one. Any other thought drained out of her brain, silence flooded her mind, and the only thing that she remained conscious of was Lia. *Lia...* With her arm hooked around her neck and her free hand on her cheek to better guide the kiss. *Lia...* Reaching for her with her tongue and retreating quickly, playfully, prompting Quinn to chase her. *Lia...* At once igniting every nerve in her body, and soothing her inner fire. Quinn reached under the light top that she wore to caress her naked back. Next thing she knew, Lia had kicked the covers off her legs and she was rolling on top of her. Quinn laced one arm around her waist. She realized when she touched her thighs that Lia was only wearing a pair of panties with that tank top. *Oh, Jesus.*

"Lia..."

"Quinn. You feel so good."

Lia sank both hands into her hair, cradling her face against her chest at the same time. Quinn experienced the tantalizing brush of an erect nipple against her cheek, and she stopped breathing. How she ached to lift that damn layer of fabric between them, to take her in her mouth, and suck the rock-hard little bud...

"You're beautiful," she whispered.

She had a sudden vision of the two of them, fully naked in each other's arms. She thought of sliding her leg in between Lia's. Slow rubbing, cupping her breasts in the palm of her hands. She would kiss her deep and slow, make Lia arch and moan softly under her, and awaken her fully. Quinn trembled at the thought of tasting her. She could go all night if Lia allowed her to. Damn, she wanted to—

"Quinn?"

Quinn tilted her head back to look into her eyes. Lia flashed her an intent smile, even as she ran the softest fingers through her hair. Cooling things down.

"You make me want to forget everything else and do crazy things with you."

Once again, behavior and words not quite matching. Quinn returned both hands firmly, safely, on top of the bed.

"That makes two of us then. Say, what kind of crazy?"

"Oh, I think that's too dangerous a conversation to be had at this point," Lia laughed.

"Mm... Yes, you're probably right."

Lia settled both hands over her shoulders, her gaze serious once again.

"Even so, I feel incredibly safe with you, Quinn. It's rare for me to feel this way."

This meant more to Quinn than she could express in words, and the kind of kiss required to demonstrate appropriately was out of the question. Beyond dangerous. She was keen to prove to Lia that she was worthy of her trust. Carefully, she moved aside from under her and pulled the light sheet back up to cover her legs. She caught a glimmer of disappointment in Lia's eyes, mixed with unconscious relief. Quinn had read her correctly. They were definitely on the same page here, and she also relaxed.

"Thanks for telling me that. I have an idea."

"Okay...?"

"It's kinda crazy, but probably not in the same way that you meant."

"Tell me," Lia chuckled, reaching for her hand.

Quinn automatically laced her fingers through hers. It felt so right!

"I'd like to take you out for dinner one night," she said. "Not fast-food after a round of duty like we already did, but a real date. And no Kevlar involved, I promise."

Lia fixed her with a gentle smile.

"You think going out to dinner is crazy?"

Ah, touché... Quinn chuckled in embarrassment.

"It is for me. I haven't wanted to ask a woman out in a long time. But you already knew that, right?"

"Yes," Lia murmured. "You told me. Although it's nice to hear you say it again. You're sexy when you blush."

"You're sexy, period."

"Even with a head injury and high on pills?"

"Totally. Now, you need to sleep, Ms Kennedy. Don't make me get bossy with you."

"Would you give me a hug first?"

"Yes, please."

Did Lia understand how much she needed this too? Quinn was not even aware of it until they held each other, simply for the pure comfort of it. Lia smelled sweet from her shower. She felt soft in her arms, but her embrace was also strong. It was Lia through and through. Quinn closed her eyes. So, then... Frantic kisses, affectionate hugs, and a dinner invite. The day had been full of surprises, including almost getting blown up. *Again...* And she had shared her story with Lia. *Unbelievable.* Everything felt easy with her. Quinn knew that she should move when she felt Lia relax into her, and her breathing deepen. In some ways, this was even more intimate than sex. *Five minutes,* she promised herself. *Five minutes and I'll go.*

••

Lia woke up some time later. It was dark in the room. All quiet outside. *Middle of the night.* The last thing she remembered was asking to be held. An outrageous demand... Showing vulnerability was never easy for her, and she knew that it must be the same for Quinn. Yet, she had met her halfway with her reply. *Yes, please...* She'd asked for it too. Now they lay together, locked in a comfortable embrace. *So wonderful...* Quinn rested with her cheek pressed over her breast, lips softly parted, fast asleep. Lia's fingers were loosely clasped around her neck. Quinn's heart beat strong and steady, just like she was. Only the bandage over her arm was a reminder to Lia that under the air of invincibility that she carried about her, the badge and the Kevlar, Quinn was definitely flesh and blood, and fragile. *Hot, too...* The memory of their first kiss made Lia smile and tighten both at the same time. As if in tune, Quinn stirred, shot her a glance, and smiled.

"Mm... I'm still here."

"Yes, you are," Lia chuckled softly. "Thanks for the hug."

"You too. Feeling better now?"

"Yes, I feel great."

"Okay."

Quinn rolled off the bed and up in one rapid move. Lia caught her bottom lip in between her teeth when she raised both arms over her head to stretch, and she was treated to a glimpse of rock-hard abs under her t-shirt. Thank goodness for the beam of moonlight coming through the open window.

"So, I'm off-duty this coming weekend," Quinn said. "Pick you up on Friday for dinner? Six-thirty?"

Lia was delighted to pick up right where they'd left off.

"Yes," she murmured with a smile. "Friday. You're on."

Quinn blew her a gentle kiss from the open doorway.

"Go back to sleep. I'll text you in the morning."

She left on that wonderful promise, and Lia let out a soft exhale when she heard the front door close after her. *Wow.* The bed was still warm where Quinn had slept, and she hugged the pillow to her chest. It smelled faintly of her; something with a hint of coconut that reminded Lia of sun-cream and the beach. *Delicious.* In the next instant, a contradicting thought came up to intrude on her experience: *I must be crazy.* Yet, all Lia could feel inside was joy, and definitely not because she was high on pills. She lay on her back to reflect. On the surface, Quinn was very similar to her ex-fiancée. At least in spirit if not looks. Brooke had been the lanky androgynous type, allergic to any kind of exercise unless it was a walk to the coffee shop. Quinn was a CrossFit fanatic, and she definitely looked the part. Other than their physical differences, both women were leaders in their chosen fields, smart, and ruthlessly committed. Drop-dead gorgeous, and with a confidence to match. But Brooke had been all fire and arrogance. Younger, too. Life, at least until that point, had not dealt her any hard blows. There had been no crushing disappointment in her career, no existential trauma in her personal life. Lia hoped and prayed that it would continue for a long time for her. Quinn was very different in that. Even before she told her about the tragedy in Iraq, Lia had sensed a deeper dimension to her character. Hurt, sadness. Pain, for sure. It was all there. She had been tried and tested in battle, literally, yet she was still standing. Still living to help others. This spoke to Lia's own recent struggles and losses. It made her feel close to Quinn in ways that several years with Brooke had not achieved. Lia spent the following days in a state of blissful anticipation and excitement at the thought of seeing her again. Nerves, too. Not surprisingly, Demi noticed.

"Is there something I should know about, my dear?" she asked her one morning.

Lia looked up from her screen, and the latest video edit that she was working on, to find her leaning with both arms over the partition.

"No," she frowned, instantly assuming that she had missed something important. "Why? What's happening?"

"You're such a reporter," Demi chuckled.

"Um, yes... You've only just noticed?"

"Don't worry, you haven't missed a scoop or anything like that."

"Right. So, what's going on?"

"I'm asking you, Lia."

"What? Nothing's going on. Why?"

"Come on!" Demi laughed. "You've been walking around with a permanent smile on your face."

"That's good, no?"

"Oh, sure. But you seem awfully distracted. You've started to wear makeup, which, in this heat, is kinda weird. Also, Quinn was in here this morning when I arrived, looking even weirder."

"Oh, yes?" Lia wondered.

"There you go, grinning again. And yes, she was. Hovering near your desk, looking extremely suspicious. Now I notice that there is a fresh rose by the side of your screen. I'm no detective with a badge, but I can't help wondering..."

Clearly, there would be no fooling Demi. And anyway, Lia was a little too happy to be motivated to try. Their respective schedules had kept them apart for the last few days, but Quinn had texted her the morning after that glorious first kiss, as promised, to check on her. This was great on its own. They'd carried on exchanging messages, which was even better, and sweet in a way that Lia had never imagined it could be. This morning, indeed, she had walked in to find a red rose, and a Post-It note with 'XO' and a smiley face written on it, waiting on her desk. She looked at the rose, touched the note, and smiled at her friend.

"You know… It's good to wonder, isn't it, Dem?"

CHAPTER
17

Quinn was amazed. If anyone had told her that she would one day experience the same kind of high as she did in combat, just from sending a woman a few text messages, she'd have laughed in their face. But doing it with Lia had her feeling super-charged. Thinking of little ways to put a smile on her face, like with the rose that she'd left on her desk, was beyond nice. Every time her cell phone buzzed in her pocket, Quinn felt a jolt of anticipation, butterflies in her stomach, and a rushing release of endorphins. She soared for a few days. Until Friday, that is, and news of a fatal shooting at a games arcade in Texas. A security guard had been killed over there during an altercation with an alleged intruder. His colleague, late coming back from a cigarette break, had not been present at the time. The news report emphasized the idea that the death of his colleague could have been averted if he had. It made much of the fact that the devastated officer would have to live the rest of his life with that on his conscience. *'He should have been the one to die!'* some people decided. It was a painful, polarizing topic. Quinn could understand everyone's frustration. Her heart went out to the deceased officer, his wife and kids, and the rest of his family. But also, to his surviving colleague as well. There was no excuse for letting down a partner, either on or off-duty, in any way, shape or form. She'd certainly never dropped the ball in that regard. Her record was stellar. Even so, natural empathy meant that she could easily put herself in this guy's shoes. It was not hard for Quinn to imagine the kind of thoughts that would haunt him at night. Hell, she'd had them all, and maybe even a few more. She was able to push the matter out of her mind during her shift, but it came flooding back on her run home from the station. Nothing specific, just general anxiety. It made her feel a little short of breath at the start of her run, and ended up with her having to stop at the bottom of the stairs leading up to her apartment. Heaving, shaking, with sweat dripping down her face... She recognized the signs, and did not panic. She just sat, closed her eyes, and tried to ride the wave as best she could. Breathing and counting down from a hundred in her head always helped. She was at eighty-seven when a person materialized in her field of vision.

"Whoa! What the hell, Wesley?"

Janet, in a pair of shorts, a maroon scrub shirt, and wearing her glasses, looked like she was coming off a shift. Before Quinn could even attempt to say anything, she grabbed her wrist in a practiced move, very different from the way that she normally tried to touch her, and tilted her head back to look into her eyes.

"Any chest pains?" she inquired sharply.

"No," Quinn panted. "I'm fine. Don't fuss."

"You don't look fine," Janet snorted, although she relaxed a fraction. "You're white as a sheet and your heart's racing. Chills. You're shaking. Is the heat getting to you?"

"I'm just—"

"You know, only an idiot would go out running in this kind of weather," Janet carried on, pressing her free hand tightly over her chest. "Don't move. Breathe into my hand. Nice and deep for me, please."

"Stop feeling me up."

"Stop being so ungrateful. Do what I tell you."

Thanks to both her counting and a good dose of annoyance, Quinn gave up arguing and went back to taking deep breaths instead. She managed one, then two. And another.

"'Kay," she muttered. "Thanks. All good, you can go."

"Nice try, but I'm not leaving yet. I'll get you settled first, and then you can tell me what it is that's giving you such drastic anxiety."

"It's the heat," Quinn automatically countered.

Janet laced a supportive arm around her waist at the same time as she laughed.

"No, it isn't. I was only saying that to calm you down and make you think of something else. You remember what I do for a living; don't you, Quinn?"

"Mm."

"You can't fool me with this stuff, so don't even try."

Once in the apartment, she half-assisted, half-dropped her onto the couch, then ran into the kitchen and came back with a glass of ice-water and a protein bar.

"Get that down you now."

"You're that abrupt with all your patients?"

Janet cut her a condescending look.

"You're not a patient, beautiful, so I have every right to grill you on this situation. Stop trying to deflect and answer my questions."

"Janet…"

"Hush. Is this a recent problem?"

"No."

"No? How long, then?"

"Dammit, Jan. It's not a problem, so just drop it, okay?"

"Getting argumentative," Janet smirked. "Good. Better than suffocating. How's Lia doing?"

Against her best intentions, Quinn choked on a mouthful of protein bar.

"What?"

"Drink your water. Don't drown. I'm only asking because rumor has it that you two are having a thing." Quinn raised a dangerous eyebrow, which did not slow the inquisitive surgeon down one bit. "And now, you're having yourself a meltdown? So, what's going on?"

"Nothing. It's not related."

"But it's true?" Janet exclaimed with glinting eyes. "You and Lia?"

"For god's sake," Quinn mumbled again. "Can't I even take a breath around here without it being news?"

"Right now, you taking a breath is good news, indeed. So, did you sleep with her?"

"No."

Janet fixed her with a confused expression.

"So, you're not having a thing. What—"

"I kissed her."

"Oh. I see. Okay. How was it? You kissed her first? And— Oh, Quinn…"

Fuck. Quinn quickly wiped the tear off her cheek but it was too late. Janet had already noticed.

"Just leave it," she instructed.

"Out of the question." Janet moved next to her and she passed her arm around her shoulders. "I'm sorry. Are you feeling okay?"

"Yeah."

"Actually, forget that, it was a dumb question. Obviously, you're not. Look, if it would help to talk about it... I'm here for you, okay?"

Quinn sighed, feeling both reluctant and grateful.

"Thanks. But everything's fine. I'm taking Lia to dinner tonight."

"Okay. A date, uh?"

"Yes."

"That's not your usual MO," Janet gently remarked.

"For sure," Quinn said with a weak chuckle. "I've been high about it all week. About her, I mean."

"Wow. Awesome."

Quinn dropped her head with a hard exhale.

"I'm going to cancel. It's crazy. I can't do this thing."

"Wait," Janet advised, as she was reaching for her phone. "I think you should take five and think carefully before you make a big mistake."

"Since when are you an advocate for serious relationships?"

"So, it's like that? Serious?"

I really need to stop talking. Quinn leaned forward with both hands stuck in her hair. She'd told Lia the full story about Iraq, and fallen asleep in her arms. Sent her mushy texts in the middle of the night, and sneaked around the office to leave flowers on her desk. The woman had been at the back of her mind 24/7. Serious? *Hell, yeah.* She was going to cry, and there was nothing she could do to stop it.

"I can't do this," she repeated through gritted teeth.

Janet rubbed her back in a surprisingly unsexual gesture.

"Of course, you can," she murmured. "Hey, what happened today to get you in such a state, anyway? It's not just pre-dinner

159

date nerves, is it?"

"I was reminded of how stupid it is to become attached to people," Quinn blurted out angrily, without thinking. "What the fuck am I doing? It's not safe!"

Janet stayed on the couch as she stood up to pace the room, watching her with a mix of sympathetic yet amused expression on her face.

"You are in deep, girl."

"You think that's funny?"

"No. I think it's gorgeous, and part of me is a little jealous. Level with me: I assume that whatever you're feeling now, that's making you lose your breath, isn't about Lia."

"I'm not going there, Jan," Quinn warned her.

"That's fine, I don't need the details. I'm just hoping to help you realize that you're full of shit."

"What are you talking ab—"

"Oh, save it, please," Janet interrupted, and her expression tightened. "We lost a twenty-year-old in the OR today, so I ain't got time to not be real with you. Got it?"

Quinn straightened up, almost snapping to attention.

"I'm sorry to hear that. Are you okay?"

"Yes, I'm fine. We did everything we could. It's not the first time that the victim of a road accident is brought in when they're already too far gone, and it won't be the last either. But these things have a tendency to focus the mind."

"Yes," Quinn nodded. "I understand."

"I know you do. But even so; sometimes, the focus needs a little adjusting when it is personal. That line about attachment and not being safe, Quinn?"

"Yeah, what about it?"

"You know it's not right."

"Negative. And I don't think so."

"Sure," Janet insisted. "Life isn't safe, eh! The illusion that you're in control of anything in this world is little more than wishful thinking. You can do your best in any situation that you find yourself in but, at the end of the day, what is supposed to happen will not fail to happen."

Once upon a time, Quinn might have told her that she was wrong about that, but she knew from experience that Janet was correct. She'd seen soldiers survive incredible odds in the field, and it applied to her as well. Lying in bed in the hospital, one of only two survivors on her team, she had done her best to find reasons, and assign meaning to what had happened. Why had she lived and not the others? How come that shard of glass had ended up in Nic's throat instead of hers? Why had Evan Alvarez bled to death in her arms, and not the other way around? Quinn could find no answers to the existential questions that tormented her. Out of desperation, she even asked the army chaplain who came to visit her one afternoon.

'God's Will', was his reply, and she immediately saw red.

"Excuse me sir, but with all due respect: Fuck that!"

He nodded as if her answer made some sense, and gave her a patient smile.

'Life is a mystery; be grateful for it. Live the best one you can in memory of the teammates that you lost. That's all any of us can, and should do, Captain Wesley'.

It was sound advice, although Quinn struggled from time to time to let go of the questions. She shot Janet a rueful glance.

"I think I like it better when you lick my abs than when you try to psycho-analyze me."

"Don't worry, I'm a great multi-tasker." Janet flashed a roguish grin. "Although I guess your abs will be off-limits from now on. Property of one Ms Lia Kennedy. Am I right, or what?"

"No," Quinn muttered, before shrugging. "Really… I don't know."

"Well, I think you're just getting cold feet ahead of tonight's date. Allowing old wounds and screwy beliefs to get in the way of happiness. You told me that you've been feeling high about her, right?"

"Yeah. She's… She feels special."

"I assume the feeling is mutual?"

"Uh-uh. Yeah, I think so."

"Then stop scaring yourself into panic attacks and give it a chance. Flow with the connection you have. Sometimes the best thing that can happen in life will. It doesn't have to be a series of tragedies."

Quinn finally cracked a smile. This was a startling idea, and one she would quite like to start believing in.

"Thanks for the reminder, Jan," she approved. "I can get a bit dark with my own thoughts sometimes."

"It happens, and you're welcome. I'll miss our naked times together if you two hook up seriously, but you are a friend and I'd like to see you happy above all else. Where are you taking Lia tonight then?

"I thought maybe O'Neill's in Carson Creek."

"Sounds great," Janet approved. "Have fun and don't forget to breathe. It helps with the kissing."

Quinn laughed.

"Roger that."

CHAPTER 18

Lia waited in front of her apartment building for Quinn to pick her up, having spent a full hour deliberating what to wear and trying on outfits. *Crazy.* But Demi's revelation that Quinn rarely if ever invited women out to dinner confirmed her own feeling that this was kind of a big deal. It sure was for her. She settled on a pair of black jeans and an emerald-green silk blouse that highlighted the amber in her eyes. Leather sandals, small golden loop earrings, and minimal makeup, completed the look. She was nervous, elated, unsure, excited. Still wondering what she was doing this for, and if it was the right decision... But recalling their first kiss, and the way it had felt to fall asleep in Quinn's arms, took care of the doubts. Lia ignored the lingering feeling that it must be more serious than that, and she took a deep breath to settle the knots in her stomach. *Just relax...* At six-thirty on the dot, she detected the growl of a powerful engine. Excitement prevailed, and she grinned at the sight of the classic muscle car that rolled to a smooth stop in front of her. Quinn was driving a red Chevy Camaro with white lines on the side and the top down. The car was eye-catching, although not as much as the woman behind the wheel.

"Hey, Lia." Quinn greeted her with a broad smile.

"Hi..."

Feeling kinda speechless, but... *Damn.* Quinn was in tight, threadbare blue-jeans, heavy black boots, and a black t-shirt with the sleeves cut off that showed off the muscles in her arms. With sparkling blue eyes, and full lips just begging to be bruised with a kiss, she fixed her with an intent stare. Laser-focused, as if Lia were the only star in her universe.

"You look gorgeous, Lia."

Without breaking eye contact, Quinn took her hands in hers and she gently kissed the back of her knuckles. Lia's skin tingled in reaction. Old-school charm, she decided, mixed with a dash of danger and forbidden from the way she looked, and the hungry expression in her eyes. Quinn was not trying to hide any of it. Her vibe was more bad girl than squared-away cop this evening, and Lia liked it a hell of a lot. It seemed like having the best of both worlds, and she instinctively stepped a little closer to her date.

"You look great as well," she murmured. She rested both hands on her chest, loving the solid feel of her under the layer of thin fabric. "I missed you, Quinn."

Lia surprised even herself at the admission, although it was true. Texting was good, but nowhere near as wonderful as being able to see her in the flesh, and lay her hands on her chest like this. It was fast becoming a favorite gesture. To catch those blue eyes instantly turn hazy and stormy; to see Quinn swallow, and witness her slow arousal; and to know for definite that she was the reason for it, too... Quinn's obvious pleasure made Lia feel powerful in ways that she had never experienced with a woman before.

"Busy week," Quinn nodded, her voice husky.

"Thank you for my morning roses, Officer Wesley."

"Oh, yeah." Quinn laughed and her face colored. "I, uh... I enjoyed doing that."

Bad girl looking shy, and Lia's heart started to race. Hell of an attractive combination... Quinn was safe, which only added to the attraction.

"So," she smiled. "You're into classic cars, uh?"

Quinn caressed her cheek.

"Generally, I am into timeless beauty."

If anybody else had tried that kind of corny line on her, Lia would have thought them desperate and irritating. But Quinn so obviously spoke from the heart, and she looked so good saying it, that all Lia could do was issue a weak warning in reply.

"Stop it," she smiled. "Or I might be tempted to drag you back to my place right now, and not let you out for the rest of the weekend."

Quinn arched a quizzical, amused eyebrow.

"Is that supposed to be a deterrent?"

"Didn't quite come out right," Lia chuckled. "But yes, it is. I want to have dinner with you tonight, ride in this great car, and take our time. You're still off-duty tomorrow, right?"

"Yes. You too?"

"Yep."

Lia unconsciously dropped her eyes to stare at her chest. Quinn's nipples were hardening. No bra, again. She licked her lips in anticipation.

"Dinner's going to be hard work if you keep looking at me like that, you know?" Quinn remarked.

"Tough," Lia laughed. "Sorry, not sorry."

"Not that I'm complaining." Quinn smiled and she held the passenger door open for her. "There's a really nice restaurant in

Carson Creek. It's a forty-minute drive away, but well worth it, and the weather's great for a slow ride."

"A slow ride, uh?"

"Yes." That luminous smile remained on Quinn's lips. "Are you up for it?"

"Definitely."

As Quinn climbed in on the other side, Lia had to bite her tongue not to come out with her own mushy line. *I don't mind where we go, so long as you're with me.* Admittedly, this was a level above and beyond what Quinn had said. Even problematic, or it could be, if she allowed the feeling to develop. Lia frowned in sudden reluctance. Again, she admired Quinn's face in profile. The determined line of her jaw, the thick, unruly blond hair she loved to hold, and that sexy smile, just tugging at the corner of her lips. She was beautiful, with a body to die for, and a soul to match. *A sure recipe for problems down the line.* And yet, there they both were. She sighed.

"Something wrong?" Quinn said softly.

Lia noticed a wariness in her gaze that had not been there only a couple seconds earlier. On impulse, she slid as close to her as the gear shift would allow, and she hooked her arm around Quinn's.

"I'm a bit nervous, you know?"

Quinn kept her free hand on the wheel as she turned to her. She held her eyes for a moment, as if looking for the answer to an unspoken question of her own.

"Hey... Me too," she murmured.

"Oh, great," Lia blurted out in relief.

"Really?" Quinn chuckled. "Why is that?"

"It's nice to know we both feel the same way. Quinn... Why are you nervous?"

Quinn rested soft fingertips against the side of her face and she smiled a thoughtful smile.

"You, uh…"

••

Everything about you makes me nervous. But it would not be fair to say that, would it? Lia may be triggering her insecurities, but the fact that there were some to activate in the first place was all on her. And anyway…

"I *was* nervous today, but as soon as I saw you, everything felt right," Quinn admitted. "Now I just want to go for a drive and enjoy dinner with you, Lia. We don't have to do anything else. Just… Enjoy. No pressure, okay?"

"No pressure," Lia smiled.

"Good."

"Would it be okay to kiss you, though?"

Quinn froze as she was about to start the car again.

"Oh, that's the good kind of pressure. Yes."

Lia had a way of kissing her that made Quinn lose all sense of anything else. Whether frantic and hungry, like the other day; or gentle and slow, like now, it was a trip every single time.

"Damn, you're good at this," she murmured.

"You know, it takes two." Lia breathed against her lips, and pulled back to regard her with glinting eyes. "Let's be easy with each other tonight."

"Alright," Quinn laughed. "I like the sound of that."

They headed West along the scenic road that followed the coast, with forest on one side and the ocean on the other. Quinn did not push the car. She wanted to enjoy easy tonight, for sure, and take her time with everything. She drove with her free hand

167

on Lia's thigh, because Lia put it there and held her in place. The gesture was at once grounding and exciting. Possessive, for sure. Quinn enjoyed feeling that vibe from Lia, which again, was a surprise.

"So, tell me about this car."

"Oh, it's a guilty pleasure."

In true reporter style, Lia zeroed-in on that one word.

"Why guilty?"

"Um... I don't know. But it feels like an indulgence."

"Yes, but I know that you work hard for your rewards," Lia stated.

Quinn shot her a sideways glance. Lia burst out laughing.

"You have a dirty mind, Officer Wesley."

"Projecting much, are you, Ms Kennedy?"

"You know what I mean," Lia smiled, caressing her wrist.

"Yeah, I do," Quinn conceded with a grin. "The car's a good thing for me. Working on it helps me to relax after hours, and I enjoy taking her on road trips when I have time off."

"Mm, I love road trips, and feeling that sense of freedom which only the open road can give." Lia squeezed her hand. "There's nothing better. What are your favorite places to get to from here?"

Quinn stole an admiring glance at her before responding. Lia seemed to have relaxed now. Watching the wind gently lift strands of glossy dark hair off her shoulders made Quinn ache to do the same with her fingers. At work, Lia kept her hair tied up. Tonight, it was loose. Carefree, as she seemed to be more and more. Very tempting. Quinn struggled to return her eyes to the road in front.

"If I only have forty-eight hours, I find myself a beach close to home to spend the night," she said.

"In the car?"

"Yep. I pack some food and a sleeping bag. I like to have a camp-fire in the evening, and it's great to get up early the next morning and go for a swim before driving back home."

"Naked swimming?" Lia teased.

Quinn tightened at the thought of chasing a naked Lia into the waves at sunrise.

"Not usually," she smiled. "But that could be arranged."

Lia absently rubbed gentle circles over the top of her wrist.

"Where else?" she asked. "When you have a bit more time."

"Then, I head out into the desert. I like it there, very much. Wide open space. Quiet. Sometimes I stay for two or three days. It's good for the soul."

"You go alone?"

Quinn picked up on the unintended sharpness of her tone, as if Lia just cared very much about the answer to that one. Once again, it made her feel good.

"Yes, I do go alone."

"Sorry," Lia grinned. "This isn't an interrogation."

"No, I'm glad you're interested. To be honest with you, Lia, I enjoy my solitude."

"Okay." Lia sounded careful, as if she sensed she might be intruded on sensitive territory.

"But I—"

Quinn's voice caught in her throat and she had to swallow. Damn, she'd not expected to feel so much emotion. For a brief moment, it was crushing. Indeed, she loved being alone in the desert. Just her and the silence, when she could be at one with the earth, the sky, and the stars. But sometimes, a deep sadness also crept into those moments of precious aloneness. Quinn understood the power of genuine, bone-deep connection. Sadly, she had also experienced the other side of the coin, multiple times. She knew the heart-wrenching pain of losing friends and teammates who felt like family. Like a part of herself. Jumping in a burning truck about to blow up would never be as scary to her as the thought of one day having to go through those feelings of despair again. This being said, her fears had already made her lose her breath once today, and almost cancel this meeting with the most attractive and interesting woman she had ever met. Quinn would not let the fears rule the day. As Janet so brilliantly put it, she would not allow any old wounds or screwy limiting beliefs to get in the way of this moment.

"Do you like being in the desert too, Lia?" she asked.

"Yes, I do," Lia answered softly. "I like pitching a tent in the middle of nowhere, and campfires under the stars."

"Maybe we could go some time," Quinn suggested, only to freeze when she realized her own words. Lia had just told her that she wanted easy. *So, what the hell am I saying?* "I'm going too fast," she corrected quickly. "I'm sor—"

"No, Quinn, no," Lia murmured, gripping her hand tighter.

Quinn was startled by the intensity in her face.

"It's okay?" she tried.

"Gosh… Yes. Absolutely. I would love to go with you."

Quinn released a careful breath. *Damn…* Lia was churning her insides like no woman ever. She nodded, feeling right on the edge. Of what, she was not too sure. Tears, perhaps… Too much emotion, probably. Happiness? *Definitely.*

CHAPTER 19

It was strange, indeed, the sense of freedom that came from just getting into a car and hitting the road. Right now, Lia felt, they may as well have been on their way to outer space. Only her and this gorgeous woman who, by some miracle, made her feel truly reborn. Quinn ignited so many feelings and desires in her which Lia had thought she'd never experience again: hope; excitement; reassurance.

"I've got to tell you something," she stated.

"Go ahead." Quinn was frowning in concentration.

"It's a bit rude, I must warn you."

Quinn clearly caught on her playful tone, because her frown disappeared, replaced by a smile.

"That's okay, I don't blush easily."

"Oh yes, you do," Lia chuckled. "And looking very sexy when it happens as well."

Quinn shot her a glance, one eyebrow raised in challenge.

"Let's see. What rude things have you got to tell me?"

"I want to touch you."

"Is that it?" Quinn grinned. "You think that's going to make me blush?"

"I'm not done," Lia whispered, staring unabashedly at her nipples under the tight tank top. "I want to rip your clothes off and put my hands on you. Everywhere. I want to caress your body and tease you for a long time, until I'm all that you can think about, and you beg me for release."

Quinn did not blush, but her nipples hardened.

"I don't beg," she said huskily.

Lia moved her hand over her thigh, enjoying the instant ripple of hard muscles that the gesture provoked.

"You will," she breathed into her ear. And she watched, in a mix of fascination and triumph, as color finally bloomed into Quinn's cheeks. "Blushing, I believe. You lose."

Quinn turned darker blue eyes to her, holding for as long as was safe before returning them to the road. Lia noticed her chest rising and falling fast, and she had to take a deep breath of her own.

"Like I said," she repeated, feeling flustered. "You make me feel a bit crazy. I'm not sure... It's not like me to say things like that."

She did not add the part that would make herself blush. The bit where she admitted out loud that Quinn effortlessly brought back all her silly hopes and dreams. Lia had thought that she must be over those naive ideas by now, of finding a woman who would drive her sexually wild and also fulfil her need for a real, stable, emotional partnership. After Brooke, she had convinced herself that this would never be on the cards for her. In turn, she had stopped wanting it. Why drive yourself crazy over things you knew you couldn't have... Right? But now, Quinn was here, talking about camping trips to the desert, and Lia was describing the start of sexual fantasies to her in detail. Quinn had not even asked! *Oh, man...*

"It seems like we are both somewhat off of our standard MO," Quinn reflected.

"Both of us?"

"Yes. You tell me sexually explicit isn't like you…"

"For sure."

"And for me, it's taking a woman out to a romantic dinner. Just for the joy and pleasure of it, with no expectation of what's going to happen afterwards, that is not the norm."

So, even in that, we complement each other… Lia flashed her a gentle smile as Quinn glanced her way again.

"I like that we can share this sort of thing."

"Me too," Quinn smiled.

She turned left off the main highway and carried on down a twisty private road that led through the forest for about half-a-mile. They emerged onto a sheltered cliff, facing the ocean.

"Wow!" Lia exclaimed, leaning forward in her seat. "That's breathtaking!"

"It sure is," Quinn replied, looking at her.

The restaurant was a cozy-looking wooden lodge with clean wraparound decking, a flagstone path that led to it, and colorful lanterns hanging from the trees. Quinn slid the Chevy into one of the last parking spots.

"Busy place, uh?" Lia said.

"Yes, but I booked ahead of time so we're good."

She came round to open the door for her. Lia took the hand that she offered.

"Thanks," she said, but Quinn did not stop there.

In the next instant, Lia found herself pressed against the car with Quinn's leg heavy in between hers. She suppressed a gasp at the sweet rush of arousal that she experienced, and her hips lifted in reaction.

"I like what you said to make me blush," Quinn murmured.

She leaned into her with her full weight. Lia laced one arm around her waist. She clasped the back of her neck to pull her even closer.

"Good. Because I meant every word."

Quinn's blue eyes flashed and they met in a hungry kiss.

Lia slipped her tongue inside her mouth. She hooked her ankle at the back of Quinn's calf. She rubbed her crotch against her thigh, knowing that it would not take very much... *I can't believe I'm doing this.* But she was, and it was good. When she lifted the front of Quinn's tank top and pressed the palm of her hand over the hot muscles in her stomach, Quinn groaned in what sounded like approval. Lia kept going up, skimming the outline of one breast, eager to feel the full weight of it. She was about to cup her when Quinn grabbed hold of her wrist.

"Stop," she ordered, panting and laughing at the same time. "Please, stop... I can't if you do that."

Lia stilled her hand.

"I like it when you say please."

She pressed her lips over the rapidly pulsing point on the side of her neck and she moved her leg, the one that was in between Quinn's, up a bit sharply. A low growl escaped Quinn's lips in reaction, which had to be the most erotically-charged sound Lia had ever heard. *She's amazing.* Quinn pushed into her twice, hard, before sagging against her and going very still. Lia froze in sheer surprise.

"Quinn?"

"Mm?"

"You didn't... Did you?"

Quinn's shoulder shook with an unsteady laugh, and she met her gaze with glinting eyes.

"No. But close. Be careful with me, okay?"

She was serious, and Lia stared back in astonishment.

"Wow…"

"Yeah," Quinn chuckled. "Everything about you, Lia."

"But are you always… Like…"

"What?"

Lia bit on her lip, feeling embarrassment creep up into her cheeks. She was so, so far out of her comfort zone…

"What, Lia?" Quinn repeated gently.

"Are you always so ready?"

Quinn threw her head back to laugh again.

"No," she admitted. "I'm usually the one in control of this type of situation, to be honest. But you make me feel… Unexpected things."

Lia exhaled, her stomach tightening with something akin to pure apprehension despite the compliment. When Quinn had started to kiss her, she had been overwhelmed by a surge of desire and need so intense that all rational thought just completely drained out of her mind. All she wanted was… *Well.* That was it, actually. She wanted, and craved to touch her. She needed to have her. To take. She knew that if Quinn had not stopped her, her next move would have been to sneak a hand down the front of her jeans. *Oh, my goodness… I almost assaulted her!* Lia shivered, suddenly light-headed.

"I'm sorry. I wasn't in control either."

"It's alright. I don't want you to feel sorry for having fun with me," Quinn said gently, her expression serious again.

"Okay," Lia nodded, albeit uncertainly.

"You really aren't used to feeling this way?"

"Definitely not."

"Well in this case, I'm glad you get to experience something a little bit different with me. Let go, Lia, and just relax. I like how you are with me."

"Okay… Yes, I like it too. I'm fine, really."

"Very fine, yes." Quinn smiled in a way that made her eyes sparkle, and Lia want to lunge at her again. "I love the way you touch me and react to me. I like knowing that I make you feel a bit out of control. You know?"

Lia softly caressed her cheek.

"Thanks for saying that, and me too. I'm not used to a woman reacting to me the way that you do either."

"I find that hard to believe," Quinn grunted. "What the hell was wrong with your ex-partner, uh?"

Lia grinned at what she knew to be a rhetorical question, although she was stunned by the reflection. For sure, Brooke never seemed to lose her breath about her. The best word to describe their sex life might have been 'Uneventful'. A total non-event, actually. Brooke did not orgasm very often. Because she told Lia that she wasn't really into sex, and that it was no big deal for her, Lia settled with that. Even so, something at the back of her mind had always wondered: why could she could not set the woman that she loved on fire the same way that Brooke did her? What was it about her that was never quite enough for her partner? How could she love her more, and better? Now was the first time it occurred to Lia that something might have been out of sync on Brooke's side and not hers.

"You ask interesting questions," she said.

"Do I?" Quinn shrugged, a bit of a dreamy smile hanging on the corner of her mouth. "Don't know how that could be, really, because you blow my brains out."

Laughing, with her confidence recovered, Lia laced a steady arm around her waist.

"Let's go, Officer. I'm hungry."

"Yeah, I noticed. So am I."

••

The owner of the restaurant was a friend, and he greeted Quinn with open arms.

"Been awhile, Wesley! How you doing, soldier?"

"Busy times at work, Hulk, but I suffered."

"Eh?"

"Missed your cooking terribly," Quinn smiled.

He threw his head back in a hearty laugh and slapped her hard enough on the back to make her cough.

"So you should. Who's your friend?"

Quinn made the introductions, and he led them to a quiet corner of the room with magnificent views over the open ocean in front.

"Tom's an ex-Marine," Quinn volunteered.

"Cool. Why did you call him Hulk?"

"Because it takes a lot to make him lose his temper, but he's fierce when he does."

"I thought it was because he looks a bit like Hulk Hogan."

"He does, doesn't he?" Quinn chuckled. "Would you like a drink?"

Lia had a glass of red wine; Quinn settled on a Budweiser. She relaxed into the moment. The dining room was full, yet the atmosphere created still managed to be intimate. Very romantic too, with the sound of evening crickets outside and candles lit on every table inside. Salty air drifting in on a warm breeze, and the heady scent of hot grass from another scorching day, made for a great combination.

"Aah," Lia sighed, smiling. "This really is summertime at its best."

"Totally, yes."

"I love this place, Quinn."

"Great, I'm glad you do."

"And I bet the swimming's pretty good out there, uh?"

"Cold," Quinn stated. "With strong currents, and the bay's full of sharks."

"Oh…" Lia grinned. "Still looks inviting from up here."

"How did you get into open-water swimming?"

"I always had a passion for the ocean. I loved going to the beach as a kid, which led to becoming a Lifeguard when I was older. There's something very primal and nurturing about being out alone in the middle of the ocean. I find it both calming and exhilarating."

"Primal and nurturing, eh?" Quinn reflected with a smile.

"For sure, yes."

"That's two words I'd use to describe you, actually."

"Mm. You sure seem to trigger the primal in me."

"Even better, then."

Lia laughed and she reached for her hand across the table.

"If you encourage me, I can't promise I'll be able to restrain myself later on."

A sudden flash of Lia, fully nude and on top of her, her skin glistening and her head thrown back, made Quinn momentarily forget to breathe.

"No pressure, but I hope so," she murmured.

Lia flashed her a sultry smile before she grabbed the menu, and promptly changed the subject.

"What are you having?"

"Steak and salad. You're an expert tease, you know that?"

"I'll have the same. And that's because you are exceedingly teasable." Lia laughed. "You set me off. I like it."

Conversation flowed over dinner. Light and playful most of the time, a bit more reflective in places, but never too much. On the whole, it was as Lia had said she wanted the evening to go: easy and fun. Quinn allowed her to drive on the way back, and she got a kick out of discovering that Lia was a brilliant driver. Fast but safe, super-confident, and very smooth with it as well. She clearly enjoyed pushing the car and testing limits. Quinn sat smiling by her side, wondering if she would be the same in bed. She suspected as much from what she had already tasted of Lia, and she hoped to find out soon, but she was also open to how the evening would go from there. Lia's call. When her date suggested stopping at the beach for ice cream, Quinn was definitely up for it.

"A different kind of foreplay," Lia announced. "Let's make this night our own, and make it last."

"Okay. Can I just ask you a favor?"

"You can ask," Lia winked, resting against her side.

"I'd like to lick ice-cream off your gorgeous lips."

"Oh, yeah?"

"Yeah." Quinn stared at the vein pulsing harder on the side of her neck. "For a start. Then I might lick a few other spots, if you give me your permission."

"Uhm," Lia purred." I think I might say yes to that."

NATALIE DEBRABANDERE

CHAPTER 20

By the time they made it to Quinn's apartment, her heart was racing harder than after a competitive workout. Lia grabbed hold of her in the hallway, before they even arrived at the door. With both arms locked around her neck, she pushed her against the wall for a passionate kiss that left Quinn feeling breathless and trembling.

"Damn, Lia..." she grunted. "You feel so hot."

"Told you," Lia mumbled, before sinking the fingers of both hands into her hair. "Not holding back anymore."

Somehow, they made it to the door. Quinn was so excited by then that she could barely see. Lia laughed when she dropped the key; twice, before managing to fit it into the lock.

"Losing your control, Officer Wesley?" she teased.

Quinn had never felt so on the edge as she did now.

"Not yet, don't worry," she promised, and pushed the door open.

Lia fell in after her and immediately tackled her again. With her hands still buried in her hair, holding on with both fists, she went straight for her mouth. God, the woman could kiss! Quinn reveled in the experience of her being so demanding and wild.

She walked them backwards blindly across the room, until her legs hit the back of the couch and she tumbled onto her back. Lia followed with the movement, landing on top of her and pinning her down.

"I want you, Quinn," she muttered. "I want you so bad it hurts."

"You can have all of me, Lia," Quinn promised. "I'm yours tonight. All night."

With a small cry of anticipation, Lia slid her hands under her tank top and ran hot fingers over her stomach. She covered her breasts, squeezed gently, and rubbed rough thumbs over her nipples in a gesture that made Quinn see fireworks behind her closed eyelids. *Oh, man!* She was wet, hard, and already so damn close to pure oblivion! She arched her back in response to Lia's demanding caress, wordlessly begging for more.

"You like that?" Lia whispered.

She bit her shoulder, grazed her teeth along the side of her neck. Quinn jerked under her again in pure pleasure and need. It seemed that her hips had acquired a life of their own, no longer obeying her, but following Lia's rhythm.

"Yes," she gasped. "I love what you're doing to me."

Lia pinched her nipple. She caught her startled moan with another deep kiss, stealing her words, before wrenching her mouth away and stilling her fingers. Quinn blinked to regain her vision. When she did, Lia was leaning over her, eyes aflame with raw hunger.

"Bedroom," she panted. "I need you naked *now*."

"Follow me," Quinn growled in reaction.

They shed clothes along the way, in between stealing kisses and becoming entangled in each other. Quinn threw her tank top across the room. Somehow, Lia was already shirtless, bra-less, and unzipping her pants. Quinn allowed her gaze to travel over perfect breasts, dark erect nipples, smooth hips, and slender legs. Lia was soft and strong, her body flawless and quintessentially female. Quinn simply had to hold her breath as she watched her nude, revealed for the first time. In awe of her beauty.

"You're so gorgeous."

"You too, baby." Lia trailed her nails along the centre of her chest. "Wicked sexy."

"Maybe we should slow down a bit. Enjoy the—"

"Later," Lia interrupted, her tone almost pleading. "Second time round. Please, Quinn, I need you now."

Quinn almost tore off her own jeans in her haste to take them off. Fully naked now as well, she laced one arm around Lia's waist and pulled her close, initiating the first contact of skin on skin. Again, the sensation made her brain sizzle. They fell on the bed, their limbs tangled, bodies perfectly fused.

"Yes…" Lia murmured. "Yes. Come here."

Quinn could have orgasmed from the commanding way that Lia wrapped her up in her embrace, and directed her mouth to her breast. She needed no invitation to take the swollen nipple in her mouth and caress it with her tongue. She sucked on it, her blood pounding. Lia was dripping all over her leg.

"You're close," she said.

"Yes," Lia groaned.

Quinn wanted to give her what she needed, but not too fast. She wanted to remember this moment, every minute detail of their first time. She brushed her fingers over Lia's heated center, parting the wet and silken folds. She was close as well, but intent on not losing control. Not yet, anyway.

"Look at me, Lia," she instructed.

When Lia did, she slid inside of her.

"Oh my god... Quinn!" Lia whimpered and laughed all at the same time. The smile that followed was at once the sexiest, most exciting, beautiful thing that Quinn had ever seen.

"Not just yet, babe," she whispered. "Ride me, please."

••

Lia could not have predicted this particular outcome. That they would end up in bed was a no brainer. Of course! The chemistry was too strong and too perfect not to. But in this way? It was the stuff of her most private and hottest fantasies. She was literally fucking herself on Quinn's fingers. Using her, shamelessly, and relishing every goddamn filthy second of it. Not only that, but the enthralled expression on her partner's face also told her how much she was enjoying herself. For Lia, this was an impossible dream come true.

"I want you to make me come," she gasped.

"I will." Quinn thrust in a little deeper, hitting the perfect spot and retreating before it would push her right over the edge. "Like this?"

Lia stopped breathing. The wave of pleasure that flooded through her was so intense. So perfect. *I had no idea it could be like this...*

"Yes," she breathed. "Right there... Mmm..."

Without being told, Quinn managed to be everywhere that she needed her to be, perfectly, all at once. Fingers teasing her G-spot, just the right amount to keep her on the edge and prolong the pleasure... Thumb over her clit, exerting the most exquisite pressure... And Quinn also had her free arm hooked around her shoulders to steady her, and keep her close. Lia was fast losing the ability to form words.

"You're gorgeous, Lia," Quinn whispered. "Ready?"

Lia could only nod, her mind dissolving into ecstasy. Quinn took her mouth in a passionate kiss and she pumped her fingers. Once. Twice. Smooth and hard at the same time. Tender. Loving. And *deep*. Lia rocked with her, precisely matching her thrusts. The third time, Quinn pushed her fingers against the precise spot that would send her into the stratosphere, and she kept the pressure on.

"Come for me, baby."

Beautiful words. An incredible command. Exactly what Lia needed to hear. Clenching around Quinn's fingers, she came hard with a short, sharp cry. But it did not end there. Waves of pleasure rolled through her, so intense and unexpected that she cried out.

"Quinn! Don't let go."

"I'm here, Lia." Quinn held her tighter. "I won't let go."

Never before had Lia experienced such a mind-shattering orgasm. Not with Brooke. Not even on her own. How did Quinn know to touch her this way, so perfectly? It was nothing short of miraculous. Out of breath, still trembling, Lia raised her head to look at her. Quinn remained in the same position, watching her with liquid, smoldering eyes.

"How?" Lia whispered. "How did you…"

Quinn curled a single finger, and it was all it took. Lia came again with a shuddering tremor, her entire world dissolving into a flash of light. When she opened her eyes a while later, Quinn lay half on top of her, one leg still firmly pressed in between her thighs.

"Hey," she smiled. "How are you feeling?"

"Did I pass out?" Lia mumbled.

"No. You were just in the land of bliss."

"Aah," Lia whispered, caressing her face. "You are so damn beautiful. I'm in the land of bliss right now."

Quinn brushed a soft kiss over her lips.

"I'm glad. Although I think you broke my fingers. You got quite a grip, uh?"

A bit steadier, Lia shook with laughter.

"Oh, I'm sorry. Can I make it up to you?"

"Take your time, I'm good for now."

Lia trailed a languid finger between her legs, making her shiver and tense.

"You're swollen. Hot." She licked traces of her arousal off her own finger, and watched all the focus drain out of her lover's eyes. "You taste of wanting me."

"I do want you, Lia."

"Then rest on the pillows."

Quinn punched one into position behind her back. She half-sat, half lay there with one leg bent, watching Lia watching her. Lia did not have to wait long to see color suffuse her face and the top of her chest.

"Blushing again," she teased. "Excited?"

"Fuck yeah," Quinn said roughly.

"Hands by your side," Lia instructed.

Wordlessly, Quinn gripped onto the bedsheet.

"I don't want to rush this," Lia said, at the same time as she straddled her body.

"You're still wet," Quinn murmured.

"Yes, I am. That's the effect you have on me."

"Me too."

Lia leaned back to caress the top of her thighs, clenching in reaction when Quinn's gaze instinctively dropped to her sex. She moved her hands to her chiseled stomach, cupped her small but full breasts in her hands, and brushed her tongue over one of her nipples. Quinn groaned.

"You like that?"

"Oh, yes."

"You're trembling."

"Yeah, you're making me," Quinn chuckled weakly.

Everything about the way that Quinn responded to her was a wonder to Lia. To realize that she could make this gorgeous woman twitch and gasp, laugh and tremble... It was incredible. Lia nibbled kisses down her neck. She caressed her breasts, and sucked on her nipples. Quinn broke the rules to run her fingers through her hair, prompting Lia to slide down the length of her body.

"Stay still," she repeated.

"Trying," Quinn replied.

Her eyes were feverish, intent, tracking her every gesture. Lia nestled in between her legs. She rubbed her fingers over the inside of her thighs, and parted her gently with her thumbs.

"So sexy..." She brushed a kiss over her glistening center. Quinn growled and her hips lifted in reaction. "I am going to take you slow."

Wordlessly, joyfully, Lia embraced her. She suckled, kissed, and licked, varying degrees of pressure and speed until Quinn was struggling for control, and almost levitating off the bed. She brought her up in layers, pausing only when she could feel her too much on the edge.

"So good," Quinn panted. "You feel so fucking good. I'm so close but I don't want to finish. Please, don't make me come just yet."

It was a big rush, hearing her say that. Emboldened, feeling empowered like never before, Lia tried a daring line.

"You'll come when I tell you to." Quinn's pupils widened at the brazen statement. She moaned, and Lia felt her pulse harder against her lips. So close, and fighting. She caressed her slowly. "Won't you?"

"Ah... Yes, Lia," Quinn mumbled. "I will."

Lia continued licking and caressing her. She relished seeing as far she could push, although she knew that her partner was going to lose control soon, no matter what. When the trembling in her legs grew to be too much, and Quinn's heartbeat had reached a dangerous threshold, she knew she had to bring her home.

"I want you to come for me now," she murmured.

At the same time, she slid her tongue into her and secured her thumb over her clitoris. Quinn arched rigidly. She stopped breathing. In the next instant, she exploded in her mouth with a strangled cry.

"More," Lia demanded.

She placed her hand over her stomach to keep her still, and started to rub heavy circles over her clit.

"Fuck," Quinn cried. "Fuck... Lia, I'm gonna—"

"Yes. Do it."

Knowing what she needed, Lia wrapped her lips around a tight nipple, and she filled her with her fingers. Only one thrust was required, and Quinn came even harder. Witnessing her full surrender, so beautiful and true, had to be the greatest thing Lia had ever experienced. Quinn spasmed under her for a long time. Eventually, she curled into her side and nuzzled her face into her shoulder. Lia pulled the light sheet over them both. She held her lover close, with the palm of one hand resting over her racing heart.

"Shh," she soothed gently. "Shh..."

The hair at the back of Quinn's neck was wet, her skin still hot and glistening, although Lia felt her shiver. No longer from arousal, she knew, and Quinn pressed herself tighter into her embrace.

"Are you okay?"

"Mm..."

Lia spotted tears shining like diamonds on her eyelashes, and her heart tightened in concern.

"Quinn—"

"I'm fine, Lia."

"Really?"

"Yes. Oh, yeah..."

Quinn spoke in a raw, naked voice, and her smile was a little broken; but if anything, the vulnerability in her eyes only made her more attractive to Lia.

"Happy tears?" she ventured.

Quinn chuckled and her eyes sparkled.

"You just destroyed me and I've never felt any better." She kissed her. "You really are an exceptional woman, Lia."

NATALIE DEBRABANDERE

CHAPTER
21

Quinn woke up with sunshine in her eyes and the smell of coffee drafting through the room. Most unusual. So was the feel of soft fingers caressing the back of her neck and going slowly up into her hair. She purred in reaction.

"Good morning, beautiful."

Lia sat on the side of the bed, hair wet from a recent shower and wearing one of her CrossFit t-shirts. Looking like an angelic apparition. Quinn lingered, head empty and her heart full.

"Good morning to you too. Hey, did you shower without me?"

"Yes, I didn't want to wake you."

"What time is it?"

"Eight a.m."

"Wow. That's a four-hour lie-in for me."

Lia leaned over to brush a gentle kiss over her lips.

"I think you needed it. You were sleeping like someone knocked you on the head."

"Mm. Someone knocked me out for sure," Quinn chuckled. She sat up and pulled Lia on top of her, straddling her lap. "You look cute in my t-shirt. Although…"

191

"You want me to take it off?"

"Reading my mind. Yes, please. Get rid of the damn thing."

Lia obliged with an amused giggle, and guided her face to rest in between her breasts. Morning-after cuddles. *I had no idea it could feel so nice...*

"Better," Quinn sighed with her eyes closed. "Much better, eh..."

"I think so too." Lia ran her fingers through her hair, gently cradling and rocking her in her arms. "Would you like a coffee, darling?"

"Normally, I would say yes, and thank you very much for making it. But this morning... Not quite yet." Quinn flashed a hopeful grin as she captured a tanned nipple between her lips. She loved the sweet whimper that the gesture elicited, and the feeling of Lia hardening under her tongue made her instantly wet.

"I could be convinced, I suppose."

Quinn moved to her other nipple.

"Convinced to do what?"

"To get sweaty with you all over again."

"I promise I'll make it worth it. Every second. And then we can shower together after."

"Sounds like a wonderful plan."

"Let me make you feel good, okay?" Quinn almost pleaded. "I'm all yours. Tell me what to do."

Lia regarded her with hazy, thoughtful brown eyes for a moment. Then, with a mesmerizing smile, she pushed her down and scooted forward to place one leg on either side of her head. Quinn licked her lips at the sight of her, already moist and open, and a beat between her own legs started to pulse furiously. *Oh, yeah.*

"Please, do it like this," Lia murmured. "So that I can watch you."

••

Once again, time and space dissolved in pleasures shared. It was too late for breakfast by the time they got out of bed, and even later after they feasted on each other in the shower.

"I think I can still walk," Lia declared as she put on a pair of shorts. "Just about. Could I tempt you with a late brunch at the beach?"

"Yes... And if you're not feeling at least a little unsteady, then I didn't do my job properly."

Lia regarded her with twinkling eyes.

"Couldn't you tell I was having fun?"

"Yeah." Quinn touched a finger to the spot on her shoulder where Lia had bitten her. Not enough to hurt, but plenty enough to thrill. "Yeah, I could tell."

"May I lean on you?"

"Yes."

"Can I borrow your t-shirt?"

"Sure."

"And drive the Chevy again?"

"Woah, woah!" Quinn chuckled. "You're going a little hard there, aren't you?"

"I don't know." Lia stared long and deep into her eyes. "Am I?"

Talking in riddles to test a few limits again... Flirting with dangerous questions. Quinn was aware of what she was doing, and she might have ignored it if it had been someone else. But Lia was too beautiful, and it felt too good, to stop this now.

"Getting mushy on me, Ms Kennedy?" she prompted.

"Little bit, I guess. But that's your fault, Officer Wesley."

"Oh, is it? How come?"

"Great sex and multiple orgasms have that effect on me."

"Ah." Quinn shrugged. "Can't be helped then, I suppose."

Lia laughed, rolled her eyes ironically, and dragged her out the door with her.

"Feed me now, or I'm really going to drop."

"Yes, ma'am."

Quinn rarely spent idle time at the beach. Usually, she was there running or working out at dawn. By the time the cafés and restaurants opened, and the crowds arrived, she was long gone. Today was totally different, and she was stunned to realize how enjoyable it was. They made their way along the busy pedestrian path, walking slowly hand in hand. Just another couple among the many people enjoying their day out. *Awesome.*

"I like being anonymous in a crowd," Quinn mused.

"What do you mean by that?"

"It's nice to blend in with people without having something to do for a change."

"Off-duty?" Lia ventured. "Like, vacation time?"

"Yeah," Quinn chuckled. "I guess that's what you call it, uh? It's been a while since I had a proper day off."

With every step, she could feel herself unwinding more and more deeply. Sex had been wonderful; the best. But this was just as good, if not better. The sense of companionship, the intimacy that came from a night of passion... Of course, Quinn enjoyed that too. She smiled again as Lia pulled her tighter against her side and laced a possessive arm around her waist. Yeah, she could get used to this kind of treatment. A warning bell sounded at the back of her mind, but she ignored it. It was so wonderful to be held... She did not mention that out loud either. Being with Lia felt very natural. Comfortable. *So damn right.* Quinn looked away toward the ocean as she swallowed a hard lump in her throat. *You know you'd better not get too used to it.*

"Hey." Lia gave her a gentle nudge to bring her back. "Still with me, darling?"

"Yes," Quinn nodded. "I'm with you."

Right here and now. The only time that she should focus on. The only thing she could ever honestly promise. Unconsciously, she tensed.

"What's on your mind?"

Ah... There was the inquisitive reporter, making a comeback. Quinn actually loved that side of Lia. She smiled, glad for the fact that her lover could not easily read her eyes behind the Oakleys.

"Debating food choices." A small white lie was probably okay, just so as not to spoil the moment. "Are you up for some tacos?"

"I could be dead and still wake up for that," Lia laughed. With a suggestive wink, she added: "Mind-blowing sex followed by tacos on the beach with a gorgeous woman... What a fantastic way to spend the weekend, uh?"

Quinn frowned.

"Are you meeting someone here?"

Lia grabbed her around the neck to deliver the sort of kiss that should be illegal in public.

"Only you, darling," she murmured.

Again, it felt like loaded talk, although the kiss promptly turned her mind to mush and did not give her a chance to reflect for long. Quinn shivered in reaction, and a stab of arousal hit her between the legs. Lia bit on her own lip, looking pleased.

"Did you like that? You did, didn't you?"

"Behave yourself, Ms Kennedy," Quinn instructed.

"Can't promise that." Lia caressed her cheek. "Especially if it makes you blush like you are doing now. Fancy going out for a paddle-board?"

"I want to do whatever keeps that gorgeous smile on your face, Lia."

"Charmer." Lia kissed her again, and she kept smiling.

Out on the water, she also teased her mercilessly about her inelegant wobbles. Quinn retorted that it was because she could not take her eyes off her, then promptly tackled Lia off her board and kissed her underwater until they both ran out of oxygen. Soon after, Lia retaliated in similar fashion. It was a playful day, full of laughter and impulsive cuddles. Late afternoon, on the hunt for a bit of shade and a cool drink, they bumped into Ethan and Jenna. The two were on foot, pushing a baby stroller along the path.

"You guys decided to skip the wedding and go straight to the baby stage?" Quinn prompted.

"Not quite," Jenna laughed. "We're on baby-sitting duty for my nephew today."

"Alright. Practicing."

"Yep, getting a taste of nappies." Ethan made a face. "I mean, not literally, of course."

"No shit, Sherlock," Quinn grunted, and Lia laughed.

"What are you two doing here, anyway?" Ethan went on, eyeing them suspiciously. "I didn't take you for the beach bum type. And I didn't see you in the gym this morning, Quinn. You sick or what?"

Lia answered before she could.

"Quinn was busy with me this morning," she stated. "I am

teaching her how to relax."

Driving me out of my mind, more like, Quinn reflected, and she just managed not to turn beetroot at the memory of how Lia had put her to sleep the previous night.

"Oh, yeah?" Ethan was still none the wiser.

"Yeah," Lia nodded rather smugly.

He paused, looking puzzled, then it must have dawned on him that the two were holding hands. Quinn suppressed another roll of the eyes as his eyes lit up. *What a cop.* Granted, he was off-duty.

"Ah…" Ethan broke into a wide grin. "Busy. Yeah, I get it. You two got busy with—"

"Ethan."

Quinn shot him a warning look, knowing full-well the sort of joking that he was capable of. Squaddie humor of the worst kind, and never mind that Lia must have heard it all before. In any case, Ethan laughed easily and he clasped them both on the shoulder.

"Hey, don't sweat it, Wesley. Wow, you guys. Cool, uh!"

"Yes," Lia agreed, and Quinn caught her smiling glance. "That's very cool indeed."

As she parked in front of Lia's apartment building later on that night, she was aching inside in a way that surprised her, and which she did her best to ignore. Lia had been very quiet on the way back as well.

"Coming up?" she asked her now.

"Yes, I'll walk you to your door."

Once up there, Lia dragged her in, of course. It did not take much effort.

"Would you like a beer?" she offered. "Ice tea? Lemonade?"

What she really meant was, '*Stay*'. Quinn could not resist a chance to extend the evening a little bit, even though she knew it had to come to an end soon. She opted for a glass of lemonade, and they both dropped side by side onto the couch.

"Ah, beach days," Lia sighed. "They're the best."

Without thinking, Quinn licked a trace of salt off the side of her neck. It kinda felt like the thing to do. She pressed a soft kiss behind her ear, delighting in the pulsing heat under her lips, and she relished the way that Lia responded, by instantly wrapping both arms around her neck, and pulling her close.

"Going to put sand all over your couch," Quinn warned.

"Doesn't matter."

Lia sought her mouth and she kissed her deeply, slow and lazy. It was different from the kisses that she had lavished on her the previous night. Not as demanding. More thoughtful, but no less enjoyable. Again, it was comforting for Quinn in ways that she had not realized she needed.

"We should shower," Lia mused, tracing the outline of her lips with a gentle finger. "But I don't want to move."

She said, 'We', and Quinn tensed again.

"Lia…" she murmured. "I have to go."

"Have to? Why?"

Good question that… As Lia gripped her tightly, grounding her in her presence, Quinn was afraid of the answer. She tried to make one up on the spot.

"Back to reality, eh," she said lamely. "I'm starting early in the morning."

"Do you mind if I ask you something?" Lia prompted.

"Yes," Quinn replied, before correcting herself. "I mean, no. Of course not, go ahead."

"When we were talking before, you told me that you were not after a relationship," Lia recalled in a gentle voice.

Quinn was on her side with her back pressed against the couch. Otherwise, she might have jumped right up and bolted for the door. She flashed Lia a quick smile, trying to control her growing agitation.

"Yes. I did tell you that." There it was, then. The sensitive morning-after stuff that she always tried to avoid by never staying the night, never mind spending the next day together. It was not a selfish decision on her part. Quinn simply hated to disappoint her partners. On the whole, few ever asked. No need, really. But Quinn should have known that Lia would be different. She was gutsy. Determined. Not one to run from delicate situations. "You told me the same thing…"

"Yes, I did," Lia agreed, and threw a leg right over hers.

Quinn had to laugh at the movement.

"Pinning me down, are you?"

"I think you like that."

"Uh-uh. I think you're right."

"So, can I finish the question?"

"Lia, I—"

"Because you said you didn't want a quick hook-up either," Lia interrupted. "And neither do I. So, I'm just wondering where that leaves us."

CHAPTER
22

Monday morning dawned grey and stormy, matching her mood. Lia had not slept well. She woke up with a headache. Worse was the fact that she only had herself to blame for the sadness that she felt. *You and your stupid questions. Way to ruin everything, Lia.* She missed finding a rose on her desk, and knowing that Quinn had thought of her like that. *You know it doesn't mean anything; so, stop it.* Lia took a deep focusing breath, grabbed her Kevlar and GoPro, and headed to the parking lot to meet her team. Back to reality – indeed. Lewiston PD ran a solid Field Training Program for their officers before they were allowed out on solo patrol, and Lia had been cleared to accompany one of their brand-new recruits on her first day in the job. The rookie officer, Eleanor James, greeted her with an eager smile as she approached her patrol car.

"Good morning, Ms Kennedy."

"Officer James," Lia nodded in return. James's uniform was perfectly ironed and her boots were shining. She was tall, lean, with coal-black hair and piercing grey eyes. She looked good, and ready for duty. "Thanks for letting me tag along with you. I appreciate it."

"No problem," James grinned. "I just finished checking the vehicle. All good to go. As soon as my FTO joins us, we can get underway."

"Who's your FTO today?"

"Officer Garrison, ma'am."

Ah, perfect. Lia was friends with Ethan outside of work now, and swimming buddies as well. At work, she knew him to be a consummate professional. Today should be good. *Make it so,* she told herself. No excuses. She noticed James's impatient glance at her watch and added;

"Feeling excited?"

"I am," the young woman chuckled. "Been waiting for this moment all my life, you know?"

"Always wanted to be a cop?"

"Yep. It's in my blood."

"Do you come from a long line of police officers?"

"Nope." A brief shadow clouded James's smooth features, but she went on briskly. "Everyone's an engineer in my family, but I'm a cop through and through. Strange, but... There you go, eh!"

"I don't think it's strange, actually," Lia reflected. "My dad was a cop, but I always knew I'd be a reporter. It's who I am and always was."

"Cool." James nodded brightly. "So we understand each other. Call me Ellie, okay?"

"Sure thing, Ellie. Lia."

"Alright." Again, James checked the time and she frowned impatiently. "I don't know what's going on. It's not like Garrison to be late."

"He might have been delayed in the—"

"Good morning," a rich, husky voice interrupted.

Lia's nervous system recognized her before she even turned around to see. *Quinn.* Her body reacted instantly, by sending a flood of blood to sensitive places. *Conditioned much, are you?* Lia suppressed a sigh and she bit lightly on her lip. Next to her, James came to attention so hard that Lia heard her spine pop. Different reason for the reaction, but definitely the same person causing it. Quinn came to a stop next to the car and flashed them both an assessing glance.

"Ethan has to be in court today," she announced. "It's a last-minute thing, so I'm filling in for him. Happy with that, Officer James?"

"Yes, ma'am!" Ellie replied with a beaming smile.

As Quinn turned steady eyes to her, Lia could not help but stare. She had never seen her in uniform before. She also never had a *'thing'* for women in uniform before. She preferred them in jeans and leather, board shorts, or simply skin, which Quinn had already demonstrated that she wore better than most. Now, Lia discovered that she also sparkled in uniform like no one else ever. She nodded to her with a brief smile.

"Quinn. Hi."

She didn't expect much more in return. They weren't alone. This was work. Also, from Quinn's reaction to her question, she suspected that the fairytale date would never be repeated. So, when Quinn lightly squeezed her hand as she went past, Lia was surprised. The touch was only fleeting, but warm beyond words. It made Lia want to grin and cry at the same time. She knew that she had to get her emotions under control, or this training day was going to be hell... Fortunately, Quinn tempered her tender gesture with a typically irritating comment.

"Put on your vest, Ms Kennedy," she instructed. "Or we'll leave you behind."

Lia would not put it past her, actually, and she scrambled to obey. Ellie got behind the wheel, with Quinn riding shotgun. Lia sat in the back. They'd barely left the parking lot when the first call of the day came through. *Disturbance at Starbucks.*

"It's your show, James," Quinn let her know.

Ellie keyed her radio mic and responded enthusiastically.

"2-Bravo-12, show us en route."

"Ten-four, 2-Bravo. A homeless guy pitched his tent on the lawn and is refusing to leave. The manager called us."

"Roger, Dispatch," Ellie acknowledged.

Five minutes later, they arrived on scene. The tent, pitched in the middle of the landscaped lawn, was hard to miss. And Lia was pleasantly surprised at Ellie's way to handle the situation. The young officer went straight into the Starbucks, came out with coffee and a donut for the enterprising camper, and sat on the lawn to chat with him for a while. Quinn stood aside during that time, not getting involved.

"How's she doing?" Lia inquired.

"Pretty good so far."

"How long is her training going to be?"

"Three weeks."

"And you're here to rate her performance?"

"My job is to offer guidance and feedback. The FTP is not a test; James is already qualified. Week One is about teaching her the procedures and policies of our department. City geography, use of equipment, personal safety. Easy stuff to begin with. It's walking pace."

"And then?"

Quinn nodded in approval, as the homeless guy started to pull down his tent. He seemed to be in good spirits, chuckling at something that Ellie had said.

"Week Two, we'll start jogging. That means being on night shift, putting her out of her comfort zone, and having to handle slightly different types of jobs."

"More dangerous," Lia murmured.

"Potentially, yes." Quinn moved on with a matter-of-fact shrug. "When she gets to Week Three, she'll be running. Able to handle ninety-percent of the calls on her own, and be confident with every aspect of the job."

"She seems at ease right now."

"Yes. It's a good start."

"Thanks for explaining how it works."

Quinn took a break from observing her charge, and keeping a close eye on their surroundings, to meet her gaze. For a split second, searing heat pierced through those guarded blue eyes. Lia was reminded of their night of passion, and her heart started to race again.

"I told Matthew we could give him a ride to the shelter in town," Ellie announced. "Is that okay?"

Quinn looked to her, cutting the connection.

"Sure thing, Officer James."

She added a quiet *'Good job'* under her breath, only meant for her colleague, but which Lia still caught. She noticed Ellie's quick flush of pleasure at the praise, and made a mental note to interview her later about how it felt to have Quinn as a mentor. For now, they kept going. The next call sent them to the liquor store, after a dispute between two customers left one of them with a bleeding nose. A regular traffic stop followed, and a visit to the skate park, after a teenager reported a couple of thieves on the prowl. A subsequent positive identification and arrest were made. Lia had a good time observing the two officers at work. Ellie was having fun doing her job, that was obvious, and Quinn was not overbearing in the role of teacher. She offered simple guidance and common-sense tips. The morning went without a hitch. At one o'clock, they rolled through Burger King and got lunch to eat in the car. Lia was thoroughly enjoying listening to Quinn, as she shared funny stories of her first times out on solo patrol, when the moment came to an abrupt stop.

"Whoa!" Ellie exclaimed. Right under their nose, a vehicle blew through the traffic light and flew like a rocket across two lanes of highway, barely avoiding causing a crash in the process. In her haste to react, Ellie dropped her fries and she banged her elbow on the door. "Ow!"

Quinn relieved her of her drink before she could dump it all over the dispatch computer.

"Check your six," she instructed calmly.

"Clear!" Ellie replied.

"Let's go then, rookie."

On that, Ellie executed a powerful extraction out of their chosen lunch spot, generating minor Gs in the process. Lia quickly pulled on her seatbelt, and she caught Quinn's eyes on her in the mirror. The officer in charge nodded quietly, and returned her attention to the front, but Lia knew what this was about. The seatbelt thing. *She's checking on me.* Quinn was not looking only after the new recruit today, for sure. Lia had no illusion about that. Quinn would behave in the same way with anybody else, man or woman, who rode with her. Even so, Lia could not prevent it from affecting her. The thought that Quinn may care a little bit more because it was her was nice to entertain, even though she knew it wasn't true.

"Is this a 10-80?" Ellie inquired excitedly.

Lia checked her list. *Ten-eighty:* chase in progress.

"Not yet," Quinn replied. "Get a bit closer and use your PA,

I don't think he even knows you're there."

Sure enough, as soon as Ellie identified herself, the vehicle in front slowed down. But the driver still kept going along at five miles an hour.

"Stop your vehicle on the side of the road," Ellie instructed.

The car veered off abruptly and stopped halfway on and off the road.

"Vehicle check, call it in," Quinn prompted.

"Oh, yeah... Sorry." Ellie was obviously flustered.

"You're fine," Quinn assured her after she made the request for more information. "What do you think this is?"

"Erratic driving, but he stopped when I asked. Shit parking skills. DUI, maybe?" Ellie ventured.

"Let's see what Dispatch has to say about the—"

Quinn stiffened and left her sentence hanging, as the driver of the vehicle stepped out and started to advance toward them. He was shouting something unintelligible, hands waving above his head at the same time.

"Sir, remain inside your car," Ellie ordered him over the PA system.

Good reaction, but the guy did not stop. Tall and thin with longish white hair sticking out, dressed in shorts and a baggy Hawaiian shirt, he reminded Lia of the Doc Brown character from the *Back to the Future* movies. Not that threatening, but you never knew; and his behavior sure was astounding.

"Sir—" Ellie started, but Quinn tapped her on the arm.

"Cover me."

She flew out without waiting for an answer, weapon drawn and pointed at the man's head. Ellie scrambled into position on her own side of the car. Behind the driver's door, as instructed. Lia held her breath and turned on the GoPro.

"Stop," Quinn ordered. "Put your hands on your car."

"I mean no harm!" the guy yelled. "Don't shoot. I'm—"

Before he could utter another word, Quinn had him against the car and into position.

"Don't move."

She was quick, safe, and efficient. As soon as she'd checked him for hidden weapons, and put him in handcuffs, Ellie relaxed her stance and holstered her Glock. Lia climbed out of the car. Quinn looked as if she'd barely broken a sweat. She was calm and in control. Powerful. *So damn sexy.* Lia suppressed a shiver of arousal.

"Don't you know you shouldn't rush at a police officer like this?" Quinn asked the guy. "You could get shot."

He stared at her indignantly.

"I would never shoot you, ma'am! First of all, I don't even have a gun!"

Lia winced. It was a damn good thing that he didn't... She could smell booze on him from ten feet away. Ellie retrieved an empty one-liter bottle of whisky from his vehicle, confirming their suspicions. After another cruiser came by to assist, and took the drunk driver away, Ellie was apologetic.

"I didn't react quickly enough. Damn! I should have—"

"Don't beat yourself up." Quinn sounded nonplussed. "It's called training for a reason, uh?"

"Yes, I suppose."

"Just tell me what you'll do differently next time."

"Talk less, act earlier," Ellie replied immediately. "Like you did. This guy could have been armed. He needed stopping. Once he did not obey my request to stay in the car, the time for talking was over."

Quinn smiled, looking pleased.

"Perfect. So, the lesson was worthwhile."

The afternoon ended on a sad note, with a welfare check on an elderly woman who, unfortunately, had passed away during the night. Ellie did her best to console her daughter at the scene.

"Yeah, that was a hard one," she confided in Lia, once back at the station. "But it's all part of the job."

"Are you happy with your performance today?"

"Quinn said she was, so I am too."

"What's next, then?"

"First of all, clean the cruiser again, since I got fries all over it," Ellie chuckled. "Then go home to eat and sleep. Get ready for tomorrow."

CHAPTER 23

Lia walked into the locker room sometime later, her mind on the video edits that she was working on and, for once, not thinking about Quinn. But there she was, getting changed out of uniform. Lia stopped abruptly. Quinn had made it as far as putting on a pair of Levi's. The buttons were still undone. She was topless, affording Lia a glimpse of the rippling muscles in her stomach. *Oh, man!* Lia could have sworn that Quinn's nipples hardened, the second that she noticed her walk into the room. As hers definitely grew tight, she gave a curt nod and went straight to her own locker.

"Hey, Lia," Quinn said softly.

That naturally deep and throaty voice never failed to make Lia shiver. She did her best not to be obvious about it.

"Hi," she replied.

"How was today for you?"

Lia risked a glance over her shoulder. Quinn had put on a polo shirt, and moved to sit on the bench to lace up her shoes. She turned to face her.

"Today was great. You're a brilliant teacher."

"Don't have to do much with someone like James."

"She's got good instincts."

"For sure. Just needs to learn to trust them."

"That should come with practice and experience, right?"

"Definitely. That's why we train."

"What else makes a good cop, Quinn?" Lia inquired, falling into reporter-mode without really being aware of it.

For sure, it was her default setting. It was also helpful not to simply stare at Quinn's gorgeous face and think of kissing her. Or get lost in flashes of memories about the other night, with all the heat-inducing urges that it implied.

"Being able to think on your feet and make quick decisions about complex situations," Quinn replied, gazing at her from the bench. "Self-awareness and interpersonal skills. Cops need to be excellent communicators. Also, genuinely care for people but keep it in balance at the same time. James was a bit rattled after that last job."

"Well, that's understandable," Lia argued.

"Sure." Quinn stood and shouldered her rucksack. "But whatever happens on patrol, good or bad, a police officer should keep her distance. It's okay to empathize, but only up to a certain point. James will learn to build her defenses."

"Like you did, uh?"

The words were out of Lia's mouth before she even realized she had said them. It occurred to her that she sounded bitter as well. That part was definitely not intentional. She watched the light wash out of Quinn's blue eyes, and her jaw tighten. *Ah, shit!*

"Quinn—" Lia gripped her wrist to hold her back as she was about to walk straight past her and out of the room. "Hey, I'm sorry... I didn't mean it."

Quinn regarded her steadily.

"What exactly didn't you mean?"

Her voice was gentle, and Lia realized that this was not said in challenge. All the same, Quinn appeared so very remote, all of a sudden. Beyond reach, even, and that was concerning.

"I didn't mean to imply that you're hiding."

"Mm. Right."

Still holding onto her wrist, Lia moved her free hand to rest on her chest.

"Quinn, I need to tell you," she murmured. "This weekend with you... It mattered a hell of a lot to me. You know?"

Quinn's lips parted with a sharp intake of breath, and Lia felt her flinch. There it was, that fire again. Emotion flared in her eyes, and Quinn covered her fingers with hers.

"Of course, I know," she whispered intently. "I—"

"Wesley!" a male voice sounded in the back. "The captain wants you."

For a moment, Quinn did not move. Lia had no idea if she was going to push her back or kiss her. It could have been either. Quinn looked so torn. So conflicted. Lia reached up to touch her face, to connect.

"Hey... Quinn, I—"

"Wesley. You get that?"

Quinn blinked hard, as if coming back to her senses.

"Yeah, got it," she snapped. With her lips pursed, she took a step back, away from Lia. "I have to go."

Lia was left to stare after her, heart pounding to breaking in her chest. *What the hell just happened?* They'd gone from easy to raw in the blink of an eye. Did Quinn feel the same way she did about the weekend? Had it meant more to her than she thought it would, and was that the reason for her detachment? Lia made her way out to the parking lot on shaky legs, struggling to make sense of the loaded exchange. A shout interrupted her difficult musings.

"Lia!"

"Hey, Dem…"

Lia stopped to allow her friend to catch up.

"Carole has been delayed at work and she won't be able to pick me up as planned. I need to get home in time for Luke. If you're leaving, would you mind giving me a ride?"

"No, not at all." *Well.* Perhaps a little bit… Lia would prefer to be alone and quiet, to think of Quinn and their latest exchange to her heart's content. Still, obsessing about her was definitely not a good idea, and this would only be a quick detour anyway. "Jump in," she invited.

"How was your day on FTP?" Demi inquired, as they drove out onto the road. "Did Ellie do okay?"

"She was excellent," Lia confirmed. "I was impressed with her skills and self-assurance. She'll be a great character to follow as part of my behind-the-scenes documentary."

"Awesome. Yes, Ellie is a good girl."

Lia smiled. Demi spoke of all the officers of Lewiston P.D., captain included, as if they were her children. *Even Quinn…* She grew pensive as her thoughts returned to her. Quinn; ruggedly handsome, battle-hardened, and hiding something, no doubt.

"That's a big sigh," Demi remarked.

"Oh, I'm just tired. It's been a full day, and then some."

"Sure? You seemed very sad just now."

"No, I'm fine. No worries."

"How was your date with Quinn? Haven't been able to ask you yet."

Lia shot her a glance and found Demi watching her with a knowing smile. Alright; she'd walked straight into that one.

"It was great," she nodded. "Quinn is awesome."

"She certainly is. You got her into bed? Was that awesome too?"

"Demi, come on!" Lia protested.

"What?" her friend chuckled. "I'm just trying to figure out why you would sound so down about it if everything is great. Sex is usually to blame for this sort of contradiction. So: what's going on with you two?"

"Nothing. We went out, had a lovely time. End of."

"Were you looking for more than just a one-off?"

"No," Lia said firmly, even as tears tickled the back of her eyes. She had not planned to discuss this, but the realization was too big to contain, and she carried on. "At least, I didn't think I did, but that was before we had dinner. A night of the best sex ever. And into the next day, as well."

"Oh?" Demi sounded surprised.

"Yeah. We spent it at the beach." Lia's heart swelled at the thought of it. "We had brunch, went paddle-boarding... All my favorite stuff. And just being together was brilliant, you know?"

"Yes, of course."

"It was so good. So unexpectedly needed. And it reminded me..."

"Of how wonderful an intimate relationship can be?" Demi prompted when she hesitated.

"I think so," Lia admitted with a sigh.

"Nothing wrong with that, is there?"

"No, but I thought I was done with this sort of thing."

"Really?" Demi laughed. "Why? Have you stopped being a real woman of flesh and blood?"

"I just thought I had outgrown the need for companionship, that's all."

215

"Pull over a second."

"Why?"

"Just, please. Pull over."

Lia complied, cut the engine, and turned to her. Demi eyed her with a mix of concern and amusement.

"What's the matter?" Lia shrugged.

"What you just said," Demi answered. "The so-called *'need'* for companionship. Do you see it as a weakness?"

"No. Of course, I don't."

"Okay. Just asking because it sure sounded that way."

"I'm sorry if it did. What I meant to say is that I don't think it's my path in life. And I made peace with that a long time ago. It's okay."

"Right. If you say so."

"Yes." Lia nodded firmly. "Now is the time to focus back on myself. Giving up on my career before was hard. Now I want to rebuild."

Demi raised a gently probing eyebrow.

"And do you think that being in a relationship would get in the way of that?"

"I don't know." Lia shrugged, impatiently now. "Anyway, it's not even a question."

"Then why do you seem so bent out of shape about it?"

"I'm not. It was great with Quinn, but... I guess I'm just..." Again, Lia stopped short. Going round in circles, always coming back to the same conclusion. *It felt different with her. I want more.* She shook her head in growing frustration. *No way.* "It's like you said, Dem: great sex messing with my mind. I'll get over it."

Demi stopped her as she was about to start the car.

"Did Quinn tell you what happened to her in Iraq?"

"Yes."

"All of it?"

"She told me about Evan Alvarez, yes. About losing most of her crew in that ambush, getting wounded, and the aftermath of it all. Horrible stuff."

"Mm." Demi narrowed her eyes. "Quinn doesn't share her most private stuff with random dates. Never, in fact. You realize that, don't you?"

"Demi…" Lia sighed.

"I'm just pointing out important facts. Are you going to see each other again? What's she saying?"

"No, we both agreed we're not looking for a relationship," Lia stated, prompting Demi to roll her eyes. "Hey. You asked, so I'm telling you, okay?"

"Yes, okay. I get it. This was just a one-off between you two, of no consequence whatsoever."

"That's not what I said," Lia grumbled, well aware that she probably sounded crazy. "Neither of us was after a meaningless connection either."

"Well then," Demi reflected with a smile. "That's what you call a paradox, my darling."

"Believe me, I'm well aware of that."

"So where does it leave you both?"

"We said we'd just leave it open."

"We, as in…?"

"Me," Lia admitted. "I said that."

"And Quinn? What's her take on this?" Demi inquired with equal patience and doggedness.

"She said she'd call me."

"Oh, dear. The girl really gave you that line?"

"It's my fault," Lia shrugged. "I backed her into a corner and left her no choice. I had no right to ask her those questions, or suggest that one night could turn into more than we agreed to."

"No right?" Demi exclaimed. "What is this, a business deal? I can't believe you said that. Tell me you're not serious."

"Nope. I am."

"Come on! You're not a robot. Neither is she. Tell you what, Lia, I'm glad you got Quinn's back against the wall. I'm sure it did her a whole world of good!"

Lia did not feel good about this conversation. Not anymore.

"Look, I'm not comfortable talking about this stuff, and Quinn, behind her back."

"Fair enough, and all credit to you. But—"

"And it was never supposed to be a *'thing'* with us, alright? I'm just shook up because it's such a long time since I was with a woman. I'll be fine. Please, do me a favor and forget we ever had this chat. Now let's get you home."

Demi looked far from convinced but, to her credit, she did not argue.

••

Quinn enjoyed the night-shift. Gliding along the darkened city streets, alone in her cruiser, she found a sense of peace and focus which was not so easily achieved during the daytime hours. Even riding with Ellie, on her second week of FTP, was pretty good. Not only was Officer James an excellent cop, but she also did not feel the need to shoot her mouth off all the time the way that some others did. Lia had spent a couple of nights with them. She knew how to be quiet too, but having her in the car was not conducive to peace of mind. Quinn was annoyed at herself for not being able to remain unaffected. Lia made her want to jump in the backseat to cover her in kisses, curl up in her lap, or roughly rip her clothes off, depending on the mood of the moment. Not her fault, for sure. Quinn did her best to avoid her in between shifts, like in the locker room or the canteen. As it was that morning, even the beach turned out to be a risky place for unwanted encounters... The sun was just rising, and she was out on a run by the water, when she spotted her in the distance. Quinn might have turned around and fled, but she noticed that Lia was sitting with her knees drawn up between her arms. Head down. She was dressed in her running gear, and Quinn instantly worried that she might have injured herself. As she approached, Lia did not even look up. *Not good.* Quinn squatted next to her.

"Hey."

CHAPTER 24

Lia glanced up, looking like she'd been a million miles away. For a second, she just stared right through her.

"Are you okay?" Quinn inquired, automatically resting one hand over her raised knee.

"Oh..." Lia broke into a beautiful, if dazzled, smile. "Quinn. Where did you come from?"

Quinn nodded behind her to the empty stretch of beach.

"Down there. You?"

"Me too, I was just out for a jog."

"Did you hurt yourself?"

"No, no." Lia gripped her fingers in reassurance. "I'm fine. Just, uh... You know."

Quinn nodded when she just shrugged.

"Having a moment?" she prompted.

"Yes... I guess I was. It's my birthday today."

"Oh." Quinn mentally kicked herself for not knowing that. Then again... She did not wish to know things about Lia. Or get involved. Or any of that stuff. Did she? All the same, she smiled warmly. "Happy birthday, Ms Kennedy."

"Thank you."

Lia was subdued, her grin tinged with sadness, and Quinn hesitated. The safest thing for her at this point would be to move on. The other day at the station, when their impromptu chat had turned more intimate than expected, had served as a warning. Lia's confession that their time together had meant a hell of a lot to her had made Quinn eager to blurt out her own truth. *You mean a hell of a lot to me, Lia.* But it was insane… She barely even knew the woman! Quinn did not want to get involved. She knew that she shouldn't. It was her rule and it was there for a reason. Already, she had allowed herself to go too deep with Lia. To feel too much. She should leave, definitely. Keep on top of the situation. *Yes. Go.* But she couldn't.

"Would you like to talk about it?" she asked.

Lia seemed a bit surprised at the question, but also relieved, and grateful.

"Okay," she murmured. "You'll think it's silly."

Quinn sat close to her, facing the rising sun over the ocean. Not even 7:00 a.m. but the sand was warming up nicely. She was hot from her run, too, and being next to Lia did not help to cool down any.

"Is the idea of turning a year older getting you down?" she ventured.

Knowing the woman, Quinn suspected that it would not be that simple or shallow a problem. But it was a good question to start with, especially as it brought an amused smile back on Lia's lips.

"No," she said. "I don't mind that at all. But my dad… He always used to call; you know?"

Emotion rose in her voice, and Quinn passed a comforting arm around her shoulders.

"It's not silly, Lia."

"Before his illness, I used to travel a lot. But wherever in the world I may be on my birthday, he always found a way to get in touch. He was a tough guy. Didn't tell me in words that he loved me very often, but he made me feel it in lots of different ways. He loved and supported me even when I did things that he did not approve of."

Sensing that she needed to talk, Quinn kept her going.

"What kind of things?" she inquired gently.

"Oh. Going to Iraq and embedding with a unit, for one. War reporting, in general." Lia rested against her. "He didn't like me taking this kind of risk."

"What about the fact that you were attracted to women? Or was that a later discovery for you?"

"Oh, no. I knew as soon as I was old enough to think about these things. You?"

"Yeah, me too."

"My dad was open-minded about gender, although he did let me know that it would be best if I found myself a good old Boston cop. Female? Fine, he had no issue with that. But a cop, definitely."

Lia laughed at the pleasing memory, but the comment was striking nevertheless. She did not seem to notice the irony of it; or perhaps she chose to ignore it. Wise move, Quinn decided.

"Sounds like he was a great guy," she approved.

"He really was to me, yes. I'm glad he's no longer suffering, but I miss him." They were very close now, foreheads almost touching. "Hey, Quinn?"

"Right here," Quinn whispered.

"Thanks for letting me tell you about this."

"That's okay. Sorry I interrupted your private moment of remembrance."

223

"Please, don't be," Lia almost pleaded, and she placed a soft hand over her cheek. "I love it when you're around."

Love... Her touch was so tender. Quinn just about managed to keep both eyes open, although she did lean into her hand. She could not help that response.

"It's this I don't like," Lia added.

"What?"

Quinn thought she might well cry at this point if Lia let go of her. *Dammit!* Never before had she felt so out of control. For sure, she'd felt a measure of it sometimes, in combat situations. But not often, until that last fateful mission. With Lia, though, it seemed to be the norm. Her mind wanted to keep her distance, to act a certain way. And somehow, Quinn always found herself doing the opposite.

"I don't like acting like nothing happened between us," Lia said in a painful voice. "Or pretending that we don't even know each other..."

"Well. When we're on patrol, I—"

"No, that's not what I'm talking about."

Lia moved her hand slightly, to rub a light thumb over her lips. Quinn stiffened. *Okay, gotta stop this.* But she was powerless to move.

"I want you, Quinn," Lia whispered urgently to her. "I keep telling myself not to... I mean, I don't want to get involved with you or anyone else! That's not what I'm here for. It was never the plan. But I—"

"Can't help it," Quinn muttered, interrupting her.

"You too?" Lia prompted. She went on without waiting for an answer. "You know, I keep thinking about the other night. I loved waking up with you in my arms. Sharing morning coffee, kissing you in the ocean, and chatting all night..."

"Lia."

"I know, it's crazy!" Lia went on, sounding a bit on the edge herself. "I don't want this but I can't stop wanting it. You know what I mean? Damn, I'm losing it. Quinn, I'm so sorry. I just—"

She made to move, to get away, but Quinn tightened her hold over her.

"Kiss me, Lia," she demanded.

Lia's eyes sparkled. She sounded out of breath.

"I… What?"

"Kiss me, for god's sa—"

Quinn never got to finish. All of a sudden, Lia was on her lap. How she moved so quickly to straddle her legs, Quinn had no idea… But all that mattered was that Lia was in her arms, and holding her in return. Quinn was surprised at the ferocity of the kiss, although it made perfect sense. Lia's embrace simply mirrored her own intensity and hunger. Her brain switched off and she lost herself in her feelings. In Lia. Warm lips, a velvet mouth, tender arms. Lia was everything and everywhere. Her fingers brushed the back of her neck and went up in her hair. Quinn slipped a hand under her t-shirt. At the feel of her lover's hot, smooth skin, a small whimper escaped her lips.

"Shh…" Lia said soothingly, and proceeded to kiss her even harder.

She did it in a way that was both urgent and joyful, exciting and calming. It was like coming home and exploring an exotic place all at the same time. Quinn laced an arm around her waist and twisted them over. She lay half on top of Lia, still involved in the passionate kiss but taking the initiative now. She caressed the inside of her thigh and felt her tremble. She skimmed her fingers under the waistband of her shorts. Lia moaned into the kiss, making her shiver in response.

"Fuck, I need you so bad," Quinn growled.

Lia still had both arms locked around her neck, holding on tight. She threw one leg back over hers. Grazed playful teeth over her lips and sucked deliciously on her tongue. Quinn was seeing fireworks.

"Me too," Lia panted. "My place. Now. We can—"

"HELP! HELP! SOMEBODY!"

The call pierced through the haze of Quinn's arousal and she glanced sharply over her shoulder. An old guy walking his dog was yelling to anyone who'd listen. In the water, she spotted a person in trouble. *Shit.* It was still early in the morning, and this part of the beach was never patrolled by the Lifeguards anyway. If you wanted to swim here, it was at your own risk.

"He's caught in a current," Lia stated as they both jumped to their feet. "Call for backup."

On that startling command, she sprinted toward the water. Quinn was not used to being told what to do in an emergency situation, but it made sense for Lia to take the lead on this one, since she was the better swimmer. Quinn grabbed her cell phone and she put in a call to the Lifeguard station, half-a-mile further down the beach. Then, she raced after her. Lia barely paused to kick off her shoes before she entered the water. No doubt her confidence in her own skills made her fearless, but Quinn was more concerned. In the space of about five seconds, the swimmer in difficulty had already drifted way further.

"Take this," she said, and put her phone in the dog walker's hand. "Stay on the line with the Lifeguards until they get here, okay?"

"Yes, Miss!" he assured her.

Quinn followed Lia into the water. Deep from the start and, only a few strokes in, she felt the rush of the current grab her and pull her away from the beach. Damn, this thing was strong! In the distance, between the waves, she could see that Lia had almost caught up to the struggling swimmer. Quinn went harder at it until she reached the spot where she had last seen them. She stopped to get her bearings then. The beach seemed very far off already... The water was cold here. Darker. Threatening. And Lia was no longer in her sights. Quinn whipped her head around. One side, then the other. She saw nothing. *Fuck!* A cold fist of fear twisted her insides.

"Lia!" she shouted.

A rogue wave caught her by surprise and she swallowed a mouthful of water. It hurt going down her throat, making her gasp and momentarily go under. *Be careful...* Quinn understood how quickly things could go downhill in this environment. One second, feeling strong; the next, in deep trouble. And where the hell was Lia?

"LIA!" she yelled again, panic rising.

"Quinn. Over here."

Quinn blew air out in relief. Lia was right behind her, and she looked just fine. In perfect control. She was supporting the swimmer, who now had his eyes closed and seemed completely out of it.

"Is he okay?" Quinn shouted over the noise of the waves.

"Will be, I got him," Lia assured. "I need you on the other side."

Quinn maneuvered according to her instructions, in order to help keep the guy stable and his head above the surface. Not such an easy task in turbulent water.

"Now we swim back?" she asked.

"Can't, the rip's too strong," Lia advised.

"So, what do we do?"

"Float until help gets here. We'll be—" She stopped as the swimmer opened his eyes, coughing and struggling instinctively against them. "Easy, easy. We've got you. Relax."

A flash of recognition and relief crossed the man's face, unfortunately soon replaced by a wince of pain. Whatever color he still had in his face drained out in an instant.

"What's wrong?" Quinn grunted.

"Argh... Cramps! Ow, my fucking legs!"

"It's alright," Lia stated calmly. "You'll survive."

Quinn shot her a quick grin over the struggling man's head. Nothing sexier in her opinion than a woman who kept her cool and her wits about her while performing a dangerous rescue. Lia caught the grin and flashed her one of her own.

"Okay, Quinn?"

"Yes, fine."

Lia's gaze was warm and affectionate. Tender, no mistake about it. It made Quinn forget her surroundings, until another wave smacked her in the face.

"Almost there," Lia encouraged.

A Lifeguard on a powerful jet-ski, dragging a rescue board behind him, soon reached their position. Not a second too early, as far as Quinn was concerned. A busy night on duty followed by a challenging run had left her feeling tired. Now, this. Fatigue made it really hard to stay afloat, let alone help somebody else. For the first time since she'd jumped in, it also occurred to her that the water was freezing. The swimmer and the Lifeguard wore thick neoprene suits, but she and Lia were in shorts and t-shirts.

"Hold on tight to the board," the Lifeguard instructed them once the swimmer was secured on top of it. "You can do that, yeah?"

"Yes," Lia replied, and she grabbed a firm hold of one of the roped sides.

Quinn reached out to do the same, but the current was too strong. She missed the board and immediately went under again. This time, it was harder to kick back up. The cold was getting to her. Her legs were numb. Damn, she was tired. All it took was that one mistake to lose contact with the jet-ski, and for it to disappear behind the crest of another wave. Amazing how quickly it happened. One more wave, another lungful of water. Quinn was in trouble and she knew it. Gathering all her energy, she managed to break through the wall of water. In the next instant, Lia surfaced next to her.

"Gotcha." She passed her arm around her waist and smiled in reassurance. "I won't let you go, Quinn."

CHAPTER 25

Once back on terra firma, sitting at the rear of the Lifeguard's buggy under a warming blanket, the swimmer was both grateful and apologetic. White as a sheet, shaking; but greatly relieved.

"I cannot thank you all enough," he gushed, including the elderly dog walker who had stuck around to watch the rescue unfold. "That current was so strong. And with my legs cramping so bad, I wouldn't have made it without you."

The Lifeguard gave Quinn a rapid once-over, checked her lungs and her blood pressure, and pronounced her good to go. He also delivered a stern warning to the swimmer about fitness levels and ocean safety, before whisking him away toward a waiting ambulance for further checks.

"Yeah, I think he'll have learnt his lesson," Lia remarked. "No matter how good a swimmer you think you are, or how fit, going out on your own in treacherous waters is never a good idea."

"You don't do that, do you?" Quinn prompted.

"I do swim alone sometimes, in better weather conditions. But only when the Lifeguards are on duty, and I always check in with them before going in. So, it's safe."

"Good."

Lia clasped her wrist, squeezing gently.

"How are you feeling now?"

"Better," Quinn nodded. "I'm glad that guy's okay, and I'm also way happier with both feet on solid ground."

Lia shot her a look.

"Even more so then: thanks for jumping in after me like you did."

"Yep."

Quinn might have said something else if the realization of what could have happened out there had not struck even harder than on the water. *Here one minute... Gone the next.* The light in Lia's eyes, the reassuring weight of her fingers around her wrist, her brilliant smile... She could lose it all in a stupid accident, in a split second, before she could react. As the notion sank in, it felt like a punch to the gut, and she let out a heavy breath.

"Quinn?" Lia was frowning. "You okay?"

"Yes." Quinn forced a quick smile, even as she struggled to recover. "All good."

"Are you sure?"

As Lia took her hand, Quinn instinctively laced her fingers through hers. *Dammit.* Despite all that was at stake, and the risk of what she stood to lose if things went wrong... She could not help but feel the pull, and enjoy it. Everything about Lia made her want to be close to her. Physically, emotionally, in all the ways possible and imaginable. Her chest tightened, like two giant hands squeezing her lungs. She ignored the sensation as best she could.

"Yes, I'm sure. Although that guy interrupted us at a crucial moment, didn't he?"

Lia quirked an amused eyebrow.

"Very inconsiderate timing on his part." Her expression shifted back to serious. "Then again, maybe not."

Even as she said that, she moved to lock both arms around her neck. Quinn rested her hands on her hips. Such a perfect fit... They stared at each other in silence.

"What do you think?" Lia whispered after a few seconds.

The words were out before Quinn could think, actually.

"I'm scared," she murmured.

••

Of all the things she might have said, it was the one that Lia expected the least. Quinn always appeared so strong and in control; unflappable, really. Out on patrol, nothing ever seemed to ruffle her feathers. She kept her cool, defused situations with a smile and a few well-chosen words. She made everyone that she came into contact with feel safe, whether it was the victim of a crime or her own colleagues. Ellie had mentioned this when Lia asked her if she enjoyed having Quinn as her PTO.

'Yeah, I do. She's so solid. Of course, I look forward to being solo; but it's great to have Quinn as a partner.'

Lia could relate. She'd moved to the West Coast wanting to be solo as well. Really, consciously, for the first time in her life. It had taken her a long time to get over Brooke. Her dad's absence hurt deeply, as evidenced by her little moment this morning. She'd been convinced that she needed time on her own to heal and re-connect to her true self. And for a while, it all went according to plan. But now, Quinn had become a part of her world. She was a threat to her solo time, but a welcome one, actually. With Quinn, Lia felt sexy, appreciated, truly seen, and powerful. To hear her admit vulnerability now evoked a fierce protectiveness in Lia. It was not the fear of losing her that she had known with Brooke; not the horror experienced through her father's illness, knowing that even her best efforts would fail at the end. With Quinn, everything felt so much more in balance, like they were on an equal footing. Both strong and vulnerable in equal measure, although in different ways. There was a sense of completeness there that Lia had never felt before with anyone in her life. It was astounding.

"I wasn't ready for a woman like you, Quinn," she reflected softly.

"Neither was I, Lia."

Quinn was still holding on to her, and Lia could feel a low-level tremor coursing through her body. She cupped her cheek and shivered too, when Quinn leaned into the touch. Lia thought of asking, but she held back. If Quinn wanted to tell her more, she would. Right now, she was tense and felt ready to run. Lia could feel her inner conflict. She realized that it could go either way at this point: either a deepening connection between them, or a clean break. She knew which one she wanted, but also that she had to be patient. There was too much at stake to try to force a resolution.

"It's okay," she murmured.

Quinn exhaled. She did not pull away.

"That weekend with you, Lia," she said. "I never wanted it to end."

Lia exhaled sharply, relief flooding through her.

"Oh, Quinn." She fought the urge to pull her tighter in her arms and show her with a kiss how much the admission meant to her. *Not yet...* Quinn clearly needed her to go slow, and Lia also owed it to herself not to rush things. "I wasn't sure of how you felt."

"Well... Our time together also meant a lot to me. And I don't... I *didn't* want it to be that way."

"Why not?"

"Because scary stuff happens when you—" Quinn winced as if she had made a mistake. She shook her head and her eyes grew hard. "Ah. Forget it. Lia. I'm sor—"

"No, no," Lia interrupted. She had to now, since Quinn had already stepped through that door. "Don't be sorry, okay? We're just talking. No judgment, everything's allowed. What were you going to say? Please... Tell me."

Just because it was comfortable, she'd rested her fingers on the side of Quinn's neck. Now, she was startled to be able to feel her pulse pick up significantly. Her heart was pounding.

"Quinn—" she started in alarm.

"It's alright, Lia. I'm okay."

Lia dropped her hand, but not the topic.

"You've gone very pale. Are you cold? Is your chest okay?"

"Yes, I'm fine. The Lifeguard checked and he confirmed."

"Is this a stress reaction, then?"

"Not a bad one. I'm really fine."

"You mean it *is* stress?" Lia insisted in genuine concern.

So much for being unflappable. And what a dumb assumption to make, anyway. Quinn was human, after all. Just because she was a leader par excellence, with a great handle on her emotions, did not mean that she didn't feel any. Lia already knew that a lot more ran under the surface with her than Quinn ever let on. She was full of fire, passion, tenderness... And still bleeding from significant wounds, no doubt. As it was, Quinn managed to take a deep breath and some color returned to her face.

"I had a really busy night, and an eventful morning. Don't worry about it."

Lia studied her face intently. This sounded like avoidance, but after spending the night on duty, Quinn was probably more than ready for a meal and some sleep, instead of a challenging swim rescue in freezing water and an emotional chat.

"Alright," she nodded. "You need to go home and rest."

She did not expect a response but it came anyway, in part reluctant and achingly truthful. And it wasn't about what she'd just said.

"You make me nervous, Lia."

Another blunt admission, to say the least, and Lia shot her an intent look.

"I would never knowingly do anything to hurt you."

"I know." Quinn fixed her with stormy eyes. "What do you want out of this, Lia?"

"You're not playing fair."

"I'm not playing. You said you weren't ready for someone like me. But here we are. So... What now?"

Lia figured that she might as well come clean about some of her own reservations.

"I moved over here just wanting to work on my career and get over past hurts," she repeated. "The last few years have been excruciating for me. I wanted to recover. And to remain single. In some ways, I still do."

Quinn bit on her lip.

"But you like me," she prompted.

Any other woman might have sounded arrogant, and even completely foolish, making this kind of a suggestion. For sure, they'd already had sex and even spent the night together... Fair to assume it would not have happened without a certain amount of 'liking' involved. But Quinn did not mean it in that way at all, it was plain to see. Lia perceived only sorrow in her expression.

Regret. She cradled her face in both hands, an attempt to soothe and reassure, and looked deeply into her eyes.

"That's a good thing, okay?"

"You really think so?"

"Of course."

"But what you just said, about not being ready..."

Lia smiled, also feeling a rush of familiar sadness inside.

"Another thing I learned in recent years is that I can plan, decide, organize, and resist all I want, but when life's ready to move, it will." She brushed a gentle kiss over Quinn's lips. "I do like you. A lot. I am not going to turn it into a problem."

••

The morning had taken on a surreal quality for Quinn. *How did I get from the station, to the middle of the ocean, to this?* Let alone losing her breath in front of Lia. *Unbelievable.* She was convinced that without the rescue earlier, they'd have ended up back at her place or Lia's apartment. Naked. In bed. *In trouble.* Of course, she already was. No matter how much Quinn tried to stay away from her physically, Lia was firmly established inside her mind. Quinn could not avoid her presence there, nor the jitteriness that it caused. Pushing herself in the gym helped, but it seemed that being with Lia was the only real antidote. Holding her. *Kissing her...* Lia talked about the inevitability of change, regardless of how one felt about it, and Quinn wondered. At first glance, her life was far from static. She worked with a team, was involved with lots of people, and no two days were ever the same for her. On close inspection, at least her own unbiased one, she realized that she'd been stuck for a while. Just work, training, sleep. With the odd sexual encounter on the side, the kind that she could easily forget. Rinse and repeat. She'd kept herself on lockdown, and somewhat safe. But was life about to yank the comfortable carpet from underneath her feet? *Probably already has...*

"Quinn?"

"Yes."

Lia caressed her arms with a gentle smile.

"We can work this out, eh? If you want to... We can."

Because she did not push for more, the temptation to open up made itself known again. *I've lost a lot of people I cared about... You make me want to care, Lia. More than I ever did about anyone.* The realization was still fresh and it carried the potential to take her breath away once more if she was not careful. Quinn held back on sharing for the time being, but Lia was steadily chipping away at her defenses. For once, Quinn did not think of running. And there was only one answer to her question, annihilating every single objection or doubt.

"Yes, I do want to work it out," she murmured.

Lia's worried brown eyes sparkled with something more than excitement. Not relief, exactly... Not just pleasure or even joy. Something more, deeper, which Quinn was careful not to label.

"Awesome. When are you back on days?"

"Next week. I'm off on Wednesday."

"How about Tuesday night, then?" Lia invited. "You come to mine; I'll cook. We can chill and be lazy together. No pressure, no expectations. Just us. Yes?"

Nothing had ever felt so right.

"Tuesday," Quinn approved. "Yes. I'll be there."

CHAPTER
26

"What on earth is wrong with you?"

Surprised at the question that seemed to be directed at her, Quinn glanced away from her red-eye coffee to discover Janet standing next to the table, eyeing her suspiciously. She replied with an easy shrug.

"Just the usual. I came in with the victim of a recent hit-and-run, talked to him, and thought I'd get myself a snack while I'm at it."

She was back to working on her own after certifying rookie Officer James as ready for solo patrol. Ellie had aced the FTP, and Quinn knew for sure that she was ready for the challenge. When it came to her presence at the hospital, it was nothing new. The job brought her around from time to time, and she often bumped into Janet when it did. It seemed her friend was after a different kind of explanation though.

"No, I mean what's going on with *you*?" she insisted.

Quinn picked up the red sauce in one hand, she grabbed the mayonnaise in the other, and poured a generous layer of both over her hot-dog.

"What do you mean?"

Janet flashed her an eager smile.

"I had to call your name three times before you even looked up, Wesley."

"Oh yeah?"

"Yep. Since when do you lounge around this place in a daydream, with a massive grin on your face?"

"Not lounging," Quinn informed her with another matter-of-fact raise of her shoulder. "I'm refueling in between jobs. It's been non-stop since I started today and I might not get another chance to do it. I'm starving, so..."

"Uh-uh," Janet grinned. "And the distraction?"

"No distraction."

"Let me ask you, then: would that be the same sort of clear unwavering focus which had Lia almost crashing into a whale during our swim session this morning?"

Quinn coughed around a mouthful of dog.

"She did what? A whale? What the—"

"Oh, don't worry," Janet interrupted, laughing. "The whale was a long way away and I got her back into the correct channel when she veered off. Just wanted to see how you'd react at the mention of her."

"How old are you, Jan?" Quinn groaned in reply.

"You're sexy when you're angry, you know that?"

"Oh, shut up."

"You got mayo on your chin," Janet observed. "I would lick it off, but something tells me you wouldn't approve. Lia's got a hold of you, uh?"

"Don't you have somewhere to be, doc? A brain to dissect? Or something?"

"Nope."

"How very tragic," Quinn grunted.

"Talk to me, woman," Janet prompted. "You and Lia?"

Quinn could not help but smile. *Me and Lia.* Yeah, that sure sounded good, and she felt herself blush in pleasure. Actually, did not care if it showed. Janet regarded her intently.

"Wow!" She dropped into the chair in front of her. "You're serious about her. Never thought I'd see the day this happened. About any woman."

To Quinn's surprise, her eyes filled with tears.

"Hey… Jan." She reached for her hand. "You okay?"

Jan flushed bright-red and she briskly brushed her sleeve over her eyes.

"Oh, now, look what you make me do."

"Me?"

"Uh-uh."

"Mourning my sexy abs, are you?" Quinn drawled.

"Shut up." Janet smacked her shoulder, but the smirk was firmly back. "Aren't you glad you didn't cancel that date like you threatened to do the other day?"

"Yes. Very glad, and I'm also grateful for your good advice. Still, don't make too much out of it, alright? It's just dinner, no expectations."

"It isn't, and I sure will make loads out of it, are you crazy? The famously aloof and un-catchable Quinn Wesley, considering a committed relationship. It's ground-breaking."

"Janet."

"What? You are, aren't you?"

"I don't know," Quinn shrugged again.

"You're so full of it," Janet snorted, and she laughed. "You should see the look on your face."

"What look?"

"Smitten." Janet's gaze softened. "Whupped. Happy."

"Alright, don't go all mushy on me, please."

"Just calling it as I see it." Janet grinned again, just as her beeper went off. "Ah, saved by the bell. ER's calling, I gotta go perform miracles."

"Good luck. Not that you need it."

Janet reached to wipe another little spot of ketchup off the corner of her mouth.

"You too, girl," she winked. "Keep me posted."

••

Tuesday dragged on for Lia, as slow and sticky as the continuing heat that clung to the city like a second skin. At least the AC had been fixed at the station. Good thing she had video edits to work on as well, even though that barely held her attention. She did a fair amount of staring at her watch, trying to decide whether it was broken or if time had really come to a standstill. She drank too much coffee and tried in vain to focus on her work. From the other end of the office, Demi flashed her an amused smile.

"Have you got a punctured lung or something?"

"No. Why?"

"What's with the constant huffing and sighing?"

"Ah, sorry about that, Dem." Lia chuckled sheepishly. In a quieter tone, she added: "I'm having dinner with Quinn tonight, at my place."

"Ooh! Lia!" Demi moved over to her desk like a shot. "And when were you planning to tell me?"

"Well... Now, I suppose."

"So, you two decided to give it another go, uh?"

"That's right."

"How does it feel?"

"Great… Amazing."

"Awesome!" Demi exclaimed.

"Yes," Lia grinned with a small shiver of excitement. "That, for sure."

Demi regarded her with a warm, approving smile.

"What are you cooking?"

"Salmon-en-croute, chocolate mousse I made this morning, and I've got a bottle of Chardonnay chilling in the fridge to go with it."

"Very nice, darling. Officer Wesley is a lucky woman."

"So am I," Lia reflected intently.

"Why don't you go home early today? You've been in here or out with the teams every day, and some nights, for what feels like way too long."

"Mm…" Lia hesitated briefly, but the suggestion made sense. Editing raw footage was one of her favorite things to do, but she'd been struggling at it for the past hour. Going nowhere fast with it. "I could do with an early finish, actually."

"Then, go," Demi declared.

"Yeah, I think I will. Thanks, Dem."

"Sure thing. And have a great evening. You and Quinn both deserve it."

Lia smiled all the way home, then put on some music and blitz-cleaned the apartment. She changed the sheets on the bed, watered the plants, and set about cooking her main. Nothing to it, really. She just wilted fresh baby spinach in a hot skillet with shallots, added cream cheese, a dash of parmesan, and the juice of a lemon. Salt, pepper, dancing around the kitchen. Next, she put a layer of the mixture on a sheet of puff pastry, added the salmon on top, a bit more spinach to cover it, and wrapped all that up with the pastry. As Bonnie Raitt sang about giving them something to talk about, Lia brushed the pastry with some egg wash, scored the top, and put her creation in the oven. *Perfect.* With an hour to kill until Quinn's arrival, she had a shower, and selected white linen slacks and a dark-pink, silk sleeveless top. Just a touch of mascara, a trace of lip gloss, and a gold bangle on her left wrist to complete the look. *Ready.* She barely glanced in the full-length mirror on her way past but did a double-take at the sight of herself smiling back. Lia noted the color in her own cheeks and the excited glimmer in her eyes. It was a long time since she'd seen genuine happiness reflected back in the mirror. She knew what her dad might say.

"Keep it up, girl," she murmured.

With fifteen minutes to go, she pulled the salmon out of the oven and left it to cool on the counter. It smelled divine. Lia set the table for two, adding a fresh rose and a candle to the display. At six o'clock, she was all set. *Any second now...* She sat down to wait. Five minutes went by. Then, ten. At six-twenty, Lia poured herself a glass of wine to help with the nerves. *Maybe she's been delayed at work.* Although Lia knew that Quinn should have been off-duty from 07:00 a.m. She was also extremely dependable, delivered on her promises, and was never late. *Maybe she forgot about us.* Lia stared out the window, feeling the familiar stirrings of disappointment. She glanced at her phone. *Should I text?* No, texts could be too easily missed. When six-thirty came and went, she stood up to pace. She grabbed her phone, unable to decide what to do. The most obvious thing, that Quinn had changed her mind, brought stinging tears to her eyes. But only for a moment.

"No, she didn't," Lia muttered fiercely.

Quinn was exceptionally straightforward and trustworthy in all the things that mattered. It wouldn't be like her to forget about dinner together tonight. And if she had been delayed, and really couldn't make it for some reason, she would call to let her know. Lia shivered with a sudden rush of apprehension. *What if something happened to her?* Without waiting a second longer, she dialed her number.

'Hi, this is Officer Wesley. Leave me a message and I'll call you right back...'

Lia hung up and tried again a few seconds later. She got the same result. This time, she did leave a brief message.

"Hey, I'm just checking you're okay. Please call me as soon as you get this."

She put the phone down and raked her fingers through her hair. Something really did not feel right. She thought of calling the station instead, but would that be over the top? *Any moment now, she's going to show up at the door and—* The phone rang. Lia lunged for it.

"Quinn?"

"Lia, it's Demi."

"Hey," Lia frowned. "Have you heard from—"

"Are you at home now?" Demi interrupted.

She sounded keyed-up to the extreme, and that in itself was concerning. Demi also was not the sort to lose her cool easily. Lia steeled herself for what she would say next.

"Yes, I'm home. What is it, Dem?" she prompted.

"Reports are just coming in of men armed with knives and guns at the beach, and inside a nearby movie theater. Shots have been fired, Lia."

Suddenly light-headed, Lia reached for the kitchen counter to steady herself. *Oh, no!*

"You should come in," Demi added. "Straight to the station, you hear me? Don't stop anywhere else along the way, because we don't know the scale of what is going on yet."

"Where's Quinn?" Lia almost yelled in return. "Is she okay? Is she—"

"Every officer has been called in, including Quinn. We have the SWAT team on their way too. Lia, are you coming in?"

Quinn was out there, tackling danger head-on, and Lia struggled to catch her breath. She recovered quickly, pulled on her running shoes, grabbed her keys, and ran out the door.

"I'll be right there, Dem."

"Hurry up, darling. And be careful."

••

Quinn had registered off-duty on time that morning. She went straight home instead of lingering at the station, had something to eat, and straight to bed. Up at two p.m. after a restful sleep, she went out for a short run, followed that up with an easy gym workout, showered, and got ready to head to Lia's. *Finally!* The two days that she'd had to wait to see her again had felt like forever. She dressed in black jeans, a white shirt with the sleeves buttoned up at the elbows, and boots. On the way to Lia's, she stopped at the florist to buy a single red rose. Why not, eh? Smiling to herself, she had just come back to the Chevy when a text message came through on her cell phone. Quinn stared at the display, the last thing she'd expected to see: *CODE RED—MAJOR INCIDENT—ALL OFFICERS RECALLED.*

"Fuck!"

She slammed her foot down on the accelerator at the same time as she radioed Dispatch.

"2-Alpha-7, back on duty. Fill me in."

The situation was grim. A group of active shooters had hit the beach area, including the strip of stores and restaurants on the other side of the street. Another armed group was inside the movie theater. SWAT had been called, but they could not be in two places at the same time. Quinn knew what it meant.

"We need you at the beach, 2-Alpha."

"On my way," she confirmed.

She just paused long enough to retrieve her weapon out of the lockable compartment built in between the two front seats. A familiar voice sounded on the emergency radio channel.

"We are taking fire on the corner of Fifth and Jefferson." It was Ellie James, who still managed to sound pretty calm and in control despite the situation. "We've got three... Uh. Correction: I think four shooters out here. We need to evacuate a bunch of people out of the area."

"Be right with you, James," Quinn replied immediately.

"Roger that, Boss," the young officer replied.

CHAPTER
27

Lines of people could be seen fleeing right down the middle of the road when she neared the place. The strip of restaurants and stores was the most popular area of the city after hours, and on a hot summer's evening, even more so. Except that now, instead of enjoying a night out, people were literally running for their lives. Quinn parked within sight of a line of police cars up ahead, and she sprinted the rest of the way on foot.

"How we doing?"

James, one of three uniformed officers at this particular location, flashed her a tense look.

"We've got four armed guys walking around. All dressed in cammo gear, so easy to identify. They didn't come past us since we've been here."

This was good news, since the road that the Police were on now was the only way in and out of the area. Ellie carried on with her hurried sit-rep, sticking to the facts.

"Casualties on the beach: ten wounded, three dead as far as we know. We've got medics and ambulances there, and some of our guys to insure cover. Ethan and Mikey have gone up ahead on their own."

In perfect timing, Ethan broke through on the radio.

"Got a fix on two of these bastards!" he announced. "They just ran inside the Domino's Pizza building and are now taking shots at the people who're running past!"

"Stay put, I'm coming," Quinn responded.

"Watch it, Quinn, we don't know where the other two are!"

"Roger that."

Quinn grabbed the spare M-4 rifle from James's vehicle and she headed up the road.

"Keep going till you see the police," she encouraged anyone coming down the other way.

There were still many, in various states of shock and panic. A few were struggling to run, or even walk. Quinn noticed that several were bleeding. Still, no one who required help was left unattended; people, virtual strangers, were helping each other to get to safety. As always in this type of emergency situation, the very best of human qualities was being highlighted in response to harrowing circumstances. Quinn experienced a rush of true love and pride for the people caught in this mayhem, which only made her even more determined to help and protect them. As Dispatch came on to say that SWAT had another team headed to the beach, she came into view of the pizza place. She spotted her two colleagues, crouching behind an ice-cream van. Not an ideal spot for cover, to say the least, but better than nothing.

"Ethan," she called. "I've got you in sight."

"Sweet, Wesley. What do you—Shit!"

A single shot was fired, bringing down an elderly woman who was trying to cross the road. Her companion immediately stopped to help her. Before another shot could be fired and get him too, Quinn lay down some cover fire.

"I've got this," Ethan stated.

"Wait," she warned, but he flew across the road toward the stranded couple. "Ethan!" *Dammit.*

A shadow moved in the doorway of the Domino's building. Finger tight on the trigger, breathing slowly, Quinn waited to be absolutely sure. Before long, she was able to discern a male figure in dark fatigues. Something glinted in the streetlight. *Gun.* Just as he was about to take out her colleague, she fired once and nailed the shooter with a bullet through the head.

"Get out of there, Ethan," she urged him.

"On it," he said tersely.

"Police!" Mikey shouted in warning to anyone who might want to chance their luck. "Hold your fire!"

He darted out of his hiding place to help someone else to safety, and a hail of bullets followed. Thankfully, not accurate. It sounded like AR-15 shots to Quinn's well-trained ears, and also as if whoever was shooting from the pizza place still had plenty of bullets.

"ETA on SWAT?" she asked into the radio.

At the same time, she laid down more cover shots to protect Mikey, and give Ethan a bit more time to retreat with the woman that he carried in his arms.

"ETA three minutes," the dispatcher replied.

"Hurry up, Eth!" she hissed.

Her partner was just about to reach cover behind a parked vehicle, when a bullet fired from the other side took him down. Quinn heard him grunt and swear under his breath. Then, some rapid breathing. Even before she could line up the culprit, Mikey reacted, and very well too. He got the shooter this time.

"Get up, Ethan!" he yelled. "Get up, man!"

But Ethan did not reply. He did not move.

"Quinn, he's down!" Mikey growled.

No. Not on my watch. I'm not losing another brother today. As more bullets whizzed across the road, Quinn tightened her grip on her weapon.

"Cover me, Mike," she ordered, and rushed to the rescue of her fallen comrade.

••

For a brief but agonizing period of time, it was not clear exactly how many shooters had invaded the city, if they were confined to the beach and the movie theater, or at other public places as well. Terrorism was suspected, and a coordinated attack. SWAT teams showed up in multiple places. There was a stand-off at the movie theater, which quickly ended with two shooters dead. A third managed to escape, although he was injured and probably would not go very far on his own. As a manhunt got under way, Lewiston residents were advised to stay at home and lock their doors.

"I'm going out," Lia declared.

"What?" Demi frowned. "No, you're not."

Even tuning in to the law-enforcement radio channels was not enough to provide an accurate representation of the situation unfolding. Just bits and pieces, more often than not delivered in code, and difficult to interpret. Being home at the time, Lia had missed out on the opportunity to ride into the thick of the action with one of the police crews, and she was going nuts waiting on the sidelines, as everything was happening.

"I need to," she insisted. "I'm a reporter, I have to find out what's going on first-hand. Also..."

She stopped, feeling breathless. Unwilling, unable to voice her fears out loud. Demi narrowed her eyes.

"Look," she stated in a firm voice. "Quinn does this work day in, day out. Don't worry about her, okay?"

The idea of Quinn injured, or in any kind of danger, made Lia feel sick to her stomach. Demi was correct, though. And Lia had seen Quinn in action. She was well-trained. One of the best. For sure, she could handle herself in this sort of crisis. Now Lia, too, needed to get on with her job.

"I have to go," she repeated. "It may not be too late to catch up with some of the teams."

She grabbed her GoPro, picked up her Kevlar vest.

"Lia, I don't think you should get involved."

"I'll be fine, Dem."

A burst of frantic radio chatter interrupted.

"OFFICERS DOWN! We need the SWAT team on Jefferson and Fifth and urgent medical assistance! I repeat, officers have been shot!"

It was Ellie James speaking. Suddenly, it occurred to Lia that she had not heard Quinn speak on the radio once, and how strange this was. As her legs shook, Demi grabbed her by the arm, her own face noticeably paler now.

"I think we should go to the hospital."

"Right," Lia grunted in reply. "Let's go."

Less than fifteen minutes later, they stood at the entrance to the ER, taking in the disturbing scene.

"Jesus, I've never seen anything like it!" Demi exclaimed in astonishment.

It looked like total pandemonium in the lobby, although Lia recognized method under the madness. One doctor in particular stood at the center of the sea of gurneys and bleeding patients, calmly assessing incoming wounded before dispatching them to the appropriate doctor for treatment.

"What are you two doing here?" Janet inquired when they caught up to her.

She sounded incongruously relaxed in the middle of this chaotic dance. Lia noticed extreme focus and fierce efficiency in her movements and directions. Sheer excellence at work, and she breathed easier for a moment.

"We've got people down," Demi responded.

Janet winced at the news but she never lost her rhythm.

"We'll be ready for them," she said, before hailing a passing doctor. "Dave, I need you in 3 with Joanne right away, I just sent her two GSW to the chest."

"Hey, Dem!" Carole, in blood-stained scrubs, showed up at her wife's side and quickly looked her up and down. "Are you okay?"

"Yes."

"Everything still alright with Luke?"

"Yes, the school has all the kids safely inside the building and extra security patrolling outside. I spoke to him earlier. He's okay."

"Excellent." Carole kissed her briefly. "Gotta run, see you in a bit."

"I'll be here, love," Demi confirmed.

The more wounded people were brought in to the hospital for treatment, the more Lia realized the magnitude of the event. Some of the more lightly injured shared frightening reports of their experience.

"Yeah, they had guns!"

"Random shooting on the beach, man!"

"One of the guys had a machete! Fucking insane!"

By then it was getting dark, but still hot and humid outside. She could smell blood in the air. Some people could be heard sobbing as they reunited with loved ones, and a sizeable crowd of onlookers and media people had assembled on the corner of the street. Then, a police cruiser and another ambulance showed up. Lia clenched her teeth as she recognized Mikey behind the wheel of the squad car. Ethan was laid out on the first stretcher to come out of the ambulance.

"He took one in the shoulder but he's stable," Mikey tossed to Demi on their way past. "Quinn's coming in with James, get a doctor on standby!"

"Okay," Demi nodded, and raced off to find someone.

So, Ellie had been injured as well? Lia rushed to the back of a second ambulance to arrive, but the woman it brought in was much older. Nobody else in there. Puzzled, she turned to see a second cruiser screech to a stop in front of the sliding doors. It was driven by an officer in plainclothes. No idea who it was. Where the hell was Quinn? Something felt terribly wrong now. Lia yanked the vehicle door open and, sadly, all her questions were answered. She gasped at the scene that confronted her.

"Oh my god... Quinn!"

Ellie shot her a wild look.

"She's in a bad way, Lia."

Quinn lay on the back seat with her eyes closed. Her face was chalk-white, except for traces of blood on her right cheek and the sides of her neck. Ellie was leaning over her with one leg on the seat in between hers, and the other one braced securely on the floor for balance. She was pressing a balled-up police jacket over the inside of Quinn's left thigh. Lia struggled to breathe at the sight of her lying so still and silent. She had never seen so much blood.

"Lia." Janet landed a commanding hand on her shoulder. "Let me have a look at her."

Lia moved out of her way but she still remained close, as Janet spoke to Ellie, whose arms had started to tremble visibly with the effort of maintaining pressure over the open wound in Quinn's leg.

"I think," she panted, "I've got my fingers on an artery."

"Don't let go." Janet pressed two gloved fingers on the side of Quinn's neck. "She hurt anywhere else?"

"No. The bullet went in her thigh. I think it's still in."

"Can you keep your fingers in place a few more seconds?"

"Sure thing," Ellie said fiercely, her eyes fixed onto Quinn's pale face.

Janet ran to the other side of the cruiser, as Carole brought up a board and a gurney.

"What can I do to help?" Lia said tightly.

"In a minute, you can lift her shoulders and help us to slide her onto the board. Nice and careful, okay?"

"Okay, I'm ready."

"Just give me a second."

Lia watched intently, her heart pounding to breaking in her chest, as Janet leaned shoulder to shoulder with Ellie and moved her own hands gently over her fingers. Quinn flinched when she felt deep inside the wound, but her eyes remained closed. Lia blinked away sweat and tears.

"Big tear in her femoral artery," Janet muttered under her breath. When Lia groaned in reaction, she looked straight into her eyes and flashed a wolfish grin. "I'm the best surgeon in the house, and this one's too stubborn to give up the fight."

"Yes." Lia clenched her fists. "I know."

A second later, Janet grinned in triumph.

"There. I've got my fingers on the spot. Officer, you can let go. Carole, let's roll."

CHAPTER
28

Janet remained on top of the stretcher as they rushed it down the corridor toward the OR, kneeling between Quinn's knees while she applied life-saving pressure to her thigh.

"Was she conscious at the scene?"

"Yes," Ellie replied. "But she fainted as soon as we got to the car. We'd run out of ambulances by then. I thought we'd better go in the cruiser than wait."

"You made the right decision," Janet approved.

"She gonna be okay, yeah?"

"Yes," the surgeon said, her voice sharp as a blade.

Lia was holding on tightly to Quinn's right hand.

"She's as cold as ice."

"That's normal with this type of injury." Carole had applied an oxygen mask over Quinn's face as soon as they got her on the gurney, stuck an IV in her arm, and now she reeled out a series of measurements. "Airway's clear. BP 130. Pulse at 105 and a bit thready."

"Somebody, find out her blood type," Janet instructed.

Demi had just caught up with them. She pulled her phone out.

257

"I'll have it for you in two minutes."

"Carole, ask Dr Wyatt—" Before Janet could finish, Quinn's eyes suddenly snapped wide open and she swung a random fist toward her face. "Whoa!"

Thankfully, she missed, and Janet never shifted her hands from the wound.

"No!" Quinn tried to remove the oxygen mask from her face, then she grabbed Janet roughly by the arm. Her eyes were blazing in fury. "Go! Get to cover!"

"Hold her down," Janet growled, in danger of falling off the side.

Ellie jumped on Quinn's left. Lia gripped her shoulder.

"Quinn, it's Lia," she called. "You're at the hospital. You're going to be okay."

"What? No…"

Her pupils were huge. She looked lost.

"It's me, babe. Hey! Quinn. Look at me."

Lia managed to get her to focus, sort of. Quinn stared at her with eyes full of pain, panic and fear, and Lia had a feeling that this was not just due to the current situation. She seemed to be somewhere else in her head entirely.

"Get out of here, leave," Quinn whispered in a raw, broken voice. "Please, just go, it's not safe…"

Lia repeated the same reassuring words to her.

"You're at the hospital, darling. You are safe. It's okay."

When Ellie re-adjusted the oxygen mask on her face, Quinn closed her eyes and her head rolled to the side.

"Gone again," Carole announced. "BP's dropping fast."

As they went through the doors of the OR, Quinn started to seize.

"Alright. Everybody out, now," Janet ordered.

"No," Lia snapped. "I'm not going. She—"

Demi wrapped a firm arm around her shoulders.

"Come on, Lia, it's alright. Let Janet and Carole handle this now."

Janet flashed her a piercing, burning look.

"She'll be fine," she promised. "I've got her."

Lia caught a final glimpse of Quinn, lying unconscious and deathly pale on the table, before Demi dragged her outside and the doors swung shut. *Don't leave me now. Please, Quinn, don't go.* Suddenly light-headed, she dropped both hands on her thighs and leaned forward, trying to recover her breath. Demi kept a careful hand on the back of her neck.

"Breathe, Lia. Are you okay?"

"Yes... Yes."

Lia forced herself to straighten up. *Get a grip, for goodness' sake!* Quinn was hurt and there was nothing she could do about it, but she was in great hands with Janet. Lia would be there for her when she came out of the OR, for sure. But for now, other people could do with a friendly face and some moral support. She could not afford not to be there for them.

"Where's Ethan?" she asked. "How is he?"

"Not so bad." Demi indicated an exam room. "Getting fixed up in there. The bullet tore through a bunch of ligaments in his shoulder, but it's nothing life-threatening. I need to call Jenna. I'll catch up with you in a bit, okay?"

"Sure, yes. You go, Dem."

Lia spotted Ellie, who'd retreated to the couch in one of the waiting rooms. She was on her own, staring into space. Looking a bit shell-shocked. Lia got a bottle of Coke out of the vending machine and she went to her.

"Hey, Officer James."

Ellie flashed her a tired smile.

"Hey, Lia." She accepted the Coke. "Thanks. You alright?"

"I'm fine. What about you?"

Ellie's uniform was dark with blood in places, and it was hard to tell.

"Yes. I wasn't hit. It was Ethan." She swallowed hard. "And Quinn… Gosh!"

She needed to tell, and Lia needed to hear. She rubbed a soft hand up and down her back.

"What happened, Ellie?"

"Ethan was helping a wounded woman cross the road when he took a round." Her eyes flashed as she explained, her jaw tight. "Quinn yelled at me and Mikey to cover for her, and she raced to the middle of the street toward Eth. She didn't even wait for us to answer. She just flew out like a missile!"

Lia pursed her lips, feeling a mix of pride and anxiety as she imagined the scene. *Oh, Quinn...*

"I'm not surprised she did that," she murmured.

"Neither am I," Ellie grunted. "Quinn's brave, isn't she?"

"Yes, she is." *And I love her so much!*

Lia flinched as it hit her suddenly. *I love her.* She glanced at the closed doors of the OR, fear kicking back in for a moment. *You've got to make it through this, Quinn…*

"She managed to drag Ethan and the woman to safety," Ellie continued. "And it was so close! She was almost there when she got shot, but she kept going until she was in the clear. She saved their lives, I'm sure of it."

Tears were running down her face, but she did not seem to notice. *She's in shock…* Lia passed a comforting arm around her shoulders.

"I think you should lie down for a bit."

"I'm okay," Ellie insisted. "Just sorry I didn't do a better job of covering for Quinn. She almost bled to death on the way over, and now… If only I'd been able to nail that shooter earlier!"

"She's going to recover." Lia held her tighter.

"Yes… Yes. Dammit, she has to!"

"She will. And precisely because you did the right things for her. Ellie, you saved her life. Focus on that, okay? Ethan and Quinn are both going to make it."

Ellie regarded her with tearful eyes.

"You're right, Lia. Sorry, I…"

"Don't worry." Lia pressed a reassuring kiss over her cheek. "Come, let's find you a place to clean up and some fresh clothes to put on."

Ellie needed looking after, and doing the right things for her also kept Lia grounded. A few minutes later, Captain Wilson showed up to check on his troops. In assault gear from head to toe, dusty and sweaty, and accompanied by the leader of the SWAT team, he'd clearly been in the thick of the action. By then, he was able to share the news that all shooters and suspects had been either neutralized or apprehended, including the one who was on the run. He checked on Ethan, had a brief chat with Ellie, but had to leave to attend to other matters soon after.

"Keep me posted on Wesley, okay?" he instructed.

"Yes sir," Demi replied. "We'll call you as soon as we hear."

The three women set about waiting. Rookie James, in clean scrubs following a well-deserved shower, stretched out over the couch and promptly fell asleep. Demi nodded with a smile in her direction.

"One hell of a woman, uh?"

"Fucking amazing," Lia answered in a tight voice.

She'd never be able to repay Ellie for what she'd done. She

knew too that she would never forget opening the car door and finding her, covered in blood and with her hands inside Quinn's thigh, keeping her from certain death. She shivered.

"How are you doing, my girl?" Demi inquired.

"I don't understand what's taking them so long."

"It's been less than an hour since they went in."

"Really? Feels like a year."

"Janet won't let anything happen to Quinn."

"I know." Lia exhaled softly. "I'm in love with her."

"I assume you're referring to Quinn, not Janet," Demi said with a gentle chuckle. "And well done, too; you finally figured it out."

"You mean that you knew?"

"Car and I both suspected. It's as obvious as the nose in the middle of your face, my dear. Quinn is just the same, she just hides it a bit better."

Lia held her breath.

"You think so?"

"I know so. Totally. I think that you both—Oh, Lia." Demi pulled her warmly into her arms. "Don't cry, darling, she's going to be just fine."

"It's hard to wait." Lia recalled the look in her lover's eyes earlier on. Quinn had seemed so lost. So frightened. "She was having flashbacks. I hate to think of her feeling scared or in pain!"

"She won't be for long. Any minute now, Janet will—Ah!" Demi stood briskly, prompting Lia to jump up as well. Ellie woke up. "Here they are..."

Indeed, Janet and Carole were coming through the doors of the OR. Both looking pleased and smiling, which could only be a good sign. Lia stepped forward on trembling legs.

"How—"

"Fine, your girl is doing fine," Janet announced before she could finish. She laughed, flashed a confident grin. "As fine as her surgeon's skills, if I may add. I can guarantee a full recovery, and no further issues."

"Oh, Janet!" Lia threw her arms around her neck for a tight, impulsive hug. She was feeling drunk with relief. "Thank you! Thank you so much."

Demi grabbed her wife for a kiss. Ellie was grinning from ear to ear.

"Can we see her?"

"She won't be awake for a while, but yes, of course. One at a time, please."

"You go first, Lia," Demi nodded.

"Come on," Carole invited, smiling wide. "I'll take you to her room."

••

Quinn did not realize immediately that she'd sustained a bad hit. She was so charged with adrenalin at the time that even a bullet in the chest might not have stopped her instantly. As it was, she was wearing her Kevlar. Sadly, it left her legs unprotected. She felt the bullet enter her thigh and some exquisite burning as it tore through her muscle. She lost her balance under the violence of the impact and landed on the ground hard. Not hard enough to knock herself out or lose track of the mission though. Ethan had taken a round in the shoulder. A civilian was on the ground, badly injured. *Get moving, Wesley.* She leaned over her wounded partner, shielding his body in case another bullet suddenly came through.

"Ethan, can you hear me?"

"Yeah. I'm okay," Ethan muttered, his face a mask of pain.

Blood seeped through the fingers that he kept pressed over his shoulder. It looked like the bullet had gone straight through. A painful injury, but not a life-ender. Quinn grabbed hold of his good arm to help him up.

"Let's move."

She lifted the unconscious woman again, and dragged them both to safety. In the background, and on the radio, she could hear that the SWAT team were in position, assuming control of the building and neutralizing hostiles on the inside.

"James, get an ambulance over here," she snapped into her mic. "Mikey, I need you to—"

She never got to finish that sentence. Her body was done, and it chose that moment to let her know. In the blink of an eye, Quinn lost her words and her legs went out from under her. She collapsed.

"Boss!"

The guys always called her 'Boss' in the field. It kinda sent her back a little, to another time, a different world... Or it would have done, probably, if the most intense pain radiating through her thigh had not kept her present in the moment. Quinn stared at her leg. Blood had already soaked through her jeans. It was pumping out of her thigh in a steady stream. *Ah, shit.* Before she could say anything else, Ellie James shoved her fingers inside her leg. It was the right thing to do, of course, although it made Quinn howl and she almost blacked out.

"I'm sorry. Stay with me," Ellie told her urgently.

"Ethan!" Quinn gasped. "Ethan first."

"We'll take care of him, don't worry."

Shots were fired in the distance. People shouted, voices she did not recognize. Oddly, the street morphed into a stretch of sandy desert. The two landscapes appeared superimposed on each other until Quinn blinked, and the vision disappeared. *It's not real. Focus!*

"No, we're not waiting," Ellie declared, suddenly very loud in her ear. Quinn was not aware that she had drifted. "Wesley! Quinn? Keep your eyes open!"

The next thing that Quinn was aware of, they were on the back seat of a car and Ellie was yelling at her to stay conscious. Two thoughts warred for attention inside Quinn's mind. One, she had to make her aware of the potential for IEDs in the road. And two, where was Lia? Was she okay? The truck was burning. Didn't Ellie realize that? *Lia and IEDs.* Quinn struggled to tell her and Ellie did not seem to hear a word anyway. She just pressed even harder on her open thigh and, for a split second, the pain flared bad enough to bring Quinn back to reality.

"Fuck," she groaned.

"Stay with me," Ellie shouted with fear in her voice.

"Lia," Quinn murmured, and she blacked out.

NATALIE DEBRABANDERE

CHAPTER
29

She was still too hot when she came to, but at least it was quiet around. Well... Almost. She detected a low hum. And some kind of machine beeping steadily on the side. For what felt like a long, fuzzy while, she stared at the green display without being aware that it reflected her own heart rhythm. Faded away again before her consciousness fully returned. In and out... Just drifting. She remembered riding in the armored vehicle when it happened. *Goddamn desert full of fucking IEDs.* She stiffened. *But, wait...* This was a long time ago, wasn't it? She was a cop now. *Ethan... Shit, it was Ethan!* She tried to move and felt pain running down her side. Something was holding her down.

"Help him," she whispered. "Ethan's hurt."

A hand came to rest on her forehead and she registered the pressure of cool fingers around her wrist.

"Quinn. Don't struggle, baby, it's okay."

She remembered being shot as well, and bleeding heavily in the back of the truck. Since when did army doctors call her *'baby'* instead of Captain Wesley? Memories clashed inside her mind, the timelines all mixed up and not making sense. She opened her eyes, blinked in the harsh glare of powerful lights. *Where am I?*

She must have spoken the question out loud because that gentle voice answered.

"You're in the hospital. Everything's alright." The hand on her forehead moved down to cradle her cheek and turn her head slightly. "Look at me, darling."

Darling. Well, yeah, this sure was no military doctor. Quinn tried her best to remember who this was, because she knew that voice and, somehow, knew that she'd missed it. From the initial grey and fuzzy background, colors and shapes slowly began to take form. One gorgeous face in particular materialized above her face, prompting Quinn to stare intently.

"There you go. You're safe now. So is Ethan."

Liquid brown eyes stared back into hers, full of reassurance and tenderness. The woman's smile was just as certain, her voice gentle and strong. Only one being like her in this whole world, and everything suddenly fell right into place.

"Lia," Quinn sobbed with a rush of emotion.

Lia tightened her hold as intense relief flew over her face.

"Yes," she grinned, the most beautiful smile ever. "I'm here, I've got you. I love you so much!"

"Lia, I—"

"Shhh… Kiss me, babe."

"Alright, alright," another voice interrupted. Janet entered the room and zeroed in on Quinn. She arched an eyebrow at Lia. "Let me look at the patient before you start giving her mouth to mouth, okay, Ms Kennedy?"

"Okay," Lia chuckled weakly.

"Hey there, Officer sexy." Janet secured her fingers around her wrist, checking her pulse the old-fashioned way. "How are you feeling?"

"Jan." Quinn managed a smile. "Hi. I'm okay."

"You know who I am, perfect. Can you tell me today's date as well?"

"It's… Tuesday, August 7th."

"We've gone into Wednesday now but close enough. Do you remember what happened?"

"Shooters at the beach," Quinn replied with a shiver. "How is Ethan doing?"

"We patched him up, he's doing fine now." As she spoke, Janet shone a light into her eyes and checked her reflexes. "The situation is under control and no one else got hurt on the side of the good guys."

"What about everyone else? How many casualties?"

"Thirteen people were killed, many more wounded."

"Shit…"

"Don't think too hard about it. I really need you to relax for now. Okay? Can you feel this?"

"Yes."

"What am I doing?"

"Touching my foot."

"Good. And now?"

"You're caressing my leg. Stop that."

Janet snorted ironically, and she glanced at Lia.

"Yeah, she'll be fine. Sense of humor still needs an upgrade, but hey… That's quite above my level of skill."

"That's alright," Lia shot gently in reply. "I like her just the way she is."

For the first time, Quinn noticed the tired look in her eyes, and traces of tears on her cheeks. Lia was still holding her hand, and Quinn rubbed her thumb over her knuckles.

"How are you doing?" she murmured.

"Better now that you're awake."

"Okay." She ignored her fatigue, the pain in her leg, and a pounding headache as well, and sat up straight. "Let's get out of here. I need to check on Ethan. And Ellie... Where is she? How's Mikey? I need to be—"

Quinn stopped short when Janet planted a firm hand in the middle of her chest and pushed her back down as she prepared to get up.

"Not so fast. You're staying the night, at least."

"There's no need, thanks. I'm leaving now."

"Absolutely not." Janet was stern, and as Quinn raised a combative eyebrow, she added; "For your information, I just repaired a major artery in your leg and spent forty-five minutes tracking microscopic fragments of bullets embedded into your thigh muscle. It was a mess."

"Oh?" Quinn frowned.

"Yes. You almost bled out on your way over, too. So, I want you to lie back, relax, and be nice. Otherwise, I'll just give you a sedative and—"

"Fine," Quinn grunted. "I'll stay."

"Good answer." Janet smiled brightly.

••

"It's my leg, not the other side," Quinn assured her. "Please, Lia, I want to feel you close."

"Would you like a cuddle?"

"Yes, please," Quinn almost pouted.

"I like you sheepish and needy," Lia remarked with a soft smile. "And it's great to see a bit more color in your face at last." Quinn always looked much younger and innocent when she blushed. With her usually piercing blue eyes still hazy from the anesthetic, and begging for a cuddle, she made it hard for Lia not to melt. The woman was cute and outrageously sexy in equal measures, and Lia gave in to the same urge she felt to climb on the bed and lie next to her. "Just tell me if anything I do hurts you, okay?"

"Okay. Will you get me some scrubs, too?"

"What for?"

"Can't walk out of here in this open gown thing they've got me in."

Amused at this blatant attempt to recruit her for an illegal escape, and not surprised in the least, Lia wrapped both arms around her shoulders and she settled Quinn's head against her breast.

"Nice try, Officer, but no can do. I want you to follow your surgeon's instructions and stay in bed until the morning. Plus, I don't think you'd be able to even stand at the moment."

"Sure," Quinn argued, albeit drowsily. "I can do it."

"Okay, tough girl." Lia gave her a fond smile. "But let's just wait a bit longer to test that theory, shall we?"

"I don't want to sleep, Lia."

"Why not, darling?"

After a pregnant pause, Quinn whispered;

"Bad dreams. Flashbacks. I get a little lost in them."

From the way that Lia had watched her thrash and mumble restlessly in her sleep earlier, she knew without a shadow of a doubt that these nightmares would be linked to her time in Iraq. She cradled her gently in her arms, brushed her fingers through her hair.

"That's alright then. We can just talk if you like. Or be quiet and simply rest. Whichever way you need is fine. I'll stay with you no matter what."

The tension she'd felt in her body eased up, and Quinn sank a little lower against her side.

"Okay," she sighed. "Thanks, Lia... I don't want you to go."

"That's nice to hear, and no need to thank me then. I'm here because I want to be. I'm not going anywhere."

Quinn finally smiled and she closed her eyes.

"I was on my way to yours when Dispatch got a hold of me about the situation. I had to scramble. I'm sorry I didn't call to tell you."

Lia caressed her cheek, smiling in genuine wonder.

"After saving a bunch of lives and almost losing your own in the process, you really don't need to apologize to me for that," she declared. "Although I appreciate the thought. Thank you. And don't worry."

Quinn raised her face to look at her.

"I'm not worried, but I want you to know that you can trust me. Did you think I'd changed my mind about dinner?"

"The thought occurred to me, yes, but I dismissed it almost as soon as it did. I know you, Quinn," Lia reflected. "I do trust you. I was more worried that something may have happened to you. Then, Demi called, and it made perfect sense. I raced to the station as fast as I could, but all the teams had already gone. So, we decided to come to the hospital instead, and help in any way we could."

"But you wanted to ride along?"

Quinn sounded reluctant. Conflicted. Lia understood why, of course, and she made sure to keep her voice gentle when she replied.

"It's my job to be in the thick of it with you all."

"Mm. Yeah. I know."

Her voice was barely audible. Lia massaged the muscles at

the back of her neck. Quinn was holding on to her with one arm across her middle, and the tension in her body was back with a vengeance.

"Are you okay with that?" Lia inquired softly.

She was clear about her own feelings now, but without total acceptance on both sides... It just would not work. She did her best not to tense in return, as she thought of all that hung in the balance at this point. Quinn took a deep breath, and she exhaled long and deep.

"I don't relish the idea of you taking that kind of risk," she admitted. "But I've seen you in action, and I know you're a real pro. I admire that side of you; your passion for the job, for life in general. I would never want to clip your wings or limit you in any way. I love the woman that you are, Lia. All of her, not just the easy stuff."

Her words were like hot chocolate after a cold ocean swim session, and Lia shivered in pleasure. She felt seen, understood, appreciated for who she was. *'All of it, not just the easy stuff.'*

"How is it that you can speak so well, and so true, after just coming out of surgery?" she laughed in delight.

Quinn flashed her that sexy grin which never failed to make Lia hold her breath in reaction.

"You're worth the effort."

"You say the most wonderful things."

"It's easy with you. I love you, Lia."

"I'm so glad... Come here, babe."

Lia kept her right arm wrapped around Quinn's shoulders. She rested gentle fingers along the side of her jaw, and tilted her head back slightly. She kissed her deep and slow, because she could. At this point, also, only a thorough kiss would express her feelings accurately.

"Mmm…"

Quinn smiled, then tensed again, but in a different way this time. Lia adored how responsive she was to her. She loved to know that she was the cause of the tiny whimper that escaped Quinn's lips. She enjoyed the small quiver in her limbs, knowing that it was due to pleasure and desire instead of pain, and that she was responsible for that as well.

"Say it again," she whispered.

"I love you, Lia."

"I love you too, Quinn."

Lia slipped a careful hand under the stiff hospital gown, needing to feel her skin. It had been clammy before, when Quinn was wrestling with dreams of another time and tragedy. But now she was just hot, and smooth everywhere that was not hard muscle. Lia pressed the palm of her hand over her heart. It beat strong; steady.

"Kiss me, please," Quinn demanded.

Lia kissed her harder, desperate for contact and connection. Quinn responded in kind, suddenly the opposite of drowsy. The rest of the world ceased to exist for Lia, time stopped, the woman in her arms her sole and only focus. Until, that is, an insistent beeping brought her back to reality. She pulled back, startled. The heartrate monitor that Quinn was linked to via a sensor on her finger had shot up to 99 bpm, from a previously stable 67. Lia looked at her, frowning in concern.

"You okay, baby?"

"Yep," Quinn chuckled.

"Blushing again, are you?"

"I guess," Quinn replied, color spreading and her blue eyes twinkling in amusement. "Because now you know exactly what you do to me."

Lia brushed a light thumb over her nipple, eliciting another shiver. The HRM hit 100. She smiled.

"Oh, this is going to be fun."

"You won't say that when Janet comes running back in the room."

"Alright, then." Lia snuggled against her side, her lips just brushing the side of Quinn's neck. "Be good, Officer. I love you."

NATALIE DEBRABANDERE

EPILOGUE

Past her initial shock at finding out that she could not return to work the next day, and a minor heart attack when her captain ordered her to take two weeks' leave out of the five that she was owed, Quinn adjusted. If time-off meant that she could spend more of it with Lia, she was all for it. She caught up on some sleep over the first week. Tinkered with the Chevy. And kept on top of her training, working all the usual body parts minus her injured leg. Lia took her on morning swims, which was great for overall recovery. Quinn cooked for her in the evenings. Lia more or less moved in with her during that time.

"Bet you never imagined I'd say this," Janet laughed when Quinn saw her to have her stitches removed. "But you really are perfect wife material, Officer Wesley."

"Bet you never imagined that I'd consider it a compliment," Quinn shot in reply. "But thank you, doc."

Janet regarded her with a pensive smile.

"So, it's like that between you, uh?"

"Hundred percent. She's the one."

"And you never saw it coming?"

"Nope. Never." Quinn chuckled. "I was totally blindsided by it. Didn't want to fall in love, but I'm glad I had no choice in the end."

"So maybe there's hope for me," Janet reflected.

"I never knew you were looking for love."

"Well... Isn't everybody, in a way?"

Quinn studied her face as she was bent over to inspect the raised scar inside her leg.

"I don't know about everybody. Are you?"

"Maybe." Janet carefully palpitated the muscle around the wound. "I see Carole and Demi, and how happy they are with Luke. Now, you and Lia found each other. And there's Ethan and Jenna as well. Is this relationship thing really all it's cracked up to be?"

"Yes." Quinn smiled as she thought of her partner. "It's fun. Safe. Exciting. Can't speak for the others but for me, it feels like home."

"Wow..." Janet carefully pulled one of her stitches. "Sounds like the stuff of romance novels. Never thought this stuff could be true in real life. I'm happy for you and Lia, Quinn."

Quinn noticed an unusual shine to her eyes and she gently touched her arm.

"Jan. I consider you one of my closest friends. You're also a gorgeous woman. Smart, funny, and kind. If you're open to the idea, you'll find your One soon enough. I'm sure of it."

"Thanks for saying that, Quinn."

"I mean it."

Smiling, a little flustered but in a good way, Janet squeezed her shoulder and returned to the business at hand.

"So, your leg is healing well. Actually, even a bit faster than anticipated."

"Can I start weight training for it?"

"Yes, as long as you're careful and don't push too hard, too soon."

"Roger that. Thanks for fixing me up."

"I'm glad I could." Janet flashed a mischievous smile. "Now get out of here, hot-shot. Before I forget that you're taken now, and start lusting after those crazy abs of yours."

••

"Hey babe. How are you doing?"

Quinn smiled at the feel of Lia coming to wrap both arms around her waist from behind as she finished the washing-up, and resting her cheek against her shoulder. She dried her hands and softly stroked the arms encircling her.

"Never better. How are you?"

"Same. Fancy an after-dinner walk? Ice-cream and sunset at the beach?"

"Anything you want, Lia," Quinn said, turning to hold her close.

"Mm…" Lia leaned into her with a smile, hands pressed flat over her chest in a favorite gesture. "That's a dangerous thing to say."

"Not with you."

"How come?"

"Because I trust you in charge."

"Oh, that's even worse," Lia chuckled, eyes glinting with laughter. She moved her leg in between Quinn's open thighs and brushed a possessive finger across her mouth. "I can be bad, you know?"

Quinn briefly caught her finger in her teeth.

"Oh, I know," she grinned. "And I love that about you."

They walked to the beach and found a quiet spot to sit and watch the sunset among many other evening strollers. A cooler breeze was blowing in from offshore, as good an opportunity as any to huddle close under a blanket. Lia sat in front, between her legs. Quinn kept both arms loosely clasped around her waist, and her chin on her shoulder, breathing the soothing scent of her.

"Are you still going back to work early next week, ahead of official schedule?" Lia inquired.

"No, I don't think so anymore."

"You don't?" Lia turned sharply in her arms. "Oh, Quinn, why not? What did Janet say to you? Are you alright?"

"Yes, fine. Janet gave me the all-clear."

"Then… What is it?"

Lia looked as if she expected bad news, and Quinn brushed a reassuring kiss over her lips.

"I just want to enjoy more time with you."

"Really? But your job…"

"It's okay. I love my job, Lia, but I love being with you even more. So, I've decided not to rush back to work and to make the most out of this extra time with you."

Lia kissed her back, slow and tender.

"Okay. That's better."

"I thought that if you're not too busy yourself, we could go away next week. Drive to the desert, sleep under the stars…"

"Oh, I forgot about that!" Lia jumped in sudden excitement. "I'd love to go there with you, Quinn! We could make a road trip of it, yes?"

"Yes, that's exactly what I had in mind."

Lia pulled her close for a fierce, hot kiss.

"I love you."

"Love you too." Quinn chuckled. "You know what else my surgeon said to me?"

"No, what?"

"That I'd make a good wife."

"Did she now?"

"Yep."

"And how would she know?" Lia growled in reply.

Quinn burst out laughing at the sure note of outrage in her voice.

"Hey, you're sexy when you're jealous."

"Uh-uh. Answer the question."

"I told Janet how you make me feel. Whole. Safe. Happy. That's when she made the comment."

"Ah." Lia blushed. "That's better, then."

"So," Quinn went on with a smile. "If maybe I asked you a question, one night under the stars, do you think it would be a good idea?"

Quinn had no clue she would say this until she did. She had not prepared a word. Did not intent to go there, really... This being said, never before had a conversation felt so right. Nor so true or meant to be. She looked at her partner, and knew that the feeling was shared.

"I think it would be an excellent idea," Lia said. "Make sure you ask, okay?"

"Okay. Wow." Quinn chuckled, feeling light-headed all of a sudden. *Just like that, eh?* "I feel like it's going to be the best trip of my life."

Lia caressed her cheek, dark eyes shining in promise.

"Road-trip to forever," she smiled. "These are the best kind, baby."

NATALIE DEBRABANDERE

DID YOU ENJOY THIS?

CHECK OUT MORE TITLES!

www.nataliedebrabandere.com

Thank You
for
Reading and Reviewing!

Printed in Great Britain
by Amazon